C. H. (Charles Hare) Simpkinson

Life and Times of William Laud

C. H. (Charles Hare) Simpkinson

Life and Times of William Laud

ISBN/EAN: 9783337054410

Printed in Europe, USA, Canada, Australia, Japan

Cover: Foto ©Raphael Reischuk / pixelio.de

More available books at **www.hansebooks.com**

LIFE AND TIMES

OF

WILLIAM LAUD

ARCHBISHOP OF CANTERBURY

BY

C. H. SIMPKINSON, M.A.

BALLIOL COLLEGE, OXFORD

RECTOR OF FARNHAM

AND EXAMINING CHAPLAIN TO THE LORD BISHOP OF WINCHESTER

WITH PORTRAIT

LONDON

JOHN MURRAY, ALBEMARLE STREET

1894

PREFACE.

AN apology is necessary when any new writer attempts to deal with a period which has been so constantly and so learnedly treated as the first half of the seventeenth century. But this, I think, is to be found in the strange misrepresentations of the career and character of William Laud, which are prevalent at the present day, and which are mainly to be attributed to the fierce invective of Macaulay and to the cold criticism of Hallam. It is owing to the far-reaching influence of these two writers that a man who was looked upon as a martyr by more than half his contemporaries, and who was revered as a saint by the great bulk of the generation which restored the Church of England after his death, is now considered by many to have been a pedant, a bigot, and a persecutor. I have tried, therefore, to show Laud as he appeared to himself, and to judge his acts sympathetically. No one, as his correspondence and his private diaries prove, was more conscious than he was of his faults and of his mistakes; but he knew he had great ideals, and was saddened and sometimes embittered by the obstinate opposition which a resolute minority of the nation offered to his reforms in the administration of the Treasury and in the development of commerce, to his far-reaching schemes for the improvement of education, and, above all, to his efforts to make worship outwardly devout, and religious teaching liberal and practical.

This opposition prevented his natural alliance with many of the great men who were working in his generation for the progress of liberty. They misunderstood him, and he misunderstood them; and this mutual misunderstanding was one cause, and a very important one, of the great Rebellion; but 250 years after his death our minds are wide enough to comprehend and admire both sides.

Three statesmen did more for the progress of Great Britain than any of their contemporaries in the struggle: Sir Harry Vane, the younger, first gave practical shape to government by Parliament; the Marquis of Argyle moulded with consummate skill the Scottish Kirk and the Scottish character; and William Laud decided the future of the English Church. None of these men are popular just at present, because they are little studied; and Vane's stiffness, and Argyle's physical cowardice, alienate our sympathies until we grow more intimate with their intentions; while Laud is disliked because he has been made, most unjustly, the scapegoat for the miseries of the great Rebellion.

The materials for a history of Laud and his times are very plentiful, though we know all too little of the early stages of his extraordinary career. His own voluminous writings tell us much about him; and the large collection of memoirs by his contemporaries, from the stately picture gallery of Clarendon, where each great personality stands out in life-like form, glowing with the colours of his passions ˙and his ambitions, down to the gossiping letters in which Garrard informs his patron Wentworth of the talk of London town, renders the period peculiarly interesting. Unhappily much of this light is lost in the last and the critical year of Laud's power, and we have to grope doubtfully among conflicting shadows, till once more his own full story of his trials and troubles and the accusations of his enemies make the closing scenes clear to us. Professor Gardiner's monumental work on the first two Stuart reigns is, of course, a guide to which all less competent students owe more than they can express.

CONTENTS.

Heylin's *Cyprianus Anglicanus;* [1] Laud's *Diary;* Wood's *Athenae Oxonienses;* Wood's *Annals of the University of Oxford;* Fuller's *Church History,* edit. 1842; Fuller's *Worthies;* Bp. Andrewes' *Works;* Neale's *History of the Puritans;* Eden's *State of the Poor;* Isaac Walton's *Lives;* Sibbes' *Works;* Hacket's *Life of Archbishop Williams;* Spelman's *Works;* Howell's *Familiar Letters;* *Autobiography* of Lord Herbert of Cherbury.

[1] This is a life of the archbishop by one of his chaplains; Heylin was admitted to Laud's intimacy in 1627, and had every means of knowing the facts of his life and the principles of his policy; it may be considered the authorised biography.

The references to Laud's *Works* are in general to Wharton's original folio edition; but when volumes vi. or vii., or the sermons are mentioned, the edition of the *Works* published in the Anglo-Catholic Library is referred to.

CHAPTER I.

A Great Man—Birth at Reading—Childhood and its Impressions—St. John's, Oxford—State of the University—Laud's Dislike of Calvinism—Causes of Success—Laud's Projects—A Grave Offence.

AMONG those signs which seem to believing men to prove the presence of God in history, we must reckon the appearance at critical opportunities of some great man, who, himself imbued with the spirit of the age, knows how to give to religious and political movements a practical and permanent shape. The seventeenth century was fertile in such leaders : John Eliot is still revered as the boldest orator of English liberty ; John Pym first gave method to party organisations in carrying the elections for Parliament ; the course of the Civil War was decided by the military and civil genius of Oliver Cromwell ; while Sir Harry Vane, the younger, found means to supply an executive such as now rules us, formed by a committee of the majority in Parliament ; and the Marquis of Argyle gave to Scottish politics and Scottish opinions a form which has lasted almost to our own days.

All these men were of gentle birth ; they rose naturally to the front as the requirements of the time called for their leadership ; but William Laud, a son of the people, had to make his own way by his own talents into that class from which rulers are selected.

He was born on the 7th of October, 1573, being the only child of his mother's second marriage, in the town of Reading. There his father was engaged in the cloth trade, for which the position of the place, on the banks of the Thames, between London and Oxford, was particularly well suited. A single entry in his *Diary* refers to this period of childhood and gives us the clue to that firm, resolute character which we are told was already built up when he first appeared in Oxford life, " In my infancy I was in danger of death by sickness ; " and it appears that through his early years he was so delicate that no one expected him to live. The sense of special preservation by the hand of Providence convinced his parents, and convinced the boy himself, that he was destined to some great future, and that a work was set him which God would help him to accomplish. This conviction gave him that extraordinary confidence in his own career which enabled him in later days to hold his own among the high-born men of England, and that

stubborn courage which seemed so astonishing in
a person of such puny frame and feeble constitution. Delicate health kept the boy from the
sports of his more robust school-fellows and
brought him to listen to the conversation of his
elders, and to think over the reminiscences of the
past and the problems of the present which
were suggested by the town and trade of Reading. His father could remember the days when
the last abbot of the now ruined abbey had been
dragged away to London and executed for his
opposition to the royal supremacy ; and could tell
of the high hopes which the Reformation had
excited in its early days, for it had seemed to promise to rid England of an ecclesiastical tyranny
which suppressed freedom of thought, and of rulers
whose covetousness stifled trade. But the Reading
cloth-makers had soon found that the nobles who
inherited the abbey lands were even more rapa-
cious and arbitrary than the Churchmen whom
they had ousted. There had been evil days' in
England when greedy regents ruled in the name
of the child King Edward VI. and pretended
to be inspired with a love for pure and Puritan
religion. There had followed days yet more evil
when half-Spanish Mary and Spanish Philip
governed England together and burnt in the
flames of Smithfield and Oxford the most eloquent
of the English bishops, the most pious of the
English clergy, and many of the most upright of

the middle class.   Only the nobles had escaped all suffering, for they changed their religion with the times willingly enough, so long as their possessions were safe.[1]   Freedom of thought and vigour of commerce were little cared for till Elizabeth sat upon the throne.

Then the great queen, most thoroughly English by descent and by temperament of all our sovereigns, had set to work to regenerate her distracted people.   She had been seriously hampered by the nobles, and the heads of the three haughtiest English houses, Percy, Neville and Howard, had been found guilty of treason during the perils of her reign, while Romanist and Puritan had done their utmost to impede the growing union of the English nation.   With her two great ministers, the Lord Treasurer Burleigh, and Archbishop Parker of Canterbury, she had built up a new England out of the ruined materials of the old.   Nobles and country gentry were compelled to obey the law.   Trade was fostered everywhere, and the spirit of adventure which was to make England supreme had been stimulated by the queen's admiration for the rough and hardy seamen who sailed the seas under her flag.

In the English Church, the last remnants of the long Roman tyranny, against which clergy and laity had so often rebelled, had been now destroyed ; but its immemorial privileges, and its

[1] See *Parliamentary History of Mary's Reign.*

ancient traditional organisation, had been diligently
preserved.   The queen had never allowed Parliament to interfere with the Church, and it was her
purpose to use its hierarchy in order to educate
and influence the masses of the people.[1]   Because
it was so genuinely English, the Elizabethan
Church system had been accepted by the great
bulk of Englishmen.   Little by little the lower
classes who loved the old ritual, and the middle
classes who delighted in the modern innovation of
constant sermons, felt they could combine, and
must combine (if England was to remain free and
once more to grow great), in the worship offered
to them by the Book of Common Prayer.

This was the English history which was being
acted round Laud as he passed his quiet childhood in Reading ; and he heard from the sober,
sensible trades-people who resorted to his father's
house that the country was still imperilled by two
extreme parties which would accept of no compromise, the Puritans and the Romanists, each a
small minority, but dangerous from their resolution and fanaticism.[2]

As he formed his opinions, and dreamed his
dreams of ambition, something told all who had

---

[1] *Cf.* the imprisonment of Peter Wentworth in 1593, which
made a great impression upon Laud (*Answer to Lord Saye's Speech
against the Bishops*, p. 58).

[2] See Heylin's *History of the Reformation*, which gives us the
history of these times written by one of Laud's pupils.

to do with him that he would one day play a great part. His schoolmaster bade his brilliant pupil never forget his humble birthplace when he had climbed to be one of the rulers of his country; and the charities of Reading attested in after years the fidelity of the boy's affections.[1] His relations and friends offered advances of their hard-earned money to ensure for the clever child an education worthy of his talents.

But if the politics of England would be the principal subject of conversation in Reading circles, the cloth trade had interests also on the continent. Those were the days of the wars of religion. France and Holland and Germany were deluged with blood shed in civil war. Italy and Spain groaned under the terrors of the Inquisition. Most intimate ties of commerce and literature bound England to France and the Netherlands; the English people were thrilled with horror at the news of the murder of William the Silent (1584), the Liberator of Holland, by Balthasar Gerard, and at the constant plots of other Romish assassins whom Elizabeth's better fortune somehow baffled;[2] while the murder of Coligny (1572) and thousands of the noblest of France in the St. Bartholomew massacre poured into London and the eastern counties crowds of refugees who spoke of that horrible night with

[1] *Things Projected*, xvi., and *Works*, vi. 470-474, and vii. 652, etc. The Grammar School and other charitable institutions were greatly enriched by him.   [2] See list in Wallington, a contemporary.

curses upon the Roman Pope for blessing the murderers.

In the chaos of French politics two statesmen saw the true path for the nation to follow out of the intricacies of religious strife. Michel de l'Hôpital, Chancellor to Charles IX., had tried to persuade king and people to build up a strong free Church, independent of Rome, yet retaining the ancient ceremonial and the ancient hierarchy, and which should train men to work and to worship together with the widest divergences of religious opinion. L'Hôpital died of a broken heart (1573); but Henry of Navarre, more buoyant and more fortunate, was already fighting and negotiating to reconstruct a strong monarchy which should compel the respect of the riotous Romanist mobs and ambitious Romanist preachers, as well as of the aristocratic Huguenots and grasping feudal nobles. These great minds cannot have failed to furnish suggestions to English statesmen, and among them to Laud, for the reformed English Church and State.

Then came the anxious days of the Armada (1588), while all England hung breathless on the issue, wondering how towns such as Reading would fare if Parma and the terrible army who had sacked Antwerp could secure a footing on English soil. It was the middle classes which saved England in those days; a few nobles might appear fitfully on the scene, but the small gentry and traders of Devon and the south coast were the real conquerors of the Armada. The lesson sank deep into the boy's heart; it fixed the political opinions of his life.

Laud was always the opponent of aristocratic rule; and he dreaded the alliance of the nobles with Papists or with Puritans through the whole of his career; for it seemed to him that events had clearly shown that the Crown was the chosen instrument of Providence for the salvation of the country. Queen Elizabeth had been anointed[1] with consecrated oil; she had been endowed by her consecration with divine powers both in Church and State; through those powers she had been enabled to deliver England from foreign interference: and therefore Laud formed an intense dislike for Puritan speakers in the Commons, and for Puritan preachers like Thomas Cartwright, who, in claiming supremacy over her as "God's silly vassal," seemed to him almost to vie in disloyalty with Cardinal Allen and Parsons at Rheims and Douay, who were despatching a constant succession of assassins to butcher her as God's enemy.

It was in 1589, in the year following the defeat of the Armada, that William Laud was sent up

---

[1] *Cf.* the expressions of old Acts of Parliament against Papal encroachments, *e.g.*, 33, Edw. III., " reges sacro oleo uncti spiritualis jurisdictionis sunt capaces ". Sir H. Spelman, the greatest authority of the day on ecclesiastical law, and subsequently a friend and follower of Laud, considers the royal unction to have given the king the government of the Church (*Works*, i. 148-154).

to the College of St. John the Baptist in Oxford.
There his first year's work was so successful that
he was elected to a scholarship : but he felt himself out of sympathy with the prevalent party in
the university.   If the Elizabethan Church settlement was being sincerely accepted by the mass of
the English people, it was not as yet the religious
profession of the leading men of the university of
Oxford.   With all her wisdom in the selection of
ministers, Elizabeth had made many mistakes ;
and the worst blot upon her reputation for saga-
city is the trust which she reposed in Robert
Dudley, Earl of Leicester.   Did the queen fancy
that a man who owed her all must be absolutely
loyal ?   If so, she was deceived.   Leicester was
a man of pleasure and himself no Puritan ; but he
shared the ambitions of his class, and like many
of the new nobles whose fortunes were built upon
monastic lands, saw in the Puritan party a valuable
instrument for future aggression against the Crown.
His influence with the queen had secured for him
the coveted post of Chancellor of the University
of Oxford, which he held till his death in 1588 ;
and seconded by Elizabeth's clever secretary, Sir
Francis Walsingham, who unlike his mistress and
Burleigh and Parker looked upon the Puritans as
the most loyal of Englishmen,[1] he had thoroughly
Puritanised the university, until it had lost most of
its Church feeling and was pouring out a flood of

[1] Wood's *Annals of the University of Oxford*, ii. 227.

teachers and preachers who would in their turn
Puritanise England. The vice-chancellor was
invariably a Puritan; the Regius Professor of
Divinity, Dr. Laurence Humphry, had been a
refugee at Zurich during the persecution under
Philip and Mary and had become a firm believer
in the Calvinistic doctrine of the Divine decrees ; [1]
he wished to remodel the English Church to the
shape of that of Geneva. The most popular preacher
in Oxford was Dr. Reynolds, who was shortly to
lead the Puritan party against Bishop Bancroft in
the Hampton Court conference ; while the most
prominent of the younger tutors was Dr. George
Abbot, who afterwards as Archbishop of Canterbury did more to stimulate the growth of Puritanism
than any man of his time. All these teachers were
renowned for their personal piety, and were themselves learned and capable. But, unfortunately
for itself, Puritanism had choked the vigour of
university life by its absorbed attention to doctrinal questions. The number of undergraduates
was small. Interest in intellectual questions was
weak. Oxford had less than its usual influence
over the country. [2]

The Society of St. John's was, however, opposed
to the prevalent tone of Oxford ; and Laud found

[1] Wood's *Athenae*, i. 241, 242 ; *Annals*, ii. 240.

[2] Chancellor Hatton complains in 1590 of the neglect of
lecturing and teaching, and carelessness about university dress
(Wood's *Annals*, ii. 242).

himself in a college where loyalty to primitive
Church ideas was still in fashion, and where the
principal tutor, Dr. Buckeridge, was an accomplished student of the ancient fathers.[1]   From
St. John's, guarded by his unfailing loyalty to his
own college, Laud could look out with some contempt on a university in which drunkenness was
prevalent, and was said to be fostered by the
newly-introduced habit of smoking tobacco ;[2] in
which learning was satisfied with the study of
Calvin's Institutes ; and where the Puritan chiefs,
divided into two hostile camps of sublapsarians
and supralapsarians, argued interminably the
question whether the Divine decrees of rigid
election and reprobation dated from before or
after the fall of Adam.   About this ceaseless
strife Laud agreed with Sir Henry Wotton,[3] the
keenest observer of the day, that "the itch of disputation will prove the scab of the Church," or as
George Herbert more melodiously phrased it in
his address to the Church :—

> But when debates and fretting jealousies
> Did worm and work within you more and more,
> Your colour faded and calamities
> Turnéd your ruddy into pale and bleak,
> Your health and beauty both began to break.

From these unending wrangles he learnt the dislike which he showed afterwards to all public

---

[1] Wood's *Athenae.*
[2] Wood's *Annals*, ii. 290.   *Cf. State Papers*, vol. 182, No. 11.
[3] Walton's *Life of Wotton.*

discussion upon insoluble problems. Stimulated by the cheers of partisans and eager at any cost to foil an antagonist, the disputants grew inflated with pride and indifferent to truth, while their listeners lost the calmness of judgment which is necessary to genuine learning. Here surely, he reasoned, were to be found just limits to toleration : and in the years of his power it became his principle of government that men might be allowed to hold what they pleased, and to talk about what they pleased, but that these high matters ought to be kept out of the pulpit and the press, else they would deluge England with blood.[1]   For himself, his interest always lay in practical duties. Aristotle, the teacher who showed how character was shaped by habit, at once attracted him and became his master " in humanities ".[2]   Already a good scholar and diligent student of the classics, he was guided by Buckeridge to the study of Church history and the writings of the fathers and famous Churchmen ; and he began to equip himself to assail the Goliath of Puritanism who seemed to him to sit like a nightmare on the awakening Church of England, stifling freedom, art, learning and devotion with the huge, inert mass of its terrible doctrine of the Divine decrees.

---

[1] He was confirmed in these views by the murder of Barneveldt in 1619, which he considered a direct consequence of the Synod of Dort (see letters to Vossius).

[2] His love of Aristotle continued to the end of his life; *Against Fisher*, sect. xvi. 6.

Naturally the strongest enemy of Puritanism, Lancelot Andrewes, became the enthusiastic boy's model as a student and his hero as a religious leader. He admired Andrewes for his wide learning, which extended over fifteen languages; and for that eloquence which was now drawing thousands of Romanists into the English Church,[1] while it swayed men's souls to righteous action and to the exercise of devotion. He cordially agreed with the indignation felt by the High Churchmen against the doctrine of election as the Puritans taught it, "saying almost all of them that God from all eternity reprobates by far the greater part of mankind to eternal fire, without any eye at all to their sin. Which opinion my very soul abominates. For it makes God, the God of all mercies, to be the most fierce and un-reasonable tyrant in the world. For the question is not here what God *may* do by an absolute act of power, would He so use it upon the creature which He made of nothing; but what He *hath* done, and what stands with His wisdom, justice and good-ness to do."[2]

Nor was the little world of Oxford even in those dull days left unstirred. Foreigners began to hear of a growing interest in learning among a section of the students; and many wandering

---

[1] In the North, where he was chaplain to Lord Huntingdon (Cassan, *Bishops of Winchester*, ii. 82).

[2] Laud's *Works*, folio, i. 503. Mozley's *Laud*, 162.

scholars came to visit the once famous university
and to talk of the studies and discoveries of the
continent in the frank freemasonry of hall and
common room. A special influence on Laud's
opinions must be attributed to the arrival of
Josephus Barbatus, strange and startling figure,
a learned Copt from Egyptian Memphis, who
lectured for a few years on his own mother tongue
and described the ancient Bible lands, and dis-
coursed about the Bible languages, proving to the
men of Oxford that there was a Christianity
beyond Europe, older and more conservative than
that of Rome.[1] Such a revelation of unknown
Churches widened the ideas of Laud, as similar
opportunities had widened the mind of Luther,
and led him to study the methods by which Rome
had made herself absolute mistress of the religious
world in the West.

Under such teaching and with such principles
Laud passed successfully through his Oxford
career. He was elected fellow of the college in
1593, and in 1598 became grammar reader; in
1600 he was ordained deacon and in 1601 priest
by the Bishop of Rochester; for the see of Oxford
was at this time kept vacant in order that the Earl
of Essex might pillage its revenues. In these
years he had several times to contend against
severe illness which hindered his progress, and

---

[1] Wood's *Athenae, Fasti,* i. 166. *Cf. Argument against Fisher,*
based on the absence of the Greeks from Trent, sect. xxvii. 3.

had the grief to lose his father and his mother, to both of whom he was devotedly attached.[1] His own college had become proud of him for his classical learning and his remarkable gifts of oratory; but he was as yet unknown outside the university.

Fame was won suddenly and unexpectedly in 1602, when he was appointed divinity lecturer at St. John's. It had been the fashion of the Puritan lecturers to speak of Lanfranc and Anselm, Bonaventura and Thomas Aquinas as teachers of falsehood, while they traced the true Church through obscure and sometimes dubious sects, the Albigenses, the Hussites and the Lollards down to a sudden new life at the Reformation of the fifteenth century. Now the magnates of the university heard with amazement and horror that the new divinity lecturer at St. John's spoke of the English Church as having lived one consecutive life through its succession of bishops, derived from Roman and British sources; and that he was tracing the history of the Visible Church of Christ through the oppressed Churches of the East, and in the West through the hated hierarchy of Rome; and was even maintaining that the Roman Church was in essentials a true Church, though marred by many errors which he unsparingly denounced.

But when this blow was followed up two years

[1] *Diary, anno* 1594 and 1600.

2

later in 1604 by two theses for the degree of
Bachelor of Divinity, in which Laud defended
the positions (1) that baptism was necessary to
salvation, and (2) that there could be no true
Church without diocesan bishops, indignation
knew no bounds.   If so, Calvin and Knox were
alike unchurched, and Cartwright had been a
false teacher.   The quaint humour, the learning,
the keen dialectic, the vivacity of the man delighted the younger portion of the university.
His teaching, adopted by his pupils, repeated in
many districts, and discussed in widespread
pamphlets, was welcomed by the great mass of
the nation, who, remembering the practical piety
of their parents, refused to believe they were
doomed to everlasting death for differing from
Calvin.   But Oxford Puritanism was too strong
to be easily vanquished; and his opponents resolved that so skilful an assailant must somehow
be overwhelmed.   They reviled him as a Papist;
they scorned him as a hypocrite.   Under the lead
of Dr. George Abbot, they pelted him with
pamphlets and sermons in which there were no
limits to abuse, until, in the words of one of the
vice-chancellors, "the pulpit and sacred function
of preaching became instruments of private revenge".[1]

Such a persecution was just what Laud enjoyed.   The point in his character which most

_____

[1] Wood's *Annals*, ii. 276.

surprised men was his confidence in himself.
He was now sure that he had been saved in
infancy for the special work of God. The words
" Blessed are ye when men shall persecute you
and revile you " elated him. His position became
rapidly strengthened, and his tenets took definite
shape. But he was no mere partisan; the
Church, he clearly discerned, must embrace all
parties, accepting what was true from Rome and
from Geneva alike. The strong personal piety of
Geneva attracted him, because of that inspiring
confidence in the presence of God which had sent
out the heroes against Spain, and had comforted
Cranmer and Latimer at the stake.[1] But the
mass of the people would need a beautiful ritual,
and carefully cultivated habits of devotion; they
must be stimulated to faith and hope by attendance at the Holy Communion, and by a well-
grounded confidence in the efficacy of their baptism. Hume has given a most just account of his
intentions when he writes: " Laud and his associates by reviving a few primitive ceremonies
corrected the error of the first reformers and presented to the frightened and astonished mind some
sensible exterior observances which might occupy
it during its religious exercises, and abate the
violence of its disappointed efforts ".[2] The gene-

---

[1] *Cf.* his patronage of Dr. Richard Sibbes, author of two
well-known devotional works, *The Bruised Reed and the Smoking
Flax*, and the *Soul's Conflict.*   [2] Hume's *England*, vii. 42.

ration which had grown up with him at Oxford
held to him, and had elected him proctor in 1603,
the first year in which he was qualified, by standing, for the office.   The election was so successful
that his enemies accused him of a well-organised
canvass;[1] and long after, when he was in the
Tower, Lord Saye and Sele taunted him as a
skilful organiser of a university faction, and "fit
for factions only".[2]   In reality, Laud had known
nothing of the honour in store for him, and was
much surprised at his election.   Every one laughed
at his little stature, at his confident and somewhat
fussy manner; but a man who can be caricatured
without becoming contemptible is certain of
success, and his genial, affectionate way of ruling
was favourably contrasted with that of a very
disagreeable colleague who discharged his proc-
torship, they said, "*cum parvo* (—*â*) Laude".[3]

But at this time he was drawn into an error
which his enemies never forgot, and which he
himself could never forget or forgive.   He had
become chaplain to the Earl of Devonshire,[4]
better known as Lord Mountjoy, a soldier distinguished in the Irish wars, and a man of
that affectionate and impulsive nature which was
frequently to call out Laud's devoted friendship.   Between this nobleman and the divorced

---

[1] Wood's *Fasti.*   [2] *Speech against the Bishops.*
[3] Wood's *Athenae,* ii. 55.   [4] *Diary,* 3rd Sept., 1603.

Lady Rich, he was persuaded, in the festivities of Christmastide, 1605, to perform the marriage ceremony. The king, James I., was incensed. The party with which Laud was associated was bitterly annoyed; one of their leaders, Dr. Howson, had just published a book on the sanctity of marriage. Friendship had persuaded Laud to an action which his judgment condemned, and his principles declared detestable. The abstemious, self-controlled, ecclesiastical leader, always a severe judge of his own actions, felt that he had condoned sin. St. Stephen's day, the anniversary of the marriage, was henceforth throughout his life a day of humiliation and bitter repentance.[1]

[1] See *Devotions*.

CHAPTER II.

Life and Work in the Country—Troubles of the Peasants— Contested Election at St. John's—Revival of Music and Art—Restoration of Ceremonial at Gloucester— Influence with the King—Nomination as Bishop.

THE wrong act of unthinking friendship related at the end of the last chapter ruined Laud's prospects of any high promotion for some five years. The larger part of this period was spent by him in country livings,[1] with an occasional return to Oxford. Bishop Neile of Rochester, a man of remarkable penetration in selecting capable men,[2] had become his patron, and was determined to bring him before the notice of the king directly the scandal of the Devonshire marriage was sufficiently forgotten ; meanwhile he employed Laud chiefly in his own diocese. These years of country retirement proved invaluable for the future ; Laud seldom failed to be interested in the duty which

[1] *Diary.*

[2] Neile was the son of a tallow-chandler, a most able controversialist and attractive preacher, but no great scholar. He was a trusted counsellor of James I. Godwin : Le Neve : Heylin.

(22)

lay to his hand, and spent his time in quietly and
humbly preaching the Gospel to the poor. In his
seclusion he formed for himself some ideal of the
life of a parish priest. There were already some
fine examples in England; Copinger at Laven-
ham had 900 communicants in his parish.[1] The
generation of Laud's friends and Laud's pupils was
soon to present a series of beautiful models, such
as Herbert at Bemerton, and Sanderson[2] at Booth-
by Pannel, who are instances chosen among scores
of devoted parish priests, many highly born[3] and
magnificently learned, ministering to rich and poor
alike. It was Laud's custom to set apart each year
a large proportion of his income to provide pen-
sions for the infirm and aged. He preached and
catechised, visited the sick and relieved the miserable, formed habits of regular prayer, and continued
his diligent studies.[4] Intercourse with the country
gentry and peasantry showed him how much the
poor suffered from oppression at the hands of local
magnates, and the serious distress under which,
as Acts of Parliament prove to us, large numbers
of the people then laboured. Barley-bread was
their staple food;[5] meat they seldom tasted; the
want of fuel[6] in the South of England made cooking
a luxury of the rich and deprived the labourers of

---

[1] Fuller's *History*.   [2] Walton's *Lives, passim*.

[3] *Cf.* Barnabas Oley, Preface to *Country Parson*, p. 131, ed.
1836.   [4] *Cf.* Herbert's *Country Parson*.

[5] *State Papers*, vol. 187, No. 12, show us buckwheat eaten by
the poor.   [6] *Cf.* Monson's *Naval Tracts*, p. 489.

all variety of diet.   The guilds which had succoured them in sickness, the prototypes of the
modern club, had been pillaged by Henry VIII.,
whose covetousness had involved these in the
ruin which he had wrought on so many institutions
connected with the Church.   And while the lower
middle classes were constantly advancing in wealth
and comfort, the poorest grew poorer year by year.
Employment was often hardly to be found ; and
the terrible laws against vagrants, framed by the
aristocratic Parliaments of Elizabeth and James,
brought imprisonment, flogging and even the
gallows upon hundreds of poor wretches who
were ready enough to work if they could find any
situations. [1]   All these sorrows of the peasants
Laud kept in his mind till his opportunity should
come.   Nor did he fail to comprehend that the
poorer classes, which formed after all the great
bulk of worshippers, needed thoughtful attention
if they were to be trained in the spiritual life.
The elaborate argumentative sermons which the
famous Puritan preachers loved and their disciples
imitated, left the huge mass of the nation, as
George Fox, the Quaker,[2] has so graphically told
us, in the condition of brute beasts.[3]   They heard

[1] See Baker's *Chronicle*, 412, for riots among the poor in 1609.
Eden's *State of the Poor*, i. 119, 139, 550, 596, etc.   Wheat was
32s. a quarter and wages were about 8d. a day (Eden, i. 152).   "The
number of the poor do dailie increase" says a tract of this time,
quoted by Eden, i. 155.   Wheat rose to 50s. at Norwich in 1630.

[2] *Autobiography.*

[3] *Cf.* appalling description in *State Papers*, 182, 1.

unheeding, for the preaching did not touch their lives. Indeed the preachers themselves said: "The ignorant peasants are like Bruits".[1]

Always resolutely practical and attentive to the most minute details, Laud made up his mind that simple instruction in the elements of the faith and a dignified and reverent worship were the first requisites in every parish church. When he had the power he would try to provide these throughout the country; and he was soon to be called to greater offices, in which he could do more to carry out his projects. In 1611 he was elected President of St. John's, after a hot contest;[2] and shortly afterwards appointed chaplain to the king. His influence in the university had been already restored, and he now became the recognised leader of a party little inferior in numbers and in power to the Puritan party. Above all, it was the party of the rising generation. With it was associated the revival of beautiful worship and of learning. Men began to feel tired of fierce denunciations of Rome, "fuller of railing than of reason,"[3] of severe logical arguments to prove the eternal ruin of the vast majority of mankind.[4] A milder religious feeling was gaining strength. Preachers spoke of the free-

[1] Baxter's *Autobiography*.　　[2] *Diary* and Heylin, p. 56.

[3] Laud's *Works* (folio), i. 160.

[4] See a good instance of such Puritan preaching in *State Papers*, vol. 280, No. 54.

will of each sinner which Almighty God was
longing to fortify with His loving grace. Careful
catechetical instructions in the moral and the
spiritual life were taking the place of abstruse
sermons on Sunday afternoons. The benefits to
be derived from the sacraments were being
emphatically taught by many of the parish clergy.
The communion-table, which had stood in the
middle of the church, a convenient receptacle for
hats and cloaks while the congregation listened to
a sermon, and often treated as the natural place to
sum up the parish accounts, was in many places
moved to the upper end of the chancel, railed
round and covered with silk or velvet. It was to
worship and not to preaching that attention was
now being directed. Beautiful church music was
sedulously cultivated in cathedrals and the great
churches, especially in London ;[1] since experience
seemed to indicate that it made worshippers more
conscious of the presence of God. The awful
mystery of the Holy Communion was treated
with reverence and solemnity ; for men felt that
there Christ actually approached their souls.
And as they realised the vastness of the love
and power of God, they were less willing to
condemn their neighbours, or to conceive it
possible that their personal opinions could form

[1] Orlando Gibbons was at this time organist of Westminster
Abbey (Burney, *History of Music*).

the only narrow ledge on which mankind might creep into heaven.[1]

With this milder and more liberal tone came a revival of learning. The old fathers were eagerly studied: Greek and Hebrew were cultivated: and, as leader of the movement, Laud already cherished hopes of setting up in England a Greek printing press, and developing the study of Oriental languages by founding professorships and accumulating manuscripts. It was noticed that the discipline of the university was stricter; more attention was given to study and less to controversy; by many men the wearing of the university dress was considered desirable and important, and the use of distinctive clerical attire was becoming the fashion. The College of St. John's was enlarged, and increased in numbers. Its services became stately and musical; to the horror of the Puritans an organ was erected in the chapel.[2] But angry attacks could now be treated with calm indifference. Everybody praised Laud's administration of the college; those who had opposed his election as president were won over by his conciliatory manners; and above all by the generous fashion in which he promoted them to college offices; the fairness of his judgment and his self-sacrifice for

[1] For an instance of the highly devout life of earnest Church laymen of the day read Howell's *Familiar Letters*, i. 193, 252-4 and *passim*.

[2] *Diary.*

the advantage of the society were spoken of on all sides.[1]   The clothmaker's son had become the strongest power in the University of Oxford, and through Oxford was influencing England.[2]

Still George Abbot, now appointed Arch-bishop of Canterbury by a Court intrigue, held the ear of the king; he had taught James I. to dread Laud as fussy and meddlesome; as one who stirred controversy and loved strife: and a mysterious atmosphere of Arminian heresies and Popish tendencies gathered round the mention of his name; his promotion in the Church was stopped, lest this incendiary should set all Eng-land on fire.   But the best answer to these charges was that where Laud was known he was popular, and was becoming acceptable to all parties; and accordingly in 1616,[3] when he was already forty-two, he was named Dean of Gloucester.

The deanery was poor and obscure; but it afforded opportunities to extend the rising Church party.   By the Puritans the cathedrals were treated as remnants of Popery, and were marked out for destruction; or, if this should prove impossible, they were determined that they should be used only as convenient halls for preaching.

But now Laud was specially commissioned by the king to restore dignity of worship at Glou-

[1] Wood's *Athenae*, ii. 56.   Laud's *Answer to Lord Saye and Sele about the Liturgy*, 474.

[2] Laud was appointed Archdeacon of Huntingdon in Decem-ber, 1615.   [3] *Diary*, November.

cester Cathedral.[1]   Supported by his residentiary
canons, he removed the communion-table to the
chancel and placed it altar-wise against the eastern
wall.

Once more the ponderous nave and delicate
lofty choir were brightened with surpliced proces-
sions, while strains of sweet and inspiring music
filled men's thoughts with anticipations of a
present God.   Choristers and clergy were taught
to bow towards the altar as they entered the
chancel, and to do reverence at the name of Jesus.
It was a practice which the new dean very
strongly advocated, as reminding worshippers of
the honour due to their Saviour and of the means
by which He imparted Himself to human souls.
But these innovations, as they called them, were
detestable to the Puritans ; and the old Bishop of
Gloucester, Miles Smith, a learned Hebraist and
one of the most distinguished of the translators
of the Bible,[2] refused to enter the cathedral till
the former arrangements were restored.   To him
the change seemed a return to Popery, and the
full horror of that fiery persecution was familiar
enough to his memory, though forgotten by the
younger generation.   It was an unavoidable
collision between the new and the old.   The aged,
conservative bishop, who felt that he needed no
outward signs and aids to worship when he would
hold communion with the God of his long life

---

[1] Laud's *Works*, vi. 239, 241.   [2] Wood's *Annals*, 228.

and expected all others to meet God as easily as
he did, was irritated and incensed by the more
liberal dean, who in his turn could not give way
because he found the need of music and ceremonial to keep the mysterious presence of God
clear and real to men deafened by the bustle of
the world.

There were fierce Puritan sermons preached
in the city of which the martyr Hooper had been
bishop—Hooper who had suffered imprisonment
rather than wear the surplice ; and there appeared
even a danger of ritual riots, but they were
speedily suppressed by the civic authorities, who
welcomed the more beautiful services, were delighted to be free of the interminably long controversial sermons, and were by no means averse to
a religious teaching which seemed more tolerant
of their weakness, and made no sins of merriment
and recreation.   Laud's influence at Gloucester
does not however appear to have been very strong,
while the violent preaching of his opponents
kindled that bitter sectarian spirit which was afterwards to make the town a stronghold of Parliamentary opposition, and then to tear it asunder in
an internecine strife which Baxter describes as
rendering it one of the most unhappy places in the
country.[1] Dividing his time between the Court, the
university and the city of Gloucester, Laud continued to enhance his reputation ; now defining

[1] *Autobiography*, p. 41.

and defending the position of the English Church against Rome ; now entering upon vigorous controversy against the promoters of Presbyterianism; now explaining the Declaration of Sports by which King James encouraged recreation and amusement on Sunday after the afternoon service. Consequently the shrewd king, intensely fond of clever sermons, who had almost compelled the eloquent Donne to be ordained because he was convinced he could sway London from the pulpit of St. Paul's,[1] became increasingly interested in Laud, and in 1621 had him elected and consecrated Bishop of St. David's.

Ecclesiastical and political power had been long deferred ; he was forty-eight, and the first vigour of his life was gone ; but he had enjoyed a completeness of training such as was the good hap of none of his chief contemporaries in Church or State. He had passed through every grade in the university, had been the familiar friend of great scholars, both English and foreign, with whom he had studied the chief necessities of the time in research and in education. He had learnt how to control subordinates; how to conciliate his equals; and how to hold his own without disrespect to his superiors. In his parish incumbencies he had experienced for himself the difficulties of the country clergy, stripped of many of the old endowments[2] and thwarted by the

---

[1] Walton's *Life of Donne.* Baker's *Chronicle*, p. 427. Both writers were personal friends of Donne.

[2] All through his life he did his utmost to improve the miser-

power of the local magnates in their efforts after
a more refined worship and for more definite
instruction of their people.   He had noted the
dull, hard life of the peasants under the despotic
control of Puritan nobles and gentry,[1] who even
on Sunday permitted no brightness or enjoyment
to their dependants.   At Gloucester he had been
confronted with the growing indolence of the
cathedral chapters.   He had recognised the
various causes which were sapping the power
and influence of the bishops.   And he began to
think he saw how the strength and usefulness of
the Church could be restored ; and the means by
which Gospel preaching and solemn worship might
become both real restraints upon brutal passions
and inspirations to holiness.   At least he would
not fail from ignorance of the people he had to
govern, or want of sympathy with the masses ;
and he was convinced that God Himself had
appointed him to a great career.   Nor was he
unsupported by the approval of the nation, for
no one was more definitely marked out by the
popular voice for high office than Dr. William Laud.

able incomes of the clergy, often not £3 a year. *Cf. Accounts of
Province*, 554, etc., and his quarrel with Abbot, who cared nothing
for the clergy, *Diary*, 29th March, 1624. Sir H. Spelman tells
us that the tithes of 3845 incumbencies had fallen into lay hands,
while 5439 still remained to the clergy (*Apology*, 35).   Only 144
Benefices in England were worth over £40 a year (*State Papers*,
vol. 279, No. 7).

[1] *Cf.* laws to forbid working people to enter the alehouses, and
dislike shown by Parliament to social guilds (Eden, i. 143, 597).

Sir T. Baker's *Chronicle of the Reign of James I.*, continued for Charles I. by another hand; Laud's *Conference with Fisher*; Laud's *Letters*; Speeches in the *Parliamentary History*; Baxter's *Autobiography*; Rushworth's *Collections*; Harrington's *Works*; Herbert's *Works*; Laud's *Diary* becomes much fuller after 1621.

CHAPTER III.

Laud's Conception of the Episcopal Office—The Commons and the Constituencies—The King—Laud's Diocesan Administration—Conference with Fisher—Royal Instructions on Preaching—The Two Parties in the Church.

LAUD had long desired a bishopric. He was perfectly well aware of his talents for rule. He was bent upon carrying out in practice the great schemes which he had dreamed over in youth and steadily thought out in middle life. More than once in his letters to his friends he complains that he is being passed over for inferior men. Frankly ambitious, he never assumed that decent or prudish veil of modesty with which so many conceal their desire for high office. Nothing could have been farther from his thoughts than to hesitate about occupying a prominent place in the management of Church and State directly he could get it ; and now he rejoiced that his opportunity was come.

Elevation to the episcopate completely revolutionises a clergyman's position : at one step he becomes a ruler, and a ruler invested with a commission from Christ Himself, all the more impres-

(35)

sive to others, all the more awful to himself, because it is indefinite. The bishop dares not be disobeyed ; rather true humility of the heart dictates firmness to the most timid will ; since, ruling as Laud maintained *jure divino*,[1] he feels himself to be under the personal control of God's Spirit in directing the affairs of the Church.

Every bishop has an anxious responsibility to see that Church rights and Church privileges are not diminished under his charge. And at the crisis of national history in which Laud lived, it seemed certain to him that he was called upon by God to vindicate the influence of the Church against the magnates of the land. Without acknowledging this fixed idea, whether we call it fanatical or see in it a real mission, we can never appreciate Laud's life and character.

But in order to regain her independence the Church needed allies ; and could there be any doubt as to the expediency of maintaining the alliance which had now lasted so many years between the Church and the Crown ? The men who had helped Laud to his high position, Bishop Neile and Bishop Buckeridge, were personal friends of the king : while they were already

---

[1] *Speech against Leighton*, and *Speech on the Censure of Burton, Prynne and Bastwick. Cf. Diary*, January, 1627, where he speaks of the importance of printing Andrewes' opinion to the same effect; and *Answer to Lord Saye's Speech against the Bishops*, where Laud maintains that our Saviour had Himself instituted the episcopal office (pp. 18, 19).

disliked and distrusted by the great rival power in the State, which now began to assert itself, the majority in the House of Commons.

A combination of two important classes, the country gentlemen and the burgesses of the large trading communities, composed this majority, working at a similar policy under very different impulses. The country gentry felt and resented the curb which by the legal system of England the Crown had placed upon their authority in their own districts, but they were equally jealous of the reviving power of the Church. The great towns, in constant communication with the business circles of the City,[1] followed the lead of London, and in London James I. and Charles I. after him were personally unpopular. James from his awkwardness and conceit of wisdom, Charles from his refined tastes and stately silence, were ill-fitted by nature to gain the affections of the populace of their capital.[2] They did not, perhaps they could not, resort to those little tricks of popularity by which their great predecessor Queen Elizabeth, and their clever successor Charles II., turned the citizens of London into a royal bodyguard. In London the two first

---

[1] Baxter's *Autobiography*. Dr. Stoughton says that in the first election under Charles II., when London had elected Opposition members, ministers stopped the post for fear of the effect on the other constituencies.

[2] Heylin's *Life of Laud*.

Stuart kings seldom showed themselves, and many of its inhabitants did not even know them by sight.[1] This unpopularity had been increased of late years by the unthrifty administration of Buckingham, which had weakened credit and left the Channel at the mercy of pirates. Moreover, London was the stronghold of Puritanism ; in the early days of King James his Calvinistic bias had increased the number of Puritan preachers in the capital ; afterwards foreign intercourse, and the great immigration from Flanders and from France, had swollen the Puritan ranks.

Thus the influence of London and of the country gentry secured successive majorities in the Parliaments of James and Charles, which insisted on limiting the royal prerogative and supported the Puritan party in the Church. But men who knew the motives which decided the elections, and the restricted numbers of the electorate, could hardly regard the opinion of the Commons as endowed with that semi-sanctity with which it has been invested by many modern writers ; while there was certainly some foundation for the claim of Laud and his associates that they themselves were the defenders of the people against an overweening aristocracy[2] and a purse-

---

[1] Heylin's *Life of Laud.*

[2] Harrington's *Valerius and Publicola :* "The people then under lords dared not to elect otherwise than as pleased the lords ". The *Oceana* shows how dissatisfied thinking men were with the

proud plutocracy, which together were able to manipulate the Lower House. Even to the end, when he was imprisoned by the triumphant Commons of the Long Parliament, Laud maintained that he represented the larger and the better part of the people.[1] And already an intense distrust of the House of Commons, almost amounting to hatred, was growing up in the minds of himself and his friends. It was a fatal jealousy, but it was no unreasoned prejudice. They felt that the Commons were really intent on stifling all freedom of opinion in religion and in politics ; hostile to that growth of art, learning, and literature, which was to become the glory of the Laudian *régime ;* insisting on immunity for the vices of the upper class,[2] while they deprived the down-trodden peasants of their innocent amusements ; champions of a bitter persecution even to death of harmless Romish priests and Popish recusants;[3] while abroad the so-called popular House cared nothing for a high policy, such as should make England the honoured arbiter of the nations. Indeed, too often their conception of international relations was that of the free-booter: "We are poor," said Sir John Eliot in one memorable debate, "Spain

elections. The Parliaments of James I. passed several acts to keep down wages, evidently in the interests of the rich (Eden, i. 142).

[1] *Speech in Defence of the Bishops*, p. 42, published in 1641.

[2] See proceedings against Laud for his punishment of Lady Purbeck and others. [3] Sir R. Verney's *Diary*, p. 147.

is rich.   There are our Indies.   Break with them,
we shall break our necessities together."[1]   And it
seemed to show an incapacity for great affairs when
the Commons,[2] after insisting that the Government should declare war to help the Calvinist
cause in Germany, dealt out money with a hand
so niggardly that it was never possible to strike
any blow of importance.[3]   Indeed in the long
economical reign of Elizabeth they appear to have
lost the conception of generous giving.[4]

All men in the nineteenth century are agreed
that the Commons under the Stuarts, in spite of
their shortcomings, were guiding the Constitution
into the course which could best ensure English
greatness and English freedom.   But this was
certainly not evident in 1621.   Rather it seemed
to very many that the victory of the Commons
meant a tyrannical aristocratic Government, and
that the king was the true protector of the poor.
Therefore Laud naturally allied himself with King
James, and attempted to rebuild the power of the
Church with his support.

The character of James I. has seldom been
fairly treated by historians ;[5] the king was a

---

[1] Quoted by S. R. Gardiner, *Buckingham and Charles I.*, i. 30.

[2] In 1624.   [3] *Parl. Hist.*, vi. 103 ff. and 336.

[4] Père d'Orléans, viii. 23, shows us the foreign opinion on this
matter.   *Cf.* Carte's *Ormond*, i. 50.

[5] See among others, Baker, 426 ; Fuller ; Carte's *Ormond* on
the settlement of Ulster ; and most of James's contemporaries, for

learned scholar and fond of ecclesiastical order. Association with the writers and artists, who were attracted to the Court by the Prince of Wales and the Marquis of Buckingham, had modified his earlier predilection for Calvinism ; and, as he grew older, he grew more devout. The beautiful services which one of his chaplains, Dean Williams, had instituted in Westminster Abbey,[1] and which were imitated in the Chapels Royal, satisfied the cravings of the king, who was as sentimental as he was conscientious, for comfort and for rest. He cordially endorsed Donne's expression : "Oh, the power of church music ! that harmony added to this hymn has raised the affections of my heart, and quickened my graces of zeal and fortitude ".[2]

The sermons, at once learned and spiritual, by Bishop Andrewes, and a galaxy of famous preachers whom he had appointed to be his chaplains, provided him with that intellectual food and that philosophical support by which he was enabled to resist the enticements of the insinuating Jesuit confessors who gained over so many of his less thoughtful contemporaries. It was Andrewes whom he summoned to preach before

a very high estimate of his abilities: on the contrary, Mrs. Hutchinson, and Weldon's scandalous *Memoirs.*

[1] See Hacket's *Life of Williams* for the pretty pride with which the dean exhibited his service to the French ambassadors, as superior to theirs.

[2] Walton's *Lives,* i. 74.

him on the great festivals of the Church. It
was for Andrewes' ministration that he called
constantly on his death-bed. The king, therefore,
appeared to Laud the safest and strongest ally in
his far-reaching schemes ; and he set himself to
gain over the royal mind such an influence as his
brother-prelates, Neile the Clerk of the Closet,
and Andrewes the Dean of the Chapels Royal,
now enjoyed. He could see nothing inconsistent
in combining the office of a minister of State with
that of a bishop ; and frequently quoted the
example of many great English saints, of St.
Ambrose and St. Augustine, and of the high
priests and prophets among the Israelites.[1]

Though he was seldom consulted on political
affairs during the first years of his episcopate, the
new Bishop of St. David's became at once a man
of marked influence in questions which concerned
the Church. And as the rulers of 1621 would
soon vanish from the scene, the prim Oxford
don, whose genial humour and keen sarcasm
rendered him so conspicuous a figure at Court,
and who was possessed of the uncommon gift of
making the gayest courtier think about spiritual
concerns, would shortly rise to the first place in
the State, and have his opportunity to show
whether ecclesiastical rule was possible in England in the seventeenth century. Fuller describes
him to us as "of low stature but high parts :

[1] *Answer to Lord Saye in Defence of the Bishops*, pp. 1-22.

piercing eyes, cheerful countenance, wherein gravity and pleasantness were well compounded, admirable in his naturals, unblamable in his morals, being very strict in his conversation ":[1] evidently a person well equipped for the great task which he believed God had set him.

Before Laud's consecration an untoward event occurred which had a most serious effect on the history of the Church. Shooting in Lord Zouch's forest, Archbishop Abbot let fly his shaft into a herd of deer, and killed the keeper, who was driving them towards the huntsmen. Had he (it was the ecclesiastical excitement of the moment) by his ugly deed rendered himself irregular and forfeited his archbishopric? and if so, who would succeed him? It was natural that this question of the succession should have its unnoticed influence in forming the opinion even of the learned as to his offence. Edward Coke, the greatest of living lawyers, who loved Abbot as a Puritan, and dreaded some High Church successor, pronounced it legal for bishops to hunt, since by the common law a bishop was to bequeath to the king his pack of hounds. If he had hounds he must hunt; if he hunted such accidents could not be avoided; so argued the acute lawyer.[2]

Two clergymen stood forward in all men's eyes as likely to be primates. The Lord Keeper, Wil-

[1] Fuller's *Worthies*, i. 90. [2] Heylin's *Life*, p. 82.

liams, Dean of Westminster, was on the eve of
consecration to the great and rich see of Lincoln.
He was a man of decent personal piety, most
attentive to the outward decorum of the Church
services, a sagacious administrator, liberal in his
ecclesiastical opinions and gifted with singular
penetration in reading the signs of the times.   But
he was not trusted by the clergy : they doubted
his   sincerity   and   questioned   his   truthfulness.
They believed him capable of any intrigue to hold
his power.   It was often remarked that he tried
to keep well with all parties, and that in spite of
his professions of disinterested zeal he had accumulated in his own hands many rich benefices.
Nor did he succeed in his efforts to win the affections of the Puritans ; Lord Saye said of him :
"Were our Saviour upon earth the Bishop of
Lincoln would betray Him again, if He stood
cross to his ends ".[1]

The other candidate was the ideal bishop of
the day, Andrewes of Winchester, a man of saintly
and beautiful life, against whom, even in those
libellous times, none had ever dared to breathe a
breath of scandal : one of the greatest scholars,
and the greatest preacher of his generation ; whose
sermons are even now read with enjoyment and
admiration for their piety of reflection, their wise
counsel and their deep theological learning.
Once already the voice of the nation had desig-

---

[1] Quoted in D'Israeli's *Charles I.*

nated him as the fittest primate, when a Court
intrigue had seated Abbot in the chair of St.
Augustine.   He was absolutely free from worldly
ambition, and never sought to extend his influence
beyond the pulpit and the altar.   But Williams
had the ear of the king and the ear of Buckingham, and Court influence was again likely to out-
weigh personal merit.

Probably this dread decided the question :
High Church bishops and Puritan lawyers alike[1]
supported the legality of a royal rescript to remove
Abbot's disabilities.   He was restored to his
position, though his authority in Church affairs
was gone.   Neither Williams nor Laud would
receive consecration from a primate whose hands,
as they said, were stained with human blood ; and
they were consecrated by a commission of bishops
selected by the king.[2]

To the Puritans, who rejected all meaning in
episcopal consecration, these scruples seemed
ridiculous and superstitious.   By men who were
engaged in maintaining against Roman contro-
versialists the genuine character of English orders,
and the purity of the apostolical succession in
the English Church, they were felt to be most
serious ;[3] nor were they despised by that widespread class of thoughtful and devout laymen

---

[1] Howell's *Familiar Letters*, i. 107.

[2] Heylin's *Life of Laud*, 82.   *Diary, sub anno* 1621.

[3] See Spelman, *Works*, ii. 112.   *Cf.* Panzani's *Memoirs*.

whose influence is so conspicuous through these troubled times.[1]

At first three great ecclesiastical interests absorbed the new bishop's attention, and his treatment of them defined his position before the watchful eyes of the nation. These were (1) the condition of his diocese, (2) the growing propaganda of Romanism, and (3) the angry preaching of the Puritans. As a diocesan bishop Laud did not distinguish himself until his promotion to the see of London. Distant St. David's was hardly a diocese to which in those days an ecclesiastic full of ambition was likely to banish himself. A very few months was all that St. David's saw of her bishop during his five years' episcopate. The long journey, the rough and miry roads, the ignorant and scattered population seemed to the scholar and courtier sufficient excuses for non-residence.[2] Though later in life he became a severe disciplinarian in the matter of episcopal residence, and compelled his suffragans to give their personal attention to the round of diocesan duties, now he lived in London and the neighbourhood ; candidates for ordination had to travel up to the capital to their bishop ; confirmations must have been few and irregular, and

[1] The lives of men like Lord Derby, the Dukes of Richmond and Ormond, Lord Capel, Lord Falkland, Mr. Hyde, Herbert's friend Mr. Woodnot, etc., illustrate this.

[2] Comp. *Works*, vi. 247, and *Diary*, 24th Aug., 1625, and *State Papers*, vol. 150, No. 110.

yet the men of his school were perfectly well
aware that in the growing neglect of confirmation
lay one of the most ready handles for their Puritan
opponents.[1]   Where was the need of bishops if
baptism was complete without their blessing?
They were intriguing at Whitehall for better
preferment, men said, leaving any wolves, who
chose, to devour their flocks.   And in his latter
years there is nothing which Laud in his reports
to the king notes as a surer proof of the increasing
power of the Church than that people have come
"very thick to receive confirmation, to the number of
some thousands in the diocese of Peterborough".[2]

None the less the bishop was in constant
correspondence with his officials on matters of
discipline and administration.   There is a curious
entry in his *Diary* of indignation against a salt-
petre-maker who had desecrated the graves at
Brecon in search of saltpetre,[3] which illustrates
how attentive he was even to details.   He provided his house at Abergwilly with a handsome
chapel.   He devoted much time and money to
putting the churches of the diocese in order;
and visited and preached assiduously when his
duties at Court could be conveniently left.   There
was very little Puritanism in Wales;[4] the people

---

[1] Heylin, p. 10.   [2] *Account of Province*, 1639.

[3] *Diary*. 13th December, 1624.

[4] It will be remembered that Wales was universally on the
royal side through the Civil War.

were devout and attentive to worship.   It was not hard for a bishop to persuade himself that he was more wanted elsewhere.   But the Church suffered.

Meanwhile Laud was devoting his powers to what appeared to be the most threatening danger of the moment.   Roman Catholicism was again on the increase in England.   The king was hankering after a Spanish match for his son, Prince Charles.   Under the crafty influence of the Spanish ambassador, Gondomar, the penal laws against Romanism had been laid aside to rust.   Roman priests swarmed in England, secular priests and Jesuits, bitter in dislike towards each other,[1] and all the more diligently rivalling one another in making converts.   Hundreds of families who had conformed for a time were being reconciled to Rome, especially in the North. And at Court the Jesuits were very successful. The Papacy still exercised a magic charm over people who wished to enjoy all the pleasures and advantages of this life and yet find heaven's gate open at the last hour : and it was becoming the fashion for statesmen, courtiers and great ladies to have a Romish priest smuggled into their chamber of death.   The first hot zeal of the Reformation, the fierce, irreconcilable detestation of Rome as the Scarlet Woman and the Crowned Antichrist, was fast cooling.   And just as in France Protestantism was being steadily ex-

[1] Panzani's *Memoirs*.

tinguished since Henry IV. had said the Crown
of France was well worth a Mass, and persuaded
his courtiers to imitate his example ; so the cultivated classes of England, who shrank from Puritanism with its professed preference for what was
bare and ugly, its jealousy of music and decoration and ritual as hindrances to the simple meeting
of the soul face to face with God, were likely to
be drawn insensibly into Romanism, unless some
middle way could be attractively set before them.
"I could speak with no conscientious persons
almost, that were wavering in religion, but the great
motion which wrought upon them to disaffect, or
think meanly of the Church of England, was that
the external worship of God was so lost in the
Church (as they conceived it) ; and the Churches
themselves and all things in them suffered to lie
in such a base and slovenly fashion in most places
in the kingdom."[1]

The English religious leaders were meeting
this tendency by elaborating beautiful worship,
by disciplining the religious feeling, by declaring
without compromise the mysterious efficacy of
Holy Communion, by well-reasoned preaching.
Anglicans felt they had by no means the worst of
the arguments. "Where was your religion to be
found before Luther?" inquired a clever priest at
Rome of Sir Henry Wotton. "My religion was
to be found then where yours is not to be found

[1] Laud in *Trials and Troubles*, p. 156.

4

now, in the written word of God," replied Sir
Henry; "but do you believe all those many
thousands of poor Christians were damned that
were excommunicated because the Pope and the
Duke of Venice could not agree about their temporal power, even those poor Christians that knew
not why they quarrelled?" "Monsieur," cautiously
replied the priest in French, "excusez moi."[1]

But Buckingham was on the point of being
gained to Rome;[2] his mother was almost a professed convert;[3] and the king, always a zealous
Anglican, thought it well to organise public conferences for controversy between the courtier
Jesuit confessors, and some of the learned scholars
of the English Church.   It fell to Laud's share to
bring out in strong relief the differences between
the Churches.   This he did by challenging the
adoration of images; the invocation of saints;
the adoration of the Sacrament; the administration in one kind only; the doctrine of purgatory;
and prayer in an unknown tongue.   It was from
the Bible that he derived all his arguments; it
was the defence of the authority and sufficiency of
the Bible to which he devoted his most careful
dialectic.[4]   "Religion," he said, "as it is professed

---

[1] Walton's *Lives*, i. 187.

[2] Père d'Orléans, ix., 240 shows us the Jesuit hopes of gaining
him.

[3] *Diary*, 23rd April, 1622.

[4] See the *Book against Fisher*, and specially pp. 48-58 and 80-
95 for the authority of Scripture.   It took him so much time to

in the Church of England is nearest of any Church now in being to the Primitive Church, and therefore not a religion known to be false." The conferences were published later,[1] and exhibit the wide learning and the acute intellect of the Bishop of St. David's ; his bitterest enemies in religious opinion admitted it was the strongest book on the subject.[2] And though the Countess of Buckingham was held back from Rome only for a short period, her son, now Marquis of Buckingham, was henceforth a firm and soon a devout Anglican. Taking Laud as his spiritual counsellor[3] he was once more seen at the Holy Communion ; he entered keenly into the English differences with Rome and with the Puritans, and became a vigorous supporter of the great bulk of Englishmen, both clergy and laity, who refused to break the links with the past and to destroy the old Church constitution, while they rejected what they considered the superstitions of the middle ages and the usurped power of the Papacy. For the time the advance of Romanism was stayed ; and Laud was marked in the Roman archives as a man to be gained at any cost or to be destroyed.[4]

prepare this for publication that he had, most unwillingly, to give up preaching in his later years.

[1] *Works*, vol. ii., in Anglo-Catholic Library.

[2] *e.g.*, Sir E. Dering (Wood's *Athenae*, ii. 65).

[3] *Diary*, 9th June, 1622.

[4] Testimony of the Roman hatred is given in Wharton's edition of Laud's *Works* i. 616, in Laud's *Trials and Troubles*, p. 338,

But the Puritan party were only the more incensed against him. The Jesuits should be executed, not reasoned with, they said.[1] The concession that Rome was a part, though a corrupt part, of Christ's Church, was to them insufferable. In his later days the heaviest charges would be those which imputed to him Romanising tendencies, and made it treasonable that he had connived at the existence of seditious Jesuits, who taught that persecuting kings might rightfully be deposed.

But the Jesuits were not the only teachers who maintained the right of deposing tyrannical kings. A sermon preached by Mr. Knight, Fellow of Broadgate (or Pembroke), at Oxford, put forth the doctrine that resistance to the king was justifiable if he turned tyrant, or forced blasphemy or idolatry upon his subjects— ominous growlings of distant storms. The vice-chancellor impounded Knight, and requested Laud as an Oxford bishop to bring the matter before the king. Knight escaped with a scolding;[2] but the fierce controversial preaching of the Puritans against Papists and Anglicans was considered so dangerous that the liberty of preaching was curtailed by royal letter issued to the archbishops. Preachers were to follow

by Sir H. Mildmay, a Puritan M.P., and for Laud's own conviction of it, see pp. 16 and 162.

[1] S. R. Gardiner's *History*, *passim*.   [2] Heylin, 91.

the articles ; in the afternoon they were to cate-
chise ;[1] politics in the pulpit were forbidden ;
controversy was limited, and none but bishops
and deans were to handle in public such subjects
as predestination, election, reprobation, and the
universality or irresponsibility of God's grace.
All preachers were exhorted to pay special attention to the rules of life.[2] Little did the royal
counsellors, among whom both Williams of
Lincoln and Laud of St. David's must at this
time be reckoned, realise how impossible it was
for the passionate Puritan, convinced of his former
sin and his present election by God into a state
of indefeasible grace,[3] to shut up his beliefs in his
own heart. Even hard-working and educated
preachers like Gouge and Sibbes were harassed
by such prohibitions. As for the extreme Puritans
who would not hesitate to wade deep in blood on
their grand but hopeless crusade for erecting on
earth the reign of God's saints, they could not

[1] See for the way this was carried out the charges against
Bishop Harsnet, *Parliamentary History*, vi. 316, and Laud's
Accounts of his Province, pp. 526, 540, 541, 545 and *passim*.

[2] Heylin, 93 and 94. They were issued 4th August, 1622.

See Carlyle's *Cromwell*, letter ii. Prynne did not hesitate to
say : " Let any true saint of God be taken away in the very act of any
known sin, before it is possible for him to repent ; I make no doubt
or scruple of it, but he shall be as surely saved as if he had lived
to have repented of it ".

And see Bancroft's assertion at the Savoy Conference, in
1605, that the doctrine of predestination was producing much
wickedness of life.

suffer such shackles for an instant.   How dull
sounded now the simple moral and religious pre-
cepts of the Sermon on the Mount to the ears
of men who had wrangled over the awful question
of the Divine Fore-knowledge, and who considered the future of each man as "o'er-ruled by
fate inextricable, and strict necessity".   Certain
that they alone could be saved, what recked the
more fanatical Puritans, who were soon to be
masters in England, of the fate of the bodies or
the souls of the worthless crowd around them!
Toleration of opinion was as yet impossible;
Laud would try to enforce it and would fail.
Toleration of different forms of outward worship
and organisation was still more impossible and
was detestable to Puritan and liberal Churchman
alike.[1]   Fire and steel would have to decide
whether scholar or enthusiast should preach the
Gospel; and they would settle at the same time
whether king or gentry should control the Civil
Government.   There are moments in the life of
nations when a struggle between opposing tendencies is inevitable; and the sects must either
have been trodden into toleration of other opinions,
or left free to work out to logical limits their tenets
of election.   Moderation they could never tolerate;
and it was no Puritan, but Jeremy Taylor, a pupil
of Laud, and himself soon to be an Anglican bishop,

[1] See Bacon, essay *De Unitate Ecclesiae;* and the speeches
in Parliament, *passim.*

who was to plead with the English Government for
"the Liberty of Prophesying".

As we turn from the pages of Milton, compelled to an unanticipated sympathy with the
hero of the epic, the fallen archangel, full
of thoughts of strife and war and wrath, to
the sweet, soothing, spiritual songs of George
Herbert, the saintly poet of the Laudian movement, of whose *Temple* 20,000 copies were sold in
a few years to be the comfort of 20,000 English
households, we see vividly how irreconcilable
were these two parties. To Marshall or to
Burgess, to Prynne or even to Baxter, the
parsonage life of Bemerton was contemptibly
mean, with its gentle toleration, its simple helpful-
ness of sympathy, its humble self-forgetfulness.
The vision of God which inspired the Ironsides
at Drogheda and Dunbar was not the vision of
God portrayed in Herbert's study :—

> Then weep, mine eyes, the God of love doth grieve;
>   Weep, foolish heart,
>   And weeping live,
> For death is dry as dust. Yet, if we part,
>   Sad as the night whose sable hue
>   Your sins express; melt into dew.

In the clash of the strife between Jesuit and
Puritan in England and throughout Europe, the
school of Laud and Andrewes, and Herbert and
Izaac Walton turned their eyes upon that "dear
mother" Church of England, whom they felt to
be truly evangelical.

A fine aspect in fit array,
Neither too mean, nor yet too gay,
    Shows who is best :
Outlandish looks may not compare ;
For all they either painted are
    Or else undrest.

So the last years of King James passed
stormily along. The Bishop of St. David's had
little part to play in the wild excitement of that
strange Spanish match, which sent Charles on his
madcap journey to Madrid, and seemed likely for
a few months after his return to despatch English
armies in chivalrous career over Germany to
drive back the advancing forces of Rome.

The warmth of Laud's heart flames out in
entries in his *Diary*, in special prayers composed
for private use, in rejoicings over the safe return,
in watchfulness that the absent duke at Madrid
should not lose his power with the king ; for this
sedate, severe bishop was the most faithful of
friends, and capable of feeling and inspiring the
most sincere affection. But his hand is shown
only in the careful attention paid to the arrangements of Anglican worship in the prince's household while he was at the Spanish Court ; in order
that his Christian faith might be justified to the
ignorant and scoffing Spaniards, who spoke of the
English as pagans ; and that he himself might
compare it favourably with the sumptuous ritual
of Rome.[1]

---

[1] See in Heylin the vessels and linen to be provided for the
altar, and Howell's *Letters* from Madrid.

On 27th March, 1625, King James I. died after a short illness, and the news reached White-hall while the Bishop of St. David's was preaching before the Court a Lenten sermon, which the sobs of the Duke of Buckingham and his own emotions terminated abruptly.[1]

[1] *Diary*, 27th March, 1625.

For the projects of the aristocracy, see note A on p. 292.

FURTHER AUTHORITIES.

The Calendars of State Papers; Laud's *Sermons; Memoirs of Sir Philip Warwick;* Hamond L'Estrange's *History of the Reign of Charles I.;* Clarendon's *Life;* Clarendon's *History of the Rebellion;* Mrs. Hutchinson's *Memoir* of her husband ; May's *History of the Long Parliament ;* Macpherson's *Annals of Commerce ;* Lilly's *Life and Times.*

CHAPTER IV.

UNDER THE MINISTRY OF BUCKINGHAM, 1625-1628.

Character of Charles I. and of Buckingham—Points of Dispute between King and Commons—Nicholas Ferrar —Dr. Montague and the Remonstrance of the Three Bishops—Commission of Bishops—Sermon on Unity to Third Parliament of Charles—Death of Buckingham.

CHARLES I. ascended the throne under the most favourable auspices. The people were delighted at the breach of the Spanish match. and the preparations for a religious war. The new king was known to be scrupulously conscientious and devoutly religious. It was noted that, unlike his father, at the special request of Bishop Laud he joined in the prayers of the Royal Chapel, instead of expecting the sermon to be commenced immediately upon his entrance.[1] They heard with approval how sternly he rebuked an Irish Romanist noble who interrupted the royal devotions by loud conversation in the anteroom. Men whispered about the story that the prince had said to his favourite bishop that he could never be a lawyer since nothing would induce him to plead the cause of a rascal.[2]

[1] Laud's *Diary*.   [2] *Ibid.*, 1st February, 1624.

Scholars and writers and artists were captivated with a sovereign who was not only a patron but a genuine admirer of all that was beautiful and well written; and who himself was no mean student in literature, "a competent judge in music,"[1] and in art an accomplished critic of the styles of the great painters of the Renaissance. Rubens and Vandyke painted for him; Milton wrote masques and pastorals for his courtiers; Waller, Davenant, Crashaw and Herbert were among the band of graceful and devotional poets who expressed the feelings and aspirations of the dominant party. Manuscripts of Greek, Arabic and Hebrew were added to the libraries; and the royal collection of pictures was soon to be the best in Europe; while the faultless architecture of Inigo Jones was ready to construct palaces and porticoes and galleries for the refined pleasures of an educated society delighting in the revival of art and learning.

Dignified and silent; passionately proud of England; loving order and decent economy; upright in all his dealings, and a pure and dutiful husband,[2] Charles seemed to be the king exactly suited to the mind of the serious Englishmen who formed the bulk of the middle classes. He had none of the pedantry and none of the insolence of his father. He was brave, and intent on making his country play a chief part in the affairs of the world.

[1] Playford, quoted by Burney, iii. 361.

[2] Mrs. Hutchinson's *Memoirs*, p. 127.

Parliament seemed to him his surest and strongest ally in the struggle which he now proposed to undertake against Romanism in Germany.

Why, then, did such a king fail? Undoubtedly because of the mistakes of his early years, and the undisciplined character of his first Prime Minister. The Duke of Buckingham had been intoxicated by too facile a success. Magnificently handsome, extraordinarily attractive, quick at expedients, prolific of great ideas, he had no patience and no diligence.[1] Having made himself necessary to Charles by his assistance in the Spanish journey and the French marriage, he had been allowed to treat the new king as his equal, and felt himself privileged to despise every other Englishman. He had enriched himself and his family at the expense of the nation. "Hark how the waggons creak with their rich lading," said a shrewd observer,[2] as men who had come to Court "with the common carrier" were seen driving home with "a full train of baggage". In so doing, and by his extravagant wars, he disordered the finances and left the State loaded with a debt which all Laud's thriftiness could only gradually pay off.

Nor was Charles the man to set himself right with his people. An impediment in his speech made him dislike speaking in public, and he felt

[1] See Clarendon's *History*, i. 48-64.

[2] See Lilly's *Memoirs*, and Weldon's *Court of King James*.

that a few words from the royal pen ought to be enough to clear up all misunderstandings. But, as will appear, an explanation of the royal policy was the last thing the leaders of the Opposition desired.

Historians and essayists take pleasure in discussing how the king and the Parliament might have been reconciled ; in discoursing, as if in some nineteenth century newspaper, on the value of responsible ministers, and the advantage that a king should reign and should not govern ; in pointing out exactly where the sovereign exceeded his rights, and where the Parliament overpressed its claims. Such discussions waste ink. The king was master ; for 150 years the kings of England had been masters, choosing their own ministers, and using their Parliaments as a means sometimes to ascertain and redress the grievances of their subjects, sometimes to support their own power by the proof which the easy passage of new laws afforded that the nation was united in the decision. By the aid of Parliament, and because the nation and the king wished it, the power of the feudal nobles had been swept away. By Act of Parliament, at the suggestion of the king, the Papal authority in England had been abolished and the monasteries destroyed. By the advice of Parliament acting under the lead of her ministers, Queen Elizabeth had set forward England as the leader of the anti-Romanist party in Europe, and had succoured and founded the Republic of the Low Countries.   Yet opposition in Parliament had been crushed and often punished by the Tudor sovereigns.   Above all Queen Elizabeth had sternly repressed any interference by the House of Commons in religion.   That was a matter for the Convocation and herself; it was the advice of the spirituality which she required in spiritual affairs.

The sovereign then had so far been supreme. It was most unlikely that he would allow the curtailment of his power except under compulsion. Rather he had every intention to increase it after the manner of his brothers of France, Spain and Austria.   But the country gentry and lawyers and great merchants who composed the Commons' House were equally resolved to rule England. It was calculated that the united incomes of the members of the House of Commons trebled the revenues of the peers.   Wealthy, powerful, each in his own little corner of England strong enough to bully the parson about his doctrines and the peasant about his pleasures, the English gentlemen naturally resented a mismanagement which they felt themselves wise enough to set right; and, perhaps it was quite as natural, talked over the ill-fated precedents of Henry III., Richard II., and Henry VI., kings famous alike for their love of art and for their misfortunes.

The struggle was inevitable.   It was by no

5

means inevitable that victory should be with the Commons.[1] At present the Crown appeared the stronger; and the tendencies of the day in the European community, which exert such a magical influence over men's minds, and which are so constantly used as arguments for new movements, pointed to monarchical victory. Holland was the one prominent Republic, and there a great family was monopolising power.

The influence of the Bishop of St. David's was at once evident on the accession of King Charles. He was appointed to preach the sermon at the opening of the new Parliament, to which the king and Buckingham looked eagerly forward as pledged by the action of its predecessor to support them in their championship of the Protestant cause in Germany. He succeeded his friend Bishop Neile of Durham as Clerk of the Closet to the king, a post which at once gave him a confidential relationship to the sovereign; and soon, on the death of Bishop Andrewes, was promoted to be Dean of the Chapels Royal and to control the ritual of the royal worship. He was asked to provide the king with a list of the leading divines in England marked P. and O., Puritan and Orthodox. He was commanded to confer with Bishop Andrewes[2] of Winchester, "the great light of the Christian world" as he reverently styles him in his *Diary*,[3]

---

[1] Pere d'Orleans, ix. 237, 238.
[2] *Diary*, 9th and 10th April, 1625.
Ibid., 21st September, 1626.

as to the government and discipline of the Church,
and especially to discuss with him the position of
the Church of England towards the five articles of
the Calvinistic Synod of Dort held in 1619.

It was just about this time that Laud had the
opportunity of assisting an attempt to show the
Roman cavillers against the English Church that
his communion possessed resources for the cultivation of a devout life of retirement and self-
recollection. Nicholas Ferrar, soon to be founder
of the community of Little Gidding, came to him
for ordination on Trinity Sunday, 1625, in Henry
VII.'s chapel at Westminster. Laud gave him
deacon's orders and never ceased to take the
deepest interest in the fortunes of the Little
Gidding family.[1] Apparently Ferrar's character
and Ferrar's self-denial and asceticism deeply
impressed him ; for we find him recording in his
Diary a few weeks later a dream in which the
saintly Bishop Thornborough of Worcester stood
by him, and invited him to a quiet and simple life
of work within the limits of his own diocese. It
was one of those dreams which Laud noticed and
from which he drew practical instruction. Greatness he still sought for ; but pomp and luxury he
put decisively from him.[2]

The first Parliament of Charles I. met in
June, 1625. The king welcomed its meeting, and
demanded at once large grants for the war in

---

[1] Ferrar's *Life*, by his brother.   [2] *Diary*, Sept., 1625.

Germany, which had been undertaken at the request of the last House of Commons. A bill was proposed to enforce more reverent observance of the Sabbath, which the king accepted.[1] A solemn fast was proclaimed at the request of the Commons by order of the king and Convocation. Religious sympathy seemed firmly established between the king and Commons, and without religious sympathy in those days political concord was impossible. But three weeks after the opening of Parliament, the House of Commons, leaving the question of the German war, commenced a fierce attack on a book of Dr. Montague, Vicar of Stanford Rivers. Montague had found that some members of his flock were being stealthily seduced to Rome. He proceeded to attack the Roman doctrines, but in so doing disclaimed Puritanism and the Synod of Dort. The Commons lashed themselves into fury in a committee on religion. They accused Montague of Arminianism and of Popery. They attempted to drive him from the Church. Thereupon Bishop Buckeridge of Rochester, Bishop Howson of Oxford and Bishop Laud of St. David's petitioned the Prime Minister to protect Montague.[2] They asserted that some of Montague's doctrines were unquestionably taught

[1] Heylin, p. 129.

[2] Laud's *Works*, vi. 244. Andrewes, Mountain of London and Neile of Durham afterwards supported the former three (*Works*, vi. 249).

by the Church of England, and that some were difficult scholastic questions on which latitude of opinion must be allowed.   They took their stand on the Act of the Submission of the Clergy in the reign of Henry VIII., which allowed the king's supremacy in religious matters, acting by the advice not of Parliament but of Convocation. They maintained that the Convocation of bishops and clergy must remain the judge of spiritual causes, and that a submission to secular judges would be disobedience to the ordinance of Christ :[1] nor would the Church of England, which had thrown off the yoke of Rome, bow to the decision of a foreign synod, like that of Dort, or admit that the House of Commons could decide matters of doctrine.

It was a daring act, for it at once brought down upon these bishops the wrath of the majority in the Commons ; but Laud's convictions were too strong to fear the danger.   " I could easily," he says, " have been as gracious with the people as any, even the worst, of my predecessors.   But I have ever held it the lowest depth of baseness to frame religion to serve turns, and to be carried about with every wind of vain doctrine, to serve and please other men's fancies, and not a man's own either understanding or conscience." [2]

[1] *Cf.* Spelman's *Works*, i. 141.   "The bishops ought to exclude the temporal Lords," much more the Commons, "when it cometh to the decision of a question in theology ".

[2] *Trials and Troubles*, p. 161.

The appearance of the plague adjourned the Parliament for the moment; but meeting soon after at Oxford they proceeded to attack Buckingham and were dissolved on the 12th of August.

From Oxford Laud set out for his diocese. Sunday by Sunday, during the three months of his stay, he preached in the principal parish churches; he consecrated the chapel he had built for his own house at Abergwilly, and rejected as unfit the solitary candidate who came forward for ordination. In November he returned to London, preaching in important centres on the road, for he was zealous for the spread of religion, and could not be accused either of want of earnestness in duty or of indifference to preaching. In both these points he took Bishop Andrewes as his model. The two bishops were accustomed to attend prayers together before consulting on the needs of the Church.[1]

At the coronation, appointed for 2nd February, 1626, Laud was directed to act as Dean of Westminster. By his desire, in order to secure perfect reverence, the king rehearsed in the abbey his part of the ritual two days beforehand; and the magnificent ceremony was carried through without a touch of disorder. The king wore white,[2] the colour of holiness and humility, instead of purple. A huge crowd filled the abbey and its approaches. All were impressed with the dignity and the de-

---

[1] *Diary*, 10th April, 1625.   [2] Heylin, p. 138.

vout character of the service. Every detail of
the ceremony was well seen by the congregation.
It is characteristic of the vice-dean that this gave
him the most intense satisfaction.[1] The Ruler of
the world had been served with decency and
order.

Laud was again appointed to preach at the
opening of the second Parliament of Charles on the
6th of February, 1626. The sermon[2] was a bold
and eloquent attempt to persuade members to
avoid the two rocks on which the friendly relation
between king and Commons had previously
been wrecked. Acknowledging the weakness of
the Church, the representative of the spiritual
power, and the growing strength of the Commons
who represented the secular power, he appealed to
them to leave the Church her independence in the
day of her weakness, and not to claim the right of
dictating doctrine. Then he went on to explain
that the authority held by the king was of Divine
origin, and thus " the foundation of his people and
of all the justice that must preserve them in unity
and in happiness". Therefore they ought not to
treat the king's personally chosen ministers as
enemies. The appeal was passed over by the
new House, nor was this surprising; for the
Government was now becoming embroiled with
France as well as with Germany. Buckingham's
administration had not been successful; and

---

[1] See *Diary*, 2nd February, 1626.　　[2] *Works*, vol. 1.

renewed attacks upon him, culminating at last in impeachment, brought the Parliament to an unsuccessful close in June of the same year. The king was resolved not to abandon his servants,[1] and he had been brought up to look on Buckingham as a brother.

On the 20th of June Laud was appointed Bishop of Bath and Wells.[2] He now shared much of Buckingham's unpopularity. He was known as his intimate friend, as the chief counsellor of the Government in religious matters, and as the prominent opponent of Puritanism. Taxes were being illegally collected; soldiers billeted in towns and villages filled England with disorder. People were saying it was better to be oppressed by a foreign enemy than to be undone at home. The King of Denmark and the Palatinate were far away and aroused little interest. Even the Protestants of Rochelle were not dear enough to the English mind for any great self-sacrifice. The Puritans would rather see the Papists persecuted and executed at home and let the Huguenots perish in France. Buckingham was a mere child in the hands of Richelieu, who had now made himself the all-powerful minister in France; and the French Court knew how to play upon the feelings of the Opposition in England, finding in the Jesuits ready agents for stirring up hatred against the Anglican bishops, and being thus able

[1] *Parliamentary History*, vi. 430.   [2] *Diary.*

to keep open the breach between king and Commons. Bitter libels written against him at this time affected Laud's nerves ; one night he dreamt that he was being overthrown at Court ; another night that he was reconciled to Rome in spite of earnest protests.[1] On foreign politics, on the direction of the war, on ordinary secular administration he had no influence : the burden of other men's mistakes weighed heavily upon him.

Meanwhile in the affairs of the Church his influence had become supreme. The succession to Canterbury had been already promised to him,[2] and he was appointed Bishop of London on the 17th of June, 1627, and named one of the commissioners who should administer the affairs of the Church during the sequestration of Archbishop Abbot.[3] This sequestration was a high-handed act of the royal authority, which declared the archbishop incapable of properly performing his duties. Abbot's health had been shaken, his influence had been destroyed by his manslaughter of Lord Zouch's keeper. He had thrown down the reins and let Puritans and High Churchmen run riot in the Church. To some men this seemed well enough, for it was a method by which the Church could include all. To Laud it was intolerable. In one parish there was a solemn ritual, beautiful music,[4]

---

[1] *Diary*, 14th Jan., 1627, 8th March, 1627.
[2] *Ibid.*, 2nd October, 1626.   [3] *Ibid.*, October, 1627.
[4] See Burney's *History of Music* for attention paid to church

and earnest preaching on the moral and spiritual
duties of the people ; so simple that the people often
thought the preachers were men of slight learning :
"Our parson," said the people of Childrey to a
wandering Oxonian, "is one Master Pococke, a plain,
honest man, but, master, he is no Latiner".[1] In the
next parish some ill-paid and ill-educated curate
droned through the prayers while the congregation
were assembling : then the rector entered from the
vestry in his Geneva cloak ; with hot and fiery
eloquence he defended the high Calvinism of the
Synod of Dort, dilated on "God's absolute decrees,"[2] and comforted his followers with the conviction that their salvation was indefeasible, however
ill their neighbours might fare.[3] In such churches
the communion table was so ill guarded that on one
occasion while the congregation sat wrapt in attention to the preacher's eloquence, a dog stole in
and carried off the loaf set ready for the Holy
Supper. The story spread like wildfire, to the
horror of pious Churchmen.

Sadder by far was the utter disorganisation of
the clergy which Abbot's long neglect had allowed
to come about. Sir B. Rudyard in his place in

music, publication of metrical psalms, etc., at this time (iii., 356-
387).

[1] Twells' *Life of Pococke*, the great Eastern scholar, p. 95.

[2] Mrs. Hutchinson, p. 100. *Life of a Fifth Monarchy Man*, by
Rogers, gives a graphic description by a listener.

[3] Baxter's *Autobiography* complains bitterly that the Puritan
teachers spoke little of the love of God.

Parliament complains : " There are some places in England where God is little better known than among the Indians ".[1] Round Baxter's home[2] in Shropshire few of the clergy could preach ; many of them were addicted to drink, some officiated with forged orders, several had been ordained because they were fit for nothing else.

Nor was the work of the Church being properly discharged abroad. The efforts to Christianise the Indians in Virginia had been thwarted by the jealousy of the Puritans,[3] in spite of the efforts of Ferrar, and the eloquent hopes which Donne had expressed from the pulpit of St. Paul's that England would be the means of the world's conversion. All these troubles were attributed to Abbot's supineness and ignorance of parochial duties.

Now under the commission of bishops there was a still more general removal of the communion table to the chancel, where it was covered with rich cloths and guarded by a rail.[4] The reins of discipline were drawn tighter. Devotional books, which to many men savoured of Popery, were prepared and issued, and were much used by the ever-increasing number who found no near communion with God in the Calvinistic preaching, but longed for prayer and quiet meditation.[5]

[1] *Parl. Hist.*, viii. 164.   [2] Baxter's *Autobiography*, p. 54.
[3] See in Ferrar's *Life* the fatal influence of the Puritan Earl of Warwick upon the Virginian Company.
[4] Heylin, 162.   [5] *Ibid.*, 164.

To soothe the political excitement and give people's thoughts a fresh direction, instructions were issued to preachers to point out the terrible perils which threatened the reformed religion abroad, and to appeal for help in raising a loan which should support an army in Germany under the King of Denmark, and should equip a fleet to succour the Huguenots in Rochelle. But these efforts were of no avail. The arrogance and extravagance of Buckingham had alienated the people. They could think of little but their own grievances. Farmers whose goods were plundered; peasants whose wives and daughters were not safe from bands of undisciplined soldiers newly pressed into the service; country gentlemen who were smarting from letters under the privy seal demanding a large loan to the king; merchants who were compelled to pay customs' dues without authority of Parliament, and then found no protection for their commerce at sea,[1] cared little for an unfortunate King of Denmark or a landless elector palatine, or for Duke Soubise and Mayor Guiton, whose hot-headed rashness had driven Rochelle into unnecessary revolt.

A Parliament must meet once more, or England would be bankrupt. And how would

---

[1] See on these points Wentworth's speech, *Parliamentary History*, vii. 369, and speeches of Phelips and Seymour, 364, 362, and Rushworth, i. 449. *Cf.* the petition of the women, whose husbands had been imprisoned in Sallee for years, to the king (*State Papers*, vol. 306, No. 85; *cf.* 316, No. 52).

Parliament act? It was opened on the 17th of
March, 1628, with a sermon from Laud. Taking
for his text Ephesians iv. 3,[1] "Endeavouring to
keep the unity of the spirit in the bond of peace,"
he preached on the need of political and religious
unity. "Unity—a thing so good that it is never
broken but by the worst of men. Nay, so good
it is that the very worst men pretend best when
they break it. It is so in the Church; never
heretic yet rent her bowels, but he pretended that
he raked them for truth. It is so in the State;
seldom any unquiet spirit divides her union, but
he pretends some great abuses which his integrity
would remedy." " Now the breakers of the bond
of peace, both in Church and Commonwealth. are
pride and disobedience; for these two cry one to
another, that is pride and disobedience: 'Come, let
us break the bond'." The exhortation was taken
to heart and the early days of this Parliament
were the most hopeful of the reign. Sir Thomas
Wentworth took the lead in the Commons.[2] His
directness of purpose, moving eloquence and bold
hatred of misgovernment produced the Petition of
Right, in which the old liberties of the subject
were vindicated from arbitrary imprisonment,
from quartering of soldiery, and from illegal taxation. It was the one session of Parliament in the
reign of King Charles in which any attention was

[1] Laud's *Works*, vol. i., Anglo-Catholic Library.
[2] *Parliamentary History*, viii. 97, 107, 120, 163, etc.

given to the condition of the poor, or any laws framed for their advantage.[1]

But the House of Commons would not be content. It was far more interesting and exciting to enter upon political strife than to devise methods for the slow progress of the people. After a few weeks Wentworth lost control of them. Once more they attacked Buckingham. Once more they proposed to decide a doctrinal standard for the Church of England, and accused the two most prominent bishops, Laud of London and Neile of Winchester, of making innovations in religion.[2] Doctrine and the affairs of the Church the king was convinced were, alike by the law of the land and the law of Christ, outside their control. On this point he would not yield an inch, though he allowed Laud to defend his action before the House of Lords, who absolved him of the accusations brought against him. As for the proposed impeachment of Buckingham, Charles claimed most unwisely that his favourite must always be above attack ; nor would he sacrifice the meanest of his servants without proof sufficient to satisfy himself that they had disobeyed his orders. With singular want of tact he had promoted and would

---

[1] Eden, *State of the Poor*, i. 155.

[2] These chiefly rested on their supposed support of Dr. Manwaring, who had preached some very unwise sermons. It was proved by peers present at the time that Laud had advised the king to prevent their publication (*Parliamentary History*, viii. 213).

continue to promote the ecclesiastics[1] whom the Commons condemned.   Once more king and Commons were drifting hopelessly apart, and Parliament had been prorogued for a time, when on the 23rd of August Buckingham was assassinated by Felton at Portsmouth.   It was a blow which the king never forgot or forgave to those orators of the Commons whose furious eloquence had inspired Felton's act.[2]   And it was a bitter personal grief to the Bishop of London.   But his influence was not shaken.   It was enormously increased. The king now turned naturally to the guidance[3] of the man who had always set before him the high ideal of a Christian Government for the good of his people, and who had enforced upon him that he was anointed by God Himself to administer justice, and succour the poor, and make his nation great.   With Weston at the Treasury, and Wentworth, just created Lord Wentworth, President of the North and privy councillor, he would have henceforth to carry on the government of the country.   How would the new ministers fare?   Could they fill the empty Treasury?   Could they restore order in disturbed England?   Could they re-assert the mastery of the seas and protect the injured commerce of England?   Could they save Rochelle, or patch

[1] Montague and Manwaring especially.

[2] *Parliamentary History*, viii. 244; Baker's *Chronicle*, 442.

[3] *Diary*, 27th August, 1628.

up some peace with France? Above all, could they calm an infuriated Parliament; discover a *modus vivendi* between the king and Commons; fix the boundaries between the spiritual and the temporal; establish some new and satisfactory principle for the relations of the executive and the legislative?

It was an appalling task. Laud's affectionate nature was shattered into ill-health [1] by the death of his brilliant friend, whom he had nursed in illness, and known [2] how to calm in passion, and whom he had guided from a life of licence to some yearning for religion. He was unfamiliar with the State business. He was not well acquainted with the capacities of his colleagues. His was the greatest influence in the council, yet he had no control over the other heads of departments. It was hardly conceivable that the first encounter between Parliament and untried ministers, unpopular from previous associations and ill served in the Commons by badly chosen subordinates, could have any but ill success. Neither party could be blamed for failure under such unfavourable conditions. But if, for the third time in four years, king and Parliament parted in anger, would the king consider Parliamentary government possible? Would Parliament ever again be able to repose confidence in the king and the king's ministers?

[1] *Diary* and *Works*, vi. 257 (letter to Vossius).
[2] *e.g.*, *Diary*, 18th May, 1624.

CHAPTER V.

ATTEMPTS TO RECONCILE KING AND PARLIAMENT, 1628-1629.

Laud and his Fellow-ministers—Concessions Despised by the Commons—The Commons' Resolutions—Dissolution —Laud's Regret—His Refusal to adopt Tyrannical Measures.

THE new Government had a difficult task before it. Engaged by the king's promises in a hopeless duty, the deliverance of Rochelle, which was now held locked in the grip of Richelieu, it could but send out to certain failure the fleet which lay at Portsmouth. The peace with France[1] which followed was necessary and prudent, but could bring no reputation to those who negotiated it.

At home ministers would be compelled in a few months to face an estranged House of Commons, with an empty Treasury. They were personally unpopular with that House, having all, with the exception of Wentworth, owed their offices to the friendship and patronage of Buckingham; and Wentworth the country party detested as an "apostate".

[1] It was not actually published till 10th May, 1629 (Rushworth, ii. 23, 25).

Was it possible to prove to the Opposition, without insulting the memory of the king's dearest friend, that there was a true desire in the Executive to work harmoniously with them? At least it must be tried. The Earl of Arundel, the most representative and the proudest of the great peers, an attack upon whom had irritated the House of Lords, was reconciled to the king and called to the Council Board. Cottington was appointed Chancellor of the Exchequer, and Dorchester Secretary of State; both these appointments might prove popular, as both men had recently opposed Buckingham.

The resistance to the payment of tonnage and poundage, which was now justified by some merchants under the shelter of the Petition of Right, was very tenderly handled, and the council refused to proceed to extremities against the recalcitrants, awaiting a settlement of the question in Parliament. Weston, the new Lord Treasurer, was a cautious and prudent minister, averse to war, and economical in his management. It was openly announced that the king was willing to admit that his right to tonnage and poundage rested upon the grant of Parliament. The abuses in the quartering of soldiers were checked with a firm hand; and no opportunity was given for accusing the Government of violations of the personal liberty of the subject which had been so definitely vindicated in the Petition of Right.

The religious question was more difficult to handle. Montague, so angrily condemned in the last session, had been appointed Bishop of Chichester; Abbot and Laud were engaged in his consecration when they received the news of Buckingham's death. Montague's elevation to the bench of bishops was sure to give offence. But his book *Appello Cæsarem*, the cause of his condemnation, was called in by authority, on the ground that it was calculated to disturb the peace of the Church; so were Dr. Manwaring's sermons upon the king's prerogative.[1] A staunch Calvinist, Dr. Potter, formerly tutor to the king, was chosen for the vacant Bishopric of Carlisle.[2] This was done that it might be impossible to say that divines tainted with Arminianism were the only men who obtained promotion. Archbishop Abbot, who was even suspected of secretly plotting with the Puritan leaders, was recalled to Court, graciously received by the king, and commanded to attend the council regularly.[2] The leading bishops assured him publicly that they repudiated the tenets of Arminius,[3] whose name indeed had been brought into the debates with very insufficient knowledge. At the same time some laws against the Romanists were put in force; a proclamation was issued

---

[1] *Parliamentary History*, viii. 243, and Rushworth, ii. 43.

[2] Baker's *Chronicle*, 443; *Life and Works of Charles I.*

[3] Arminius was a Dutch professor who taught very emphatically the freedom of the human will, etc.

against the Jesuits; and another for the seizure of the Titular Bishop of Chalcedon, who was exercising episcopal functions in the Pope's name in England.

It was hoped that a reissue of the king's instructions on preaching, which prohibited the open discussion of burning questions of doctrine, would calm men's minds before Parliament met in January, 1629. In fact the king and his ministers were prepared for wider toleration than had yet existed in England, and at the same time were most anxious to meet the Commons half way. They would repress Popery so far as it was possible without bloodshed. They would give Puritans and Calvinists a share in the control of the Church, so long as they observed the Anglican discipline and did not refuse to live in peace with divines of broader views. Actions, not opinions, were to be controlled by law. The king and the bishop alike refused to go farther, and they would not execute Roman priests, nor imprison men who did not acknowledge the Divine inspiration of the Dutch Synod of Dort.[1]

Laud had established relations with several members of the House in the previous session; he had obtained the king's consent to a new Act for the observance of Sunday:[2] he had succeeded in getting an Act for the re-establishment of

---

[1] See Laud's Epistle Dedicatory of *Book against Fisher.*

[2] *Parliamentary History*, viii. 243.

Sutton's Hospital at the Charterhouse passed
through both Houses :[1] he had further persuaded
Sir Benjamin Rudyard, one of the most temperate
and capable members, to introduce a bill for the
better endowment of some of the miserably provided livings in England, a matter which he always
had greatly at heart.[2]   But there still remained an
atmosphere of suspicion, the natural consequence
of the daring and uncertain policy of Buckingham.   Laud and Weston had been his followers ;
the king had been his friend.   The Commons
would only trust a ministry selected by themselves ; and would only feel confidence when they
had inaugurated a policy of persecution against all
who did not agree with them.[3]

This temper was shown immediately Parliament met.   Selden, the greatest lawyer in the
House, declared that the Petition of Right had
been infringed by the punishment of Savage
in the Star Chamber.   This Savage had acknowledged himself an accomplice in the assassination

---

[1] Cf. Parliamentary History, viii. 243, with Works, vi. 1-4.

[2] Cf. Sir B. Rudyard's speech, Parliamentary History, viii.
165, and Diary, 12th April, 1626, and Things Which I have Projected,
x.   Rudyard's speech is not reported by Rushworth, who is not
always trustworthy in relating matters to the credit of the
Royalists.

[3] See the refusal to give a copy of charges (made against him
in the House) to a Roman priest.   He had to get them through
a Puritan acquaintance (Parliamentary History, viii. 292).   Père
d'Orléans bitterly asserts (viii. 231) that persecution of Romanists was the only sure means of popularity with the Commons.

of Buckingham, and, according to the brutal
practice of the day, had been sentenced to have
his ears cropped.   The impetuous Phelips claimed
privilege of Parliament for a merchant member
whose goods had been seized—an extension of
privilege which was certainly most unusual.   The
Government vainly asked the Commons to settle
down to the discussion of supply, promising to
remedy any breach of the Petition of Right, and
to redress all grievances.   Sir John Eliot once
more gained the leadership of the Opposition,
and led the House in an eager attack upon the
levying of tonnage and poundage ; on the respite
from execution granted to Romish priests;[1] and on
the innovations, as he styled them, in religion.

Unhappily for England, Eliot was an idealist,
little versed in the business or the practical requirements of the time.   In the complications of
foreign affairs he took scanty interest. [2]   In
religion he posed as the strictest of Calvinists,
and as the stern persecutor of every opinion
which his party pronounced unorthodox.[3]   The

---

[1] He complained fiercely that a priest condemned under the
sanguinary laws of Elizabeth had not been executed (*Parliamentary History*, viii. 304; *cf.* 302, 305, 325).

[2] He had never understood that France was now decidedly
more powerful than Spain (speech in *Parliamentary History*, viii.
158).   For the enfeebled state of Spain as compared with France,
see *Hist. Gén. d'Espagne*, vol. viii., and Howell's *Letters*.   Some of
the Puritans realised the danger later.   *Cf.* Ludlow's strictures on
Cromwell's policy, in strengthening France, which he inherited
from Eliot (ii. 559).

[3] Yet his religious works published in prison were so broad

difficulties of carrying on Government without money to supply fleet or army, or even to provide pay for the judges and the other officials, with a heavy load of debt incurred in wars which had been undertaken at the wish of the Commons—all these were nothing to him. Passionately earnest, magnificently though somewhat bombastically [1] eloquent, knowing how to stir the feelings of the House, perfectly careless of danger to himself and free from self-seeking, filled by study with a conviction that the Commons had lost many powers which they had once wielded, Eliot was the least fitted of leaders to save England from civil war. Even his friend John Pym, the future leader of the Long Parliament, shrank from his extreme measures. But he carried all before him.

At his instigation the House formed itself into a committee of religion. The king's instructions to preachers were severely handled. He would hinder, some members declared bitterly, the preaching of the Gospel. "Oh, Mr. Chairman," said Eliot in speaking of Montague's mild Arminianism, "this breaks the hearts of all, for if God be God let us follow Him, and if Baal be God let us follow him, and no longer halt between two opinions."[2] How could they exist if they might not

in their views that we must believe he was carried away by the impulse of the hour.

[1] See speeches in *Parliamentary History*, *e.g.*, viii. 311.

[2] *Parl. Hist.*, viii. 296.

hear Sunday by Sunday that they, the chosen few, were to be saved, while the preacher fulminated forth terrible denunciations on the fate which awaited their ecclesiastical opponents, garnished with many pointed allusions to Midian and to Moab? No doubt such fanatical Puritans were but a small minority in the Commons, as they were certainly a small minority of the great and serious party which is usually described as Puritan. The important point was that for the moment their influence was supreme. The numerous supporters of the Court were too timid for open resistance; they never attempted to take a division which would have shown the existence of differences among the members; and the religious fanatics swept along the whole House in their wake, for all leading politicians in the Opposition felt it to be their interest to support them. It was resolved that "we the Commons now in Parliament assembled do claim, profess and avow for truth the sense of the Articles of Religion which were established in Parliament in the reign of our late Queen Elizabeth, which by public act of the Church of England, and by the general and concurrent exposition of the writers of our Church, have been delivered to us, and we do reject the sense of the Jesuits and Arminians".[1]

The Commons were soon made conscious that

[1] *Parliamentary History*, viii. 274.

their resolution was ridiculous. What precedent
could they quote for laying down the rule of faith
in England, so evidently the privilege of Convocation? What was the public Act of which they
spoke so loudly? Who were the Arminians
against whom they fulminated? The most prominent High Church preachers always declared
that they cared nothing for the tenets of the Dutch
professor Arminius. The leaders of the Opposition
answered by putting forward as the tests of ortho-
doxy the Lambeth Articles composed in 1595 by
Archbishop Whitgift and a few friends,[1] the Irish
Articles, which certainly could not bind the
English Church, the acts of the Synod of Dort,
and books of Calvinistic professors at the universities. It was evident that they had got out of
their depth. It was evident also that they were
setting up an intolerable tyranny in England. It
was certain that the Church would not submit to an
assembly of country gentlemen and lawyers, elected
after all only by groups of well-to-do citizens and
prosperous gentlemen and farmers, and in no
sense representative of that huge inanimate mass
of artisans and labourers, who would one day
claim a right to be heard.

Nor was the Puritan party in the House safe
from the charge of inconsistency. Rudyard said
sadly in committee: "I observe that we are
always very eager and fierce against Papistry,

[1] Fuller, *Church History*, *sub anno*.

against scandalous ministers and against things
which are not in our power ; " but "an adversary
may say that we choose our religion because it is
the cheaper of the two, and that we would willingly
serve God with somewhat that costs us nought ".
"Scandalous livings cannot but have scandalous
ministers." "It will lie heavy upon Parliament,
until somewhat be effected." [1]

But all this could not check Eliot ; he was
resolved once more to attack and imprison Montague, who should be declared no legal bishop.
Prebendary Cosin of Durham should be punished
for his ritual practices at Durham Cathedral, and
for his book of devotions so popular among the
members of the Court, which was now impugned
in the House as savouring of Romanism.   Gossip
was quoted against Bishop Neile of Winchester,
that he had forbidden his canons to preach against
the Pope ; and Oliver Cromwell had an old story
from 1617 of some anti-Puritan sayings of this
Popishly-inclined prelate. [2]   One of the canons of
Winchester—so a member had heard—used to
cross two napkins on his dinner-table and then
humbly do reverence to the cross.   Evidently he
was an emissary of the Pope. [3]   Hotter and hotter
grew the debate.   Romish priests, it appeared,
had actually been protected by the judges against

[1] *Parliamentary History*, viii. 165.
[2] *Ibid.*, 289, 293.
[3] Nicholas, *Notes*, quoted by S. R. Gardiner.

witnesses who swore that "common rumour" pointed them out as having celebrated mass in England.

What clearer evidence could be needed that the ministers were bringing England back under the Roman yoke? They would impeach Weston, the Lord Treasurer, whom Eliot described as an oppressor of the deepest dye, ransacking history to find tyrants ferocious enough to compare with this cold, accomplished English gentleman, whose prime ambition was to make himself a competent fortune. All the ministers, all the officials should be swept away. In vain the Speaker declared that the king had ordered him to adjourn the House. He was held down in the chair by main force, while resolutions were passed that :—

"Whosoever shall bring in innovation in religion, or by favour seek to extend or introduce Popery or Arminianism, or other opinions disagreeing from the true and orthodox Church, shall be reputed a *capital* enemy to this kingdom and commonwealth ".

" Whosoever shall counsel or advise the taking and levying of the subsidies of tonnage and poundage, not being granted by Parliament, or shall be an actor or an instrument therein, shall be likewise reputed an innovator in the government, and a capital enemy to this kingdom and commonwealth."

"If any merchant or other person whatsoever shall voluntarily yield or pay the said subsidies of tonnage and poundage, not being granted by Parliament, he shall be likewise reputed a betrayer of the liberty of England and an enemy to the same." [1]

So it had come to this that any man who disagreed with the religious opinions of a chance majority of the House of Commons must expect to pay the penalty with his life.

The intolerant resolutions were carried by acclamation ; the House declared itself adjourned ; and the members poured out to proclaim what they had done. The breach between king and Commons was complete. Of necessity the Parliament was dissolved. It seemed impossible that the two powers could exist longer in the State. Eleven years would pass before Parliament would meet again. Laud notes in his *Diary:* " The Parliament, which was broken up this 10th March, laboured my ruin ; but God be ever blessed, for it found nothing against me ". No one was more conscious than he how terrible was an impeachment by the House of Commons, and that few men, however complete their innocence, could hope for acquittal.[2] He was glad that it was gone and that a breathing space was left for work

---

[1] *Parliamentary History*, viii. 332, and Baker's *Chronicle*, 443.

[2] The impeachment of Cranfield in 1624 was considered by most calm observers to have been very unfairly managed (*Parliamentary History*, vi. 132 onwards; *cf.* Howell's *Letters*, etc.).

which seemed to him all-important.   During the
next eleven years he was to exercise the chief
authority in England.

But before we proceed to describe the administration of Laud, let us pause for an instant to consider the accusation brought against him that he
was an enemy to liberty.   His letters to the
famous foreign scholar Vossius,[1] to whom he often
poured out his heart, show his sincere sorrow at
the failure of the Government to come to terms
with this Parliament, in which he had tried so
hard to secure unity by every allowable concession.   But to Laud there was an institution, the
interests of which towered above all other interests.
The Church of God had been commissioned to
save the world ; it held its authority direct from
the Lord Jesus Christ ;[2] men's temporal needs
could not be weighed for a moment against the
spiritual.   Herein lay his strength to influence the
future, but his weakness in winning his way
during his lifetime ; for a devout and scrupulous
Christian seldom becomes successful as a statesman ; and an ecclesiastical leader too often forgets
in the apparent interest of the Church some important principles of political progress.

Next to the Church Laud reverenced the
king.   Reading literally the Biblical command to
" honour the king," he looked upon him as com-

---

[1] *Works*, vi. 265, 278, 294, 300, etc.
[2] *Speeches against Leighton and Prynne*, and *Works, passim.*

missioned from on high for the work of government.[1] The king's solemn consecration by the Church gave him the right to interfere in Church affairs.[2] He was its supreme governor on earth, bound, however, to rule by the advice of the bishops and clergy, and having no right of himself to declare doctrine.[3] But God had given no such sacred office to the House of Commons. Here Laud reaffirmed the Tudor theory,[4] that Parliament was a body intended to represent to the king the needs and desires of the constituencies ; and to bring before the king grievances caused by the misconduct of provincial and central officials, or by ill-framed or obsolete laws. He had tried to effect a reconciliation between king and Commons when he first came to be chief counsellor ; and every action of his administration had been intended to prove his sincerity. But the Commons had flung the king's professions of loyalty to the constitution back in his face ; they had miscon-

---

[1] It should be remembered that when statesmen spoke of the king as "absolute," they meant only that he had no rival or superior, such as pope or emperor. *Cf.* Sir T. Davys, Solicitor-General, to the Irish Recusants, in Carte's *Ormond*, i. 39.

[2] See note on page 10.

[3] "That God hath entrusted into the hands of His priest " (*Speech for the Liturgy*, p. 510, folio).

[4] *Cf. Works*, vii. 631. Answer to the remonstrance of the Commons drawn up by Laud for the king : " Let us see moderation and the ancient Parliamentary ways and we shall love nothing more than Parliaments ".

strued all his acts ;[1] they had set themselves up as rulers of the Church contrary to the law of Christ ; contrary to the law of the land they had tried to wrest from the king the reins of civil government ; and by claiming a right to interpret and administer laws[2] had invaded also the province of the judges. In this manner the Lower House had become dangerous for the moment to the liberties of Church and people; but Laud felt[3] it was desirable to restore the regular course of Parliaments so soon as the confusion of ideas about its functions had been properly cleared up. And this he might have accomplished if he had obtained a free hand in administering the Government, and if he had not trusted too much to his own honesty of purpose, forgetting that equally honest men were misjudging him day by day.[4]

Several courses now lay open to Laud in order to secure a majority in the House of Commons. He might gain the leaders and make it their interest to assist the Government. The sincerity of the Opposition seemed doubtful both to him and to the king ; and as three of the most prominent

---

[1] There is no real proof that the king had tried to delude the Commons in his first ill-expressed answer to the Petition of Right.

[2] *Parliamentary History*, viii. 307.

[3] *Trials and Troubles*, 172.

[4] See the bitter feeling in Mrs. Hutchinson's *Memoirs*, p. 129. Sir T. Roe writes of him in 1634 as "very just, incorrupt and above all mistaked by the erring world". Sir T. Roe was a political opponent. *Cf.* the Jesuit historian, Père d'Orléans, ix. 266: "Laud was a zealous Protestant for his own sect".

members of it, Digges, Littleton and Noy, soon accepted office, there was some cause for this scepticism.   Selden they were sure they could gain at any time ; Coke's blind love of money would make him an easy acquisition ;[1] even Eliot they believed to be eager for office, but the ghost of the murdered Buckingham forbade such an alliance. If this course had been successfully adopted, there was little question that the Commons, forsaken by their leaders, would have voted for the king with a facility equal to their former rugged distrust ; for it was the practice of the Stuart Parliaments never to come to a division if they could avoid it, in order to present at all costs an appearance of unity.[2]   But underhand ways were impossible to the open-minded probity of Laud.

Or the Government might have manipulated the elections as Queen Elizabeth's ministers and Queen Mary's had often done ; and Wentworth was soon to show in turbulent Ireland how easily a House of Commons could thus be managed.[3] Or they might have compelled submission by executions and imprisonments ; there were striking contemporary examples abroad ; Richelieu taught his enemies to fear him by the execution of Mont-

---

[1] See instance of Coke's rapaciousness, *State Papers*, vol. 280, No. 12.

[2] See *Parliamentary History*.

[3] *Cf.* Cromwell's management of elections, Ludlow, ii. 498, 578, and especially 600-602 and 617 ; and for reigns of Edward VI. and Mary, Heylin's *Reformation*.

morency,[1] and the tragic fate of Calderon struck terror into the opponents of Olivarez;[2] but severe punishments became rare under the ministry of Laud, who prayed several times a day that he might be enabled to forgive his enemies, and often interceded for the pardon of libellers.[3]

These limitations to his action, set, as he believed, by the laws of God, caused him to risk failure. He was thoroughly convinced that his life was in constant danger from assassins; and that his execution must follow the victory of his opponents.[4] But he had no fear of death if by dying he could secure for the Church freedom of thought and liberty to work out her constitution and her worship upon the primitive lines. And if it could so happen that he should seal his principles with his blood, it was certain that these would become a part of the intellectual and spiritual inheritance of the English race.

In his attempt to free the Church and make it once more a power in England, now and again passion blinded his eyes when he found himself thwarted by an ignorant hatred of learning and beauty; and his indignation led him to sanction some occasional acts of oppression which in his better moments he sorrowfully reprobated. But

---

[1] Howell's *Letters*, i. 242.

[2] *Hist. Gén. d'Espagne*, viii. 76.

[3] *State Papers' Calendar*, 1629-31, p. 362.

[4] Letters to Vossius and to Wentworth.

none the less he consistently observed the evangelical command which one of his own Oxford
disciples, Henry Vaughan, has so exquisitely
rendered :—

> Who with the sword doth others kill,
> A sword shall his blood likewise spill ;
> Here is the patience of the saints
> And the true faith which never faints.

The Strafford Letters; Laud's *Accounts of his Province to the King;* Ludlow's *Memoirs;* Panzani's *Memoirs,* edited by Father Berington, show us the dissensions among the Roman Catholics and their efforts at Court.

CHAPTER VI.

PRINCIPLES OF GOVERNMENT, 1629-1633.

Quiet in England—Fatal Indifference to the Desire for Popular Government—Protection of the Poor—Royal Instructions for Better Government of the Church—The Feoffees—The High Commission as a Court of Morals—Growing Devoutness.

THE passionate proceedings and unmeasured violence of the Commons at the close of the last session in 1629 had by no means commended them to the good sense of the people;[1] and apparently the majority of the members were heartily ashamed of the conduct of their more noisy and ambitious colleagues. On the whole it was felt to be just that Sir John Eliot and other leaders should be imprisoned for misdemeanour in refusing to adjourn at the king's bidding, and in holding down the Speaker forcibly in his chair. When brought to trial a few months later they were condemned by the courts and sentenced to considerable fines.

Eliot evaded payment of the heavy sum imposed on him by a transfer of his property to

[1] *Autobiography* of Sir Symonds D'Ewes, a strong Puritan and member of the Long Parliament.

trustees, and died a few years later while still in prison.   To the others the king was willing enough to show mercy.   For Eliot, who had led the assault upon Buckingham, and had, so he always believed, been the indirect cause of the assassination, he could feel no pity.   A release, which might have saved the great patriot's life, was mercilessly refused.

With these proceedings Laud had little to do ; nor did he exercise any commanding influence over foreign politics.   The king, having no resources for war abroad, was compelled to look on while the battle was fought out in Germany between Romanist and Protestant.   He could only assist the reformed princes with occasional small grants of money, with the sympathy of himself and the nation, and by permitting the enlistment of troops in his dominions.[1]   Laud, who had the most intense horror of war and bloodshed, and who, even in such a cause as this, refused to counsel armed interference,[2] did his utmost to draw the Calvinists and Lutherans of Germany into one Church, whose numbers might defy persecution : it was a great grief to him that this attempt proved unsuccessful.   The nation, in so far as its voice was expressed in Parliament, had shown no sincere desire for foreign war.   Herself

[1] There were many English and Scotch regiments in the army of Gustavus (*State Papers*, *passim*).

[2] Letters to Wentworth, *passim*.

at peace, England attracted to her shores an increasing commerce, partly from her own colonies, chiefly at the expense of the Low Countries; and London was fast becoming the greatest port of the world.[1] Some of the merchants resisted the payment of tonnage and poundage; but their opposition was gradually overcome because the judges upheld the king's claim to these customs. At the same time the law courts proved their independence by checking any attempts to interfere with the personal liberty of individuals, so distinctly vindicated by the Petition of Right.[2] The state of things was unsatisfactory, but not intolerable. Society gradually settled down,[3] and after a time even John Pym accepted office under the Crown as Lieutenant of the Ordnance; while Selden wrote books in defence of the foreign policy of the Government.[4] Charles and his ministers indignantly disclaimed any projects of military despotism, and their sincerity was self-evident since the Court itself remained defenceless and unguarded. There were no troops to repress a rising against tyrannical acts; and the incidents of the early days of the Long Parliament were soon to show how completely the royal authority

[1] London at this time became the bank for Spanish payments to the Netherlands (Continuation of Baker's *Chronicle*, 447, by Edward Philips). *Cf.* Howell's *Letters*.

[2] Rushworth, ii. 80.   [3] *State Papers*, vol. 162, No. 18.

[4] Wood's *Athenae*, ii. 36 and 181. Selden's *Mare Clausum* gained him the thanks of Laud and other privy councillors.

was devoid of force to resist even a well-organised demonstration by the populace of London.

This want of military force is probably forgotten by those historians who speak of the eleven years which followed as if they were a Reign of Terror. Indeed, through these years there were no political executions, and no executions for religion.[1] The atrocious but familiar punishment of the pillory, with its accompaniments of flogging and ear-clipping and nose-slitting, was resorted to now and again ;[2] men were accustomed to see these barbarities constantly employed as deterrents against ordinary criminals ; but to state that the name of each political sufferer is still a household word is enough to prove those sufferers few. Imprisonments which seldom [3] lasted long, and fines which were constantly remitted, were the more usual sentences of the courts.

Under the economical administration of Weston, the firm hand of Wentworth, and the decided and distinctly liberal policy of Laud, which fostered trade and encouraged learning,

---

[1] The " Romish Recusant" in his *Life of Laud* (Kegan Paul, 1894) speaks of one priest executed in these years. He admits it was contrary to the orders of the Government and gives no details or references.

[2] The Parliament had used it against its own enemies (*cf. Parliamentary History*, vi. 110) ; and did again, Carlyle's *Cromwell*, ii. 487.

[3] There were occasional cases of prolonged imprisonments, at times it would seem because fanatical prisoners refused to be released. See an extraordinary case, *S. P.*, vol. 427, No. 107.

the nation prospered, and rose to a height of
wealth and comfort which it had not previously
attained.   But this gave men all the more desire
for a share in the Government, and an influence
upon the progress of the State.

And here lay the first error of the administration.   Charles, Weston, Cottington, even Wentworth and in some degree Laud, fancied the
people would be satisfied with material prosperity.
They forgot that while this absolutely contents
the majority of men, the world is ruled by small
minorities of the active and the restless, and that
if these are not repressed by force, or enlisted by
interest on the side of stability, difficulties are
certain to arise.   But at present there seemed an
astonishing ease in carrying on the Government.
Weston found means to meet necessary expenditure.   Shortly the revival of an old law was to
provide the State with a powerful fleet and make
England mistress of the narrow seas.

Puritanism appeared to have been flung off like
a nightmare with the dispersion of the terrible majority in the Commons.   The mass of the people
welcomed the festivals and the sports, which the
Laudian bishops and clergy taught to be lawful on
Sundays,[1] after the community had duly discharged
its service to God.   When Chief Justice Richard-
son tried to suppress these on the western circuit,

---

[1] The Declaration of Sports was republished in 1632 (Baker's
Chronicle, 454).

he was summoned before the council, confronted
with the strongly expressed opinion of the Bishop
of Bath and Wells and his leading clergy, that
village festivals were a source of peace and harmony, where mirth seldom degenerated into de-
bauchery ; and, having been sternly scolded by
Laud for interfering outside his province as a judge,
departed weeping, " choked," as he said, " by a
pair of lawn sleeves ".

In every community the country gentry, despotic so far, found themselves confronted by the
clergyman who had the Star Chamber at his back.[1]
This famous court, composed of judges and privy
councillors, was by statute commissioned to interfere in all those cases where justice could not be
had at common law, and was designed to be the
protector of the weak and the ignorant.   In aristocratic Yorkshire, Wentworth, now Lord President of the North, compelled the haughtiest nobles
to obey the law courts, and respect the rights of
the poor, and his mode of action was being copied
by the Government throughout the country.   For
it was one of Laud's strongest convictions that, as
all men are equal in the sight of God, so ought

---

[1] See for the nobles' hatred of the Star Chamber Lord
Andover's speech in moving its abolition, March, 1641 (*Parliamentary History*, ix. 189); for its support of the clergy, *S. P.*, vol.
325, No. 1, etc.; for its defence of the poor against the great, *S. P.*,
vol. 277, Nos. 45 to 48, and *cf.* 278, Nos. 26 and 27 and 325, No.
5 ; for oppressions by great men after its abolition, Lilly's *Memoirs ;*
for its action as a court of equity, its chief duty, *S. P.*, vol. 313, No. 33.

they to be equal in the eye of the law.[1] The care
of the poor he considered to be the special duty
of the king, and during the bad harvests of 1629
and 1630 caused great pains to be taken to prevent the indigent from suffering, by forbidding the
export of corn, and through instructions issued to
the justices and other officials.[2] He himself was
munificently generous at all times ; it was his custom in every parish and benefice which he held to
allot a large part of the income to the poor, and at
Lambeth in later years he was adored by his poorer
neighbours.[3] Certainly much required to be done
if all Englishmen were to share in the prosperity of
England. Therefore orders poured out from the
Privy Council under the inspiration of the Bishop of
London, sometimes unwise, constantly unsuccessful, but always proving a distinct desire to render
the lives of the lowest class of Englishmen more
comfortable. Men might laugh at a command that
Friday should be observed as a fast day, but they
could not deny the importance of the object when
they were specifically asked to distribute the

[1] Instructions to judges, Rushworth, ii. 80, 261, 294.

[2] See full reports from Norfolk justices in 1630. *State Papers*,
191, 44 and *passim;* Rushworth, ii. 197 ; *Strafford Letters*, i. 459.
In 1631 a special commission to protect the poor was sent out,
Rushworth, ii. app. 82 and ii. 333, S. R. Gardiner, *sub anno.* For
the protection given to the poor and to charities by the Star
Chamber, *cf. S. P.,* 6th February, 1635.

[3] See also constant allusions in *Diary* to the weather as affecting the poor, *e.g.*, 20th March, 1631, and 17th July, 1632.

money economised among the starving. Or the builders might be annoyed at a set of directions, the germ of our Building Acts, that no new houses should be erected unless they were built of solid materials and provided with larger windows ; but evidently such a change must benefit the health of the poorer classes. The improvement of criminals was not forgotten, nor the due training of children, nor the raising of rates for the relief of the indigent under the famous statute of Elizabeth ; and the officials were specially commanded to watch over the proper apprenticing of boys when their parents could not afford them a good start in life.[1] Such administrative improvements were evidently the result of the years spent by the new chief minister in country parsonages. And as he knew the ignorance of the officers by whom most of these changes would have to be carried out, he obtained a proclamation from the king ordering the nobles and gentry to leave London for their own counties, and there to devote themselves to the guidance and protection of the poor under the jealous supervision of the Star Chamber.

Regulations were also issued for the proper payment of workmen in the employment of the State,[2] and of the seamen who were pressed for the

---

[1] Eden, *State of the Poor*, 1372, 156-164, and long reports of justices to the Privy Council in the *State Papers*.

[2] *State Papers*, vol. 280, No. 17.

royal fleet,[1] while customs were remitted in bad
times on the necessaries of life, so that the poor
might be sufficiently supplied.[2]   England was to
be governed with scrupulous economy, strict
justice and diligent attention to the rights and
comforts of all.   But these plans of Laud and
Wentworth were often frustrated by the pleasure-
loving nature of the queen, by the irresolute
character of Charles and his expensive delight
in the artistic and beautiful, by the corrupt proceedings of several of the ministers, and by the
indifference or hostility of the local magnates.

Meanwhile Laud's special province was the administration of the Church.   Though he was not
yet archbishop, he was the king's most trusted
counsellor, and the king, by the advice of the
bishops, could compel Archbishop Abbot to
execute the law.   And if the Bishop of London's
purpose could be accomplished, the Church would
once again be made so rich and so powerful as
to be able to hold its own in political affairs
against any attack which could be reasonably
anticipated, and to guide the destinies of the
nation.

Though Laud's *Diary* shows us his constant ill-
health in the years 1629 and 1630, during which he
was unnerved by the sudden loss of Buckingham,
no weakness could reduce him to inaction.   In

[1] *State Papers*, vol. 285, No. 40.
[2] *Ibid.*, vol. 285, No. 39.

December, 1629, the king, at the request of the
Bishop of London, and the new Archbishop
Harsnet of York, issued to the archbishops a
series of instructions,[1] the object of which was to
temper and sharpen the weapon of Church influence
so that religion might be fostered and the monarchy
find a powerful ally against the authority of the
nobility and gentry. Brought up among the
commercial classes, trained in the free society
of the university, and successful there by the
power of persuasion and the force of moral
influence, Laud was not ignorant that it would be
impossible to govern England unless he could
draw the people to his side; and this he was
convinced could be done through the pulpit and
the press. But the powers of the Church could
not be effectively used until he had reformed the
bishops. The episcopal appointments had of late
been carefully made, men of strong character
being consecrated to the vacant sees, mostly distinguished for learning and piety, and trained as
parish priests to understand the difficulties of the
society with which they had to deal. Such experience was now felt to be essential in a bishop; for
his want of acquaintance with parochial duties, which
left him ignorant of the people and of the poor,
was often alleged as a main cause of Archbishop
Abbot's failure,[2] and for the relaxation of moral

---

[1] Heylin, 188, and Rushworth, ii. 7 and 30. *Cf. State Papers*,
vol. 153, No. 41.   [2] Fuller, iii. 473.

and devotional discipline under his administration.
The younger generation of parish clergy for the
most part were set upon improvements in public
worship, and opposed to the discussion of meta-
physical religion; and, as the prominent Calvinist
preachers preferred the independence of the lecturer
who had no cure of souls, it was difficult to find
even an occasional Calvinist for promotion to the
bench, in order to prove that no party would be
passed over, and that the new Government was
determined to practise a strict neutrality with
regard to doctrinal views.[1]

But, in spite of what had been done, some of
the older and less devout bishops still looked upon
a bishopric as a worldly advancement, and were
constantly watching for a chance of a richer diocese. The instructions were therefore first directed
to compel the bishops to reside in their diocesan
houses, in order that they might travel through
their dioceses, confirming, conferring with clergy
and laity, preaching, inspecting the condition of
fabrics, and enforcing the reverent observance of
public worship.[2]   Laud, who had by no means been
absorbed in the diocese of St. David's, now gave
an example to his colleagues by himself preaching
at Paul's Cross on the anniversary of coronation
day.   He also set his face most resolutely against
the evil practice of enriching relations by granting
beneficial leases, and of making a private fortune

[1] Appointments of Potter, Morton, etc., show this.
[2] *Cf. State Papers*, vol. 153, No. 40.

from the revenues of the see ; and did all he could to control his colleagues into a like un-selfishness.[1]

But if it was all-important that the bishops should become leaders of opinion through the exercise of personal influence, there was nothing more disastrous to the progress of the Church than the condition of the parish clergy.   Baxter[2] and others describe to us the disgraceful character of large numbers of incumbents, ignorant, avaricious, often immoral, who had been ordained during the lax administration of Archbishop Abbot.   In future (such were the directions of the king at Laud's suggestion) men must be carefully ex-amined and tested before they were admitted into holy orders,[3] and, so far as possible, the clergy should enjoy a university training.   A high standard of self-sacrifice was expected of them ; Laud was horrified on hearing of a debate at Oxford as to whether or no the parish clergy were compelled by their office to administer the sacraments to those dying of the plague.[4]

The independence of the clergy needed also to be protected.   The man who lived in the house and sat at the board of some great country gentle-man might enforce penance on an ignorant milk-

---

[1] *Works*, vi. 389.   *State Papers*, vol. 270, No. 6.

[2] *Autobiography*, p. 32, and Rudyard's speech, *Parliamentary History*, vi. 422.   *Cf. State Papers, passim.*

[3] *Cf. State Papers*, vol. 308, No. 39.

[4] *Cf. Ibid.*, vol. 174, No. 45.

maid who had been led astray, and might thunder
denunciation against an immoral plough-boy ; the
vices of the squire would go unreproved, and his
high-handed acts might even appear to be sheltered
by Church authority.   Laud's own mistake in
earlier life showed him the dangers to which great
men's chaplains were exposed.   If the clergy were
to be the champions of the poor, if they were to
be the upholders of the equal laws of God against
vice in high places and in low, the system by
which so many were engaged as chaplains of great
country houses must be repressed.   In future no
one under the rank of nobleman was to be allowed
a resident chaplain.[1]

Puritanism would need careful handling.   In
many places it had been the custom for years to
disregard the rubrics.   These were now to be
strictly enforced.   Popular lecturers, paid by
Puritan congregations,[2] must read prayers in
a surplice and no longer sit by the vestry fire
till the moment was come to ascend the pulpit.
Even the congregation would have to attend
worship if they wished to hear the preaching.
Nor did the instructions forget the necessity
for simple teaching.   Disputatious and dogmatic
sermons were leaving no place for the guidance of the Gospel[3] in the duties of ordinary

---

[1] Heylin, 191.

[2] The lecturer could be dismissed at a fortnight's notice
(*Accounts of Province*, 527).   [3] Hobbes' *Behemoth*.

life. The afternoon sermon was ordered to be replaced in every church with catechising by question and answer on the elements of faith and practice. The Lord's Prayer, the Creed, and the Ten Commandments were once more to take their old position as the foundation of Christian instruction. The directions against preaching controversially and handling the subjects which divided Calvinist and Arminian were also to be obeyed. On such dangerous themes, the pulpit must observe a masterly silence.

It was natural that these instructions should be carried out very irregularly. In many dioceses the bishops still winked at disregard of the law ; some bishops enforced them with exasperating harshness,[1] while in the diocese of Canterbury they remained a dead letter. It argues well for the personal influence of Laud that in the diocese of London there was very little opposition, and that few clergy needed to be coerced even with censure. It was the bishop's practice to send for contumacious incumbents, and quietly persuade them to be silent on the burning controversies.[2] Even Dr. Gouge, the chief Puritan preacher in London, acknowledged and appreciated his conciliatory

---

[1] *Cf.* Wren of Norwich later on ; speeches against him in *Parliamentary History*, ix., and May's *Long Parliament*, p. 82. May's authority is greatly discredited by his application for a monopoly from the Crown, which was refused, to his great indignation.

[2] *Accounts of Province*, 526.

treatment.[1] But with the rich citizens of London Laud was less popular than with the clergy, since he was determined to enforce the full payment of the tithes which the great men of the city had hoped to confiscate to their own use, after the fashion of many of the country landlords.[2]

Meanwhile Laud was dealing in another direction a strong blow to secure the necessary elasticity for the Church.[3] In 1626 a body of clergy and laity had organised a fund for the buying up of tithe impropriations[4] which had fallen into the hands of laymen, and restoring them to religious uses. But these men, called the feoffees, being of the Puritan school, were naturally anxious to retain the control of the clergy whom they provided, and therefore kept the funds and the appointments in their own hands. There was a lecturer at St. Antholin's in the city under this system, paid for by the tithes of Presteign in Radnorshire, itself a parish very ill provided with clergy: this lecture became a great gathering place for those who disliked the present conduct of Church affairs.[5] Similar lectures were set up in important centres through

---

[1] *State Papers*, 19th October, 1631, Gouge's letter.

[2] *Cf. State Papers*, vol. 291, No. 101.

[3] Heylin, 198; Fuller, iii. 361.

[4] Out of 9284 parishes in England, the tithes of 3845 had been impropriated, chiefly by laymen, after the Reformation (Baker, 451).

[5] Heylin.

the country. The clergy who held these lectureships were paid servants of the feoffees, and
could only hold office so long as they preached
acceptable doctrine. The Court of Exchequer[1]
decided that such a trust was illegal, and confis-
cated the impropriated tithes to the king's use ;
they were restored to the parishes to which they
had formerly belonged. Shortly afterwards, by
Laud's advice, Sibbes, the most eloquent preacher
and most spiritual writer among the feoffees, was
promoted by the Crown to the charge of Trinity
Church in Cambridge : a post in which he exercised immense influence.

Such appointments made it evident that there
was no desire to crush independent thought and
teaching.[2] But if he could effect it, Laud was
determined to rescue patronage from bodies of
trustees, who by their very existence are intended
to hinder those modifications in teaching and
worship which the ever-changing condition of
society demands; and by his determined action he
secured liberty for the Church to advance with the
times. People who only saw the immediate advantage of an increased income for the clergy, and had
no sight for the future, blamed him bitterly ;[3] but
the wisdom of his course has been made plain by
experience.

[1] In 1632. *Cf.* Heylin, 200, and *Diary*.
[2] Warwick's *Memoirs*, 88.
[3] Garrard to Strafford ; Baker's *Chronicle ;* Prynne's *Works ;*
Mrs. Hutchinson ; May's *Long Parliament*.

At the same time the rights of the clergy against powerful laymen were vindicated by the action of the High Commission Court. This court had been instituted by Parliament[1] under the Tudors to exercise the royal jurisdiction in ecclesiastical matters, and was composed of bishops, privy councillors, and lawyers. Before it, in these years of Laud's supremacy, were brought cases of flagrant immorality among that class which was too great and powerful to be locally dealt with ; and here, by royal authority, such punishments were meted out to them as the inferior courts of the bishops and archdeacons inflicted upon the poor and humble. Among others Lady Purbeck (who had forsaken her husband for Sir Robert Howard) and her paramour were fined and imprisoned by the High Commission.[2]

This was a cause of some indignation ; but much more anger was felt some time later when a severe sentence was passed against a distinguished lawyer in this court.[3] Sherfield, Recorder of Salisbury, one of the Opposition leaders in the last Parliament, being annoyed by a window in

[1] Pym admits this in his speeches in Parliament of 1628. *Cf. Parliamentary History.*

[2] *Cf.* case of Lord Dudley in April, 1635 (*State Papers*), of Sir Giles Alington (Baker, 450); and of Mr. South of Grantham (Laud's *Account of his Province* in 1634 ; and *State Papers, passim, e.g.*, vol. 312, No. 45, and vol. 424, No. 39).

[3] Laud's *Works*, vi. 13 ; Heylin, 215, and accusations against Laud by the Commons.

the Church of St. Edmond, Salisbury, which represented God the Father, and to which he thought some of the worshippers did reverence, persuaded the vestry to order its removal. But as the Puritan Davenant, then Bishop of Salisbury, in annoyance at such open disregard of his authority, forbade the vestry to proceed, Sherfield shut himself into the church, and smashed with his stick the offending window. He was summoned before the High Commission, fined and compelled to apologise publicly to the bishop. Great men could no longer be a law unto themselves, and felt and said that England was losing her freedom. Laud would hear more of his tyrannical oppression of Sherfield and of Sir Robert Howard when the day of retribution dawned..

Such sentences as that on Sherfield might be brought up with some fair excuse, when the predominant party had lost its ascendency, as proving an unfair bias in this court against the Puritans. But a study of the acts of the High Commission shows us other causes for its unpopularity. Gentlemen of ancient name and high repute in their counties who were sentenced to stand in a white sheet, and do public penance in their own parish church for ugly acts of immorality, were not likely to allow themselves or their friends to forget the stern measure meted out to them by the Church, when the opportunity of revenge was come.[1] Evil-

[1] *State Papers*, vol. 324, fol. 1 and 10, and vol. 325, No. 53.

doers of every kind who had been imprisoned or fined ;[1] comfortable corporations who had been scolded severely for providing a handsome cemetery for themselves while they buried the poor in some distant corner of the parish ;[2] husbands obliged to provide alimony for their deserted wives ;[3] simoniac patrons and clergy who had been mercilessly reprimanded by the archbishop, while they lost the fruits of their transactions ;[4] all these cherished a bitter feeling against the coercion of the High Commission and fed their animosity secretly ; until at last they began to feel this well-founded and patriotic as they read in the public prints the attacks upon the hated court for prohibiting the circulation of libellous or unorthodox books,[5] and dispersing conventicles of Anabaptists.[6]

The courts of High Commission and of Star Chamber became unpopular in the country ;[7]

---

[1] *State Papers*, vol. 261, fol. 314 and 315.

[2] *Ibid.*, vol. 324, fol. 16.

[3] *Ibid.*, vol. 261, fol. 312, 268 and *passim*.

[4] *Ibid.*, vol. 261, fol. 320.

[5] *Ibid.*, vol. 261, fol. 257 and 273.

[6] *Ibid.*, vol. 261, fol. 264, where the Puritan Dr. Gouge is being supported in his efforts " to reclaim schismatics ".

[7] Contrast the usual account of these courts with the tables given by Dr. S. R. Gardiner; from 18th February, 1634, to 19th May, 1636, six clergymen were suspended for preaching against ceremonies, etc., and five for crimes. A study of the records in the *State Papers* shows how little of the business of the court had to

they were specially obnoxious to the lawyers who formed a large proportion of the House of Commons ; and they were swept away without opposition in the early days of the Long Parliament. Happily they were never revived, for they served to confuse the functions of judge and minister, because in them ministers were allowed to sit as judges of their own administration ; and the Long Parliament itself was to give the best proof, in its many acts of tyranny, of the injustice which such a confusion of the judicial and executive is sure to cause.   Yet thoughtful men regretted them as filling a place else left vacant in the judicature of England, and it was some time before a further development of the judicial system could discharge their duties.   A great judge spoke of the startling growth of fraud and perjury in the law courts since the abolition of the Star Chamber ;[1] and the chroniclers indicate the ugly increase of immorality and horrible sensual offences, as well as of blas-

do with the repression of Puritanism. Its work was chiefly for morals, *e.g.*, *State Papers*, vol. 147, No. 66. *Cf.* Clarendon's *Rebellion*, book iii.

The largest receipt in one year for fines in the Star Chamber was £7375 in 1635, a startlingly small sum when compared with the fines levied by the Long Parliament. The *State Papers* show the general mildness of treatment.

Selden (*Table Talk*, quoted by "Romish Recusant" in *Life of Laud*) reminds his listeners that there were more laymen than clergy in the High Commission.

[1] Sir M. Hale, quoted by Sir P. Warwick, p. 175. The business of the Star Chamber was mainly with private suits which could not be decided in the ordinary courts.

phemy and practices of magic,[1] which was coincident with the fall of the High Commission Court.

Meanwhile, a spirit of outward devotion and reverence was growing through England. In the North especially, where the comparative ignorance of the people made sermons without worship less endurable, and where the simple peasantry welcomed the renewal of the old stately forms, the revival of ritual was marked. This was particularly irritating to Puritan travellers. Tracts spread broad-cast in the South asserted that an image of our Saviour had been set up in Durham Cathedral for worship. In vain did Cosin, the most influential of the canons, laughingly point out that it was a part of Bishop Hatfield's somewhat barbaric tomb which a traveller's tale had magnified into an image of the Saviour. Men believed the story ; that was enough. Evidently the court was fast leading the nation back to Rome. Was it not years since the last Jesuit had been hung, drawn, and quartered? Were not new churches being built in London, and solemnly consecrated too, as if there were a special holiness in such places?[2] Were not the communion tables being everywhere moved to the east end and placed "altarwise"? Was not St. Paul's Cathedral, that "rotten relique of Popery," being fast repaired and beautified at a cost which

[1] Lilly, *Memoirs*. See in Rogers, *A Fifth Monarchy Man*, the strange desire for magic and necromancy felt often by the Puritans.

[2] *Diary*, 16th January, 1631.

men said was mounting to £100,000? Had not
Nicholas Ferrar at Little Gidding founded a community for devotion and meditation which was
nearly as bad as a Popish monastery? Were not
pious men from time to time summoned before the
High Commission and forbidden to preach the
comfortable doctrine of strict predestination? The
queen was a Papist: the king was a Papist at
heart; soon a new legate would sail solemnly up
the Thames, as Pole had done seventy years
before, and the fires of Smithfield would be
relighted.[1]

---

[1] Prynne's *Hidden Works of Darkness*. Ludlow's *Memoirs*, i. 6.
State Papers, vol. 148, No. 66, and vol. 161, No. 39. The presence
of Panzani, who was commissioned by the Roman Court to come
to England at the end of 1634, seemed to support these accusations.
He was sent by Urban VIII. to settle the angry quarrels between
the seculars and regulars; to arrange about the appointment of
a bishop in England, much opposed by the Jesuits, but greatly
desired by the laity, whose children were left unconfirmed; and to
represent the Papal views to the queen. He also interposed in
the disputes about the legality of an oath of allegiance which
most lay Romanists were willing to take, and the refusal of which
exposed them to conviction for high treason; but which was disliked at Rome, since it acknowledged the rights of a Protestant
king; see Berington's edition of Panzani's *Memoirs*.

CHAPTER VII.

*St. Paul's Cathedral—Church Extension—The Archbishop-
ric—The Project of a Patriarchate and Opposition to
Puritanism—The Eastern Counties—Going too Fast—
The Reform of the Treasury—War with Corruption—
England Mistress of the Seas—Prosperity.*

As Bishop of London, Laud had the best of
opportunities for showing to all England what
was his conception of Anglican worship and
Anglican teaching. The grandest of the cathedrals of England had been neglected for years.
St. Paul's, the mother Church of the richest city[1]
in the world, was perishing day by day because
there were no endowments for its repair. Such
a condition of things was insufferable to the man
who now took the lead as champion of light and
beauty, of art and learning. The sight of the
miserable little tenements which the greed and
carelessness of the chapter had allowed to grow
like hideous excrescences upon the walls of the
great building, and which not only hid its beauties,

---

[1] In Charles I.'s reign London seems at last to have outstripped
her rivals, Amsterdam, Genoa and Venice. See Howell, who knew
each city well.

(123)

but irritated the reverent and devotional feelings with which pious men should approach one of the most sacred places in England; the turmoil of buying and selling, of gossiping and news-telling, which had converted the long, stately nave of Bishop Maurice into " Paul's Walk," a noisy centre of business and dissipation; the disused and dilapidated choir, no fit home for the celebration of the most solemn mysteries of God, filled the new Bishop of London with indignation and impatience. The king was invited to the city on a state visit. After service and sermon he proceeded to inspect the cathedral. In his train came many a student of architecture, many a creative artist; greatest of all that architect whose severe and faultless method still draws our sympathies away from the predominant Gothic, Inigo Jones, English born and Italian bred, the king's surveyor.[1]

The inspection was decisive. Something must be done, and that promptly. Lord Brooke and the Puritan leaders might grumble out the hope that all the cathedrals, so long the homes of idolatry, would soon be demolished; but their vandalism found little favour even with the puritanically disposed citizens of London, who could not refuse affection to the church of their ancestors. It was soon evident to Inigo Jones,

---

[1] See Rushworth, ii. 90-93, for the repair of St. Paul's; *State Papers*, vol. 188, Nos. 27 and 37.

to whom the work was committed, that more than £100,000, an immense sum in those days, would be wanted to put the cathedral in order. Then there would be internal fittings to secure full dignity of worship ; and further, Laud, ever attentive to a wise policy which should not harshly offend those who could not agree with him, stipulated for a great portico at the west end ; in which the merchants might meet, and the newsmongers might gossip, without making the house of God a house of merchandise.

The Bishop of London, out of his already over-burdened income, guaranteed £100 a year, and would give anything more that he could scrape together. The work which his predecessors had only talked over, he was determined to carry through. By his widespread influence, citizens, ministers, great nobles, clergy of more fortunate cathedrals all over England, contributed liberally. By the 16th of December, 1632, shortly after the repair had been decided upon, between £5000 and £6000 had been paid into the Chamber of London.

The restoration was immediately commenced at the choir, and so cordially was it taken up by the nation that in 1641 considerably over £100,000 had been collected. And this did not include several magnificent private gifts. When Inigo Jones brought to the king the plans which he had prepared for the great western portico, Charles declared it so beautiful a conception that, for the honour of God, and the embellishment of his capital, he would himself undertake the whole cost, which amounted to nearly £11,000.[1] A friend of the bishop, Sir Paul Pindar, expended £10,000 upon the decoration and fittings of the interior ; other gifts followed, and the work was pushed on so energetically that the cathedral was just ready for the full glory of worship when Laud fell.

Modern feeling is inclined to stand aghast at the strange blending of the classic and the Gothic which Inigo Jones had wrought, but it is noticeable that there seemed nothing incongruous or inartistic about it to the great body of nobles, scholars and artists who filled the Court of Charles, and who delighted in the stately ceremonial services celebrated with all the pomp of vestment and procession and genuflection which Bishop Laud now introduced into London. St. Paul's was crowded with worshippers, and became the centre of worship in England. The most earnest and eloquent of English preachers might be heard there, or at the neighbouring Paul's Cross, Sunday by Sunday.[2] In these sermons disputation on hard school questions was the only forbidden ground. The preachers were not expected to confine themselves to one set of theological opinions so long as they instructed their hearers in the spiritual mysteries, and in the moral duties. Many distinguished men became

[1] Laud's letter to the lord mayor, vi. 369.   [2] Works, vii. 369.

famous at St. Paul's. It was here that Jeremy
Taylor's eloquence was first heard.[1] The beautiful music,[2] the poetical hymns,[3] the solemn cele-
brations of holy communion, the all-pervading
air of reverence were gradually to train men, so
the bishop hoped, to a religion of the heart as
well as of the mind, a holy habit of intercourse
with God, a strong delight in duty.

While the restored St. Paul's was the most
famous monument of Laud's episcopate in
London, the restoration of other churches was not
forgotten, nor the building of new churches in growing suburbs.[4] These it was his custom solemnly
to consecrate[5] with a ceremonial, originated or
revived by Bishop Andrewes, which was bitterly
satirised by the Puritan pamphleteers. What
good was done, they scoffingly asked, by these
bowings and scrapings and mutterings? Did he
imagine that God was only to be found in a spot
over which certain incantations had been used?

And herein lay indeed one of the chief points

---

[1] Bishop Heber's *Life of Taylor.* Laud's *Works*, vi. 437.

[2] Burney's *History of Music*, iii. 356-387, for church music of
the time.

[3] See "Hymns" in Howell's *Letters;* George Wither's *Hymns;*
Sandys' *Paraphrases*, etc.

[4] Similar proceedings went forward in other dioceses. Archbishop Neile reports that, in the diocese of York, £6500 was
expended during 1635 on the restoration of churches (*State Papers*,
vol. 312, No. 84).

[5] *Diary*, 7th June, 1631, 17th July, 1632, 26th May, 1632.

of difference between the two schools of thought.
To the Puritan the church was a preaching house,
in which some well-trained speaker pressed upon
the listener's mind a conviction of sin, and the
means to gain the forgiveness of an angry God.[1]
For this purpose there was no need of beauty :
" I want the chapel cheap," said the Puritan Lord
Bedford, as he conferred with Inigo Jones on the
building of a new church for Covent Garden, "in
short, I would not have it much better than a
barn ".[2] The nobler side of their preference for
ugly churches is brought home to us by Milton :
" Tell me, ye priests, wherefore this gold, wherefore these robes and surplices over the Gospel ?
Is our religion guilty of the first trespass and hath
need of clothing to cover her nakedness ? . . .
Ye think by these gaudy glisterings to stir up the
devotion of the rude multitude ; ye think so because ye forsake the heavenly teachings of St.
Paul for the hellish sophistry of Papism. If the
multitude be rude the lips of the *preacher* must
give knowledge, and not ceremonies."[3] But to
Laud the church was the hallowed spot in which
a poor weak human soul came into the presence

---

[1] Prynne's *Works.   Cf*. Cromwell, letter i., and Carlyle's comments; Rogers' *Fifth Monarchy Man ;* and *State Papers*, vol. 267,
No. 90, where a Puritan preacher asserts that " preaching is the
ordinary means ordained by God to salvation," and therefore
urges the *necessity* of two sermons every Sunday.

[2] Cunningham's *Life*, 35.

[3] *The Reason for Church Government*, book ii. chap. ii.

of his Maker and his Father for prayer and
praise. His school dwelt on the importance of
having a fixed place for devotion where the train
of spiritual thought could quickly be resumed.
When the worshipper entered, he should bow
reverently to the holy table, collecting his thoughts
in prayer; not because the Saviour was there
present in the consecrated elements (this was
a distinction from Romanism which Laud continually emphasised),[1] but because it was the table
of Christ, and symbolised the covenant of grace
which He had made with His people. And this
reverent feeling should be deepened by every
external aid; by magnificent architecture, by
melodious music, by solemn ritual, by careful
decorum of demeanour, all valuable habits for assisting the worshippers to realise that God Himself
was present. The sermon was to be subordinate.
No one took more pains about preaching, or was
more diligent in finding and promoting preachers
of talent, and most of the great preachers of the
Restoration were first brought forward by him; but
he would have no one preach who would not pray.
It was a point of principle as much as of discipline
that the lecturers should lead the prayers of the
congregation whom they were about to instruct.
The bare sermon as the only worship of the day
was hateful to Laud. After communion in prayer,
teacher and taught could understand each other.

[1] *Cf. Book against Fisher*, sect. xxxv.

9

This war, therefore, against the Puritan lecturers he carried on by gentle means, but with iron will. The Vicar of St. Botolph's without Aldgate had agreed that his parishioners might appoint a lecturer at their own charges to do half his work, if they would first increase his vicarial stipend by £30 a year. Both parties were considerably surprised to find that the bishop considered them in this comfortable arrangement to be buying and selling the charge of souls.[1]

On the whole the diocese of London settled down comfortably enough. A few lecturers were deprived for nonconformity, and paid out the bishop for the inconveniences which they endured by the savage libels which they published against him. Laud's affectionate nature always suffered from bitterly expressed dislike : he writhed under the charges of hypocrisy, dishonesty, and even of acts of immorality which they did not hesitate to invent ; but he suffered in silence, for he felt he was performing his duty to the Church and nation. Occasionally he considered the libels too serious to be left unanswered. Sometimes they could be refuted by his acts, as when he publicly celebrated the marriage of one of his chaplains in reply to the accusation that he considered celibacy obligatory on the clergy.[2] Sometimes his chaplains were instructed to publish books on great questions of

---

[1] Cf. State Papers, vol. 177, No. 34.   [2] Heylin, 212.

principle.[1]   Once and again some specially malig-
nant charge against the Church, which he could
not treat as a mere personal accusation, induced
him, as in the case of Prynne and of the detestable
punishment inflicted on Leighton,[2] to permit trial
and sentence in the Star Chamber, unless the
offender chose to appeal to the more severe justice
of the King's Bench.

The Opposition grew more angry as the success
of the new ecclesiastical policy proved more conspicuous, and as Laud's power with king and
people increased.

On 6th August, 1633, he came to visit Charles
at Greenwich. " My Lord's Grace of Canterbury," said the king, " you are very welcome."
Abbot was dead,[3] and the long-expected primacy
was vacant.   The last obstacle to the reform of
the Church of England had been removed (so both
Charles and Laud felt) by Providence : and their

[1] Jeremy Taylor's *Works*, v., "Episcopacy Asserted"; Heylin,
etc.

[2] Young Leighton, son of this savage libeller, was carefully
looked after by Laud; he was afterwards the saintly Archbishop
of Glasgow.   The king would have pardoned Leighton if he had
not broken out of prison.   Leighton horrified people by applying
to himself the prophecies of the sufferings of Christ; he called
the bishops "men of blood," and advised his readers to repeat
Felton's praiseworthy act (Rushworth, ii. 55).   I can find no contemporary proof of Neale's assertion in his *History of the Puritans*
that " Laud took off his cap and thanked God for the sentence "
on Leighton ; which seems to be taken from Leighton's *Epitome*,
published many years later, quoted by Dr. Gardiner, i. 184.

[3] See Carte's *Ormond* for the carelessness of the archbishop
in his latter years in the discharge of his duty, i. 5.

joy was probably shared by the majority of Englishmen: *exultat ecclesia*, writes Sir Thomas Roe in congratulating Laud.[1] For indeed all seemed to be going well. England had never been more free from disturbances. Trade had never been so vigorous. London was becoming more and more the chief emporium of the world's commerce.[2] The king had just been crowned in Scotland, and Laud, after a personal visit to the chief towns and much conversation with the chief people, had come to the conclusion that a liturgy might safely be introduced into that country.

The Church had welded England into one in the old days; her influence had made Wales a part of England. Was it not possible that in the Church life would be found the necessary force of sympathy to combine the whole population of the two islands into one nation, with one king, one form of worship, one legal code, and since Laud and Wentworth always looked forward to the full revival of the Tudor Parliamentary system—one Parliament? Could the archbishop help adding in his own heart that of this magnificent empire, already extending over the world, he would be first patriarch;[3] and, as men had said of old about Anselm (it was a tale he loved to tell), *Papa alterius orbis*, Pope of a second, of an English

---

[1] *State Papers*, 20th August, 1633.
[2] *Cf.* Ranke's *England*, ii. 55.
[3] See the Père d'Orléans, ix. 249.

world; but no tyrant Pope, rather the constitutional leader of a free, liberal, learned Church, strong in organisation, dignified in worship, devout in prayer, champion and deliverer of the poor, which might do for the West what Alexandria and Constantinople had failed to do for the East? Even wider schemes than this—for a general reunion of Christendom[1] which would leave Rome isolated in its corner of south-western Europe—were already being sketched out. Emissaries from Canterbury were working to reconcile Lutheran and Calvinist in Germany, and to establish some agreement between the German Protestants and the Anglican community; while, at the same time, Pococke, Laud's new Arabic reader at Oxford, was negotiating on his behalf with Cyril Lucaris, the learned patriarch of Constantinople, and Graves, his agent in Egypt for the collection of hieroglyphics and manuscripts, had opened correspondence for him with the patriarch of Alexandria. The affection and admiration felt for Laud by the leading foreign scholars seemed to promise that at least the foundations of unity could be laid, and the

---

[1] See letters to Pococke, *Works*, vi. 521, etc., and Twells' *Life*, 49-72. Sir T. Roe's embassy to the Sultan in 1621 had gained many privileges for the Greek Church, and commenced that intercourse which brought us the Alexandrine MS. of the Bible (*Athenae*, ii. 52). The patriarch, Cyril Lucaris, during Pococke's sojourn in the East used to attend English worship (Twells' *Life*, 49).

historic episcopate, meeting in general council, might yet recover its liberty from the autocratic Popedom. Schemes for foreign missions to the Indians in America, and even to the Mahommedans of Turkey, floated before his eyes.[1]

Wentworth, the strong, decided, clear-sighted statesman, to whom Laud clung with an affection not unmixed with such admiration as a shy, sensitive scholar must naturally feel for the man of war and action, had restored Ireland to order, and was on the eve of summoning a Parliament. He had curbed the power of the great nobles, and had commenced the reform of the Irish Church, always a most dear object to the heart of the new archbishop.

The law apparently, so the judges had decided, would bear out all the king's acts: and without guards and without police, without executions and without wars, [2] Charles seemed to be growing as potent in England as Louis XIII., his brother-in-law, was in France; and to be in a fair way to rule his country according to his own will, unless he preferred the old English custom of periodical Parliaments. And if the king was strong, what honour was reflected upon Laud, the chief architect of his fortunes? Two years later the position of Charles' great minister seemed so secure and so magnificent that Sir Thomas Roe writes to the Queen of Bohemia about him: "Being

[1] Twells' *Pococke*, 77.
[2] Correspondence of Laud and Wentworth, *passim*.

now so great he must choose and make new ways
to show he knows and can do more than others,
and this only hath made Cardinal Richelieu so
glorious ".[1] But it was not fame which the archbishop coveted ; he desired to perfect the English
Church and State according to his own ideals ;
and this could only be accomplished by hard work
at the details of administration and the most diligent attention to the wants of the people. Two
purposes specially interested him at this time : he
was determined to complete the reform of the
Church, and to purify the administration of the
Treasury from the corruptions which the Lord
Treasurer, Weston, had fostered for his personal
advantage.

The first of these objects could be secured by
a visitation of the whole province of Canterbury,
diocese by diocese, on his own authority as
metropolitan. For three years, beginning in
1634, the vicar-general, Sir Nathaniel Brent,[2] was
sent to every diocese in the South of England
to reform abuses and to enforce the law. The
clergy were compelled to attend to their duties ;
immoral clergymen were brought before the
High Commission and deprived ; communion
tables were removed to the upper end of the
chancel ; and communicants obliged to receive the
holy sacrament kneeling.

[1] *State Papers*, 5th April, 1635.
[2] For Laud's instructions see *State Papers*, 22nd February, 1634.

Two large dioceses caused the archbishop special anxiety. Williams, Bishop of Lincoln, opposed his claim to visit, and, though the courts supported the metropolitan, it was quite clear that the directions for placing the communion tables in the chancel, and for suppressing such lectureships as were held at the will of lay patrons, would not continue to be carried out when the vicar-general had departed. Worse still, the morality of the county of Lincoln was shown to be in a grievous condition ;[1] and, in this diocese conspicuously, great numbers of people were found by the visitor to have been excommunicated for neglect in paying the fees due to the legal officials of the bishop. Laud directed the excommunications to be taken off and watched his opportunity to put the diocese into safer hands. He felt keenly the disgrace brought upon the Church by the use of spiritual penalties for pecuniary gain.[2]

The diocese of Norwich was the most difficult to govern in all England. Large numbers of foreign settlers had poured into it from France and Holland, flying from Roman persecution. So great was the compassion felt for them that the bishop had given up his episcopal chapel for a French service.[3] These new-comers had added by their industry and technical skill to

---

[1] *State Papers*, 9th September, 1634, and Laud's *Accounts of Province.*

[2] *Accounts of Province*, 555.   [3] *Ibid.*

the riches which made Norfolk rank next to Middlesex in wealth among the counties of England;[1] but they remained foreigners in a strange land, with no interest in its religious and social progress :[2] and they stirred a strong feeling against ceremonial of any kind. There was a commercial danger also, for now that Holland had established her freedom they, and many English with them, were being tempted across the North Sea by liberal offers from the rulers of the Republic.[3] Such departures seriously injured trade and engendered discontent. At the same time Puritanic feeling in the diocese was developed by the close connection between Norfolk and London, where most of the commercial families had representatives.[4] And yet, when the rebellion came, Norfolk proved to be less Puritan in its sympathies than many writers have supposed. Lynn was devout in its churchmanship and resolute in its loyalty.[5] Long lists of malignants were presented to the Parliament for fines ; and a riot in Norwich in 1648 could only be extinguished by numerous executions,[6] while Colchester was the

---

[1] Mason's *Norfolk*, 303 ; Drayton's *Polyolbion*, xx. 12.

[2] This was probably the chief reason for Laud's attempt to break up the foreign congregations (*State Papers*, 19th December, 1634, and *passim*).

[3] Mason's *Norfolk*, 409 ; Laud's *Accounts of Province*, 549.

[4] State papers, wills, deeds, etc.

[5] Mason's *Norfolk*, 282, 410.

[6] *Ibid*, 304.

last retreat of the conquered Royalists.   It was the
military genius and the swift blows of Oliver
Cromwell which forced the eastern counties into
the famous Association.   For Laud's work had
been carefully done in the diocese of Norwich.
Bishop Samuel Harsnet, the baker's son of Colchester,[1] a good scholar and a hard-working
clergyman, though despised for his low birth by
the country gentry, had enforced the royal instructions about catechising and reverence in worship.[2]
Then on Harsnet's elevation to York the Prime
Minister had attempted to win over the Puritans
of the eastern counties by sending them the
witty Bishop Corbett, whose gay humour lights up
many a dull page of contemporary documents, and
whom Wood describes as "a quaint preacher and
therefore much followed by ingenious men":[3] and
later he hoped to hasten the establishment of Church
ritual by the appointment as Corbett's successor of
the stern Bishop Matthew Wren, of "a severe, sour
nature, but very learned,"[4] who proved so strict a
disciplinarian that in 1638 he was moved to Ely,
and succeeded by Montague, the hero of many a

---

[1] Morant's *Essex*, book ii. 121.

[2] *Parliamentary History*, vi. 312-319, for absurd accusations
brought against him by a man who wished to be Archdeacon of
Norwich.

[3] Wood's *Athenae*, and *State Papers*, vol. 150, No. 80.   Garrard
describes his death-bed: "prayers ended, he gave them all good-
night and died" (*State Papers*. Sept. 18, 1635).

[4] Clarendon's *Rebellion*.

Parliamentary debate and the author of *The New Gag for an Old Goose*, written against Romanism, a keen disputant and bright and educated preacher. The rule about the position of the communion table was enforced with decision. But Laud's advice to his suffragans was to be cautious ; and he accepted the objections urged by many clergy against communicating at the rail, as a reason for introducing the practice gradually and after persuasive instruction ; though he pointed out that no difficulty had been experienced in bringing up over 2000 communicants at St. Giles', Cripplegate, to the east end with reverence and solemnity.[1]

Upon the mass of the inhabitants the combination of clever preaching and strictness had had its effect ; but Wren's severity drove the more determined men into revolt. Three thousand people, it was said in Parliament, had fled to Holland,[2] and though the records prove that only 1350 emigrated between 1630 and 1640, and that many of these went for purposes of trade,[3] evidently others resented what they felt with justice to be a persecution. At one time, out of the 1500 clergy in the diocese no less than thirty were suspended for nonconformity ;[4] and one case shows in a most

---

[1] *Accounts of Province*, 557. *Cf. State Papers*, vol. 417, No. 31.

[2] Speeches against Wren, *Parliamentary History*, 1641, and Clarendon's *Rebellion*, i. 316.

[3] Mason's *Norfolk*, 409.

[4] *Accounts of Province*, 542.

unpleasant light the occasional tyranny of the High Commission Court.

A popular minister, Ward of Ipswich, was imprisoned for several years for attacking the Prayer Book.   It was an injudicious act, for such a punishment was startlingly excessive.[1]   The English community, so indifferent to logic but so impatient of personal wrongs, discussed the harsh treatment of the pious Ward of Ipswich.   Perhaps he was a little mad, people said, in his melancholy fits, but he had helped many souls.   They missed his ministrations; they resented his sufferings. Did the archbishop in the vast number of details which he had to supervise forget Ward of Ipswich and his indignant congregation?

Indeed, it is in cases like these that we see the future peril of the Government.   The few years in which ceremonial Puritanism had been allowed to conduct the services as it pleased, under Abbot and Buckingham, had accustomed men to ir-reverent and slovenly worship.   The English race had formed a dislike to kneeling.   To a large proportion of sincerely religious men, outward reverence has often appeared unnecessary, and even a hindrance to faith.

But to Laud this seemed entirely contrary to reason.   " I evidently saw," he says, " that the public neglect of God's service in the outward face of it, and the nasty lying of so many places dedi-

---

[1] *State Papers, passim,* and *Accounts of Province,* 1634-5-6, etc.

cated to that service, had almost cast a damp upon
the true and inward worship of God, which, while
we live in the body, needs external helps, and all
little enough to keep it in any vigour.   And this
I did to the utmost of my knowledge, according
both to law and canon, and with the consent and
liking of the people ; nor did any command issue
out from me against the one or without the other
that I know of." [1]

But outward reverence enforced by men of
very superficial religion opened the way for
dangerous and natural criticism.   The vicar-general
was not the archbishop ; men might ridicule Laud
for his prim manners and small stature ; yet, after
all, they soon found his religion was genuine, and
that he was no self-seeker.   Brent followed the
fashion ; high Anglican to-day, he would be furious
Puritan [2] when Pym and his colleagues ruled in
England.   The lawyers, who presided in the ecclesiastical courts, and whom the bishops in spite
of every effort could not replace with more spiritual
men, [3] were mostly like Brent, eager to use their
offices for profit ; the Church got the discredit of

[1] *Trials and Troubles*, p. 224.   *Cf.* support given to the removal
of the nonconformist minister of St. Catherine Cree by the congregation, *State Papers*, vol. 261, fol. 282 and 291 ; a similar case at
Ware, vol. 261, fol. 298, etc., etc.

[2] He gave evidence against Laud at his trial (Wood's *Athenae*,
i. 161).

[3] *Cf.* the troubles of the saintly Bishop Bedell of Kilmore
(*Life*).

these men's acts through no fault of her own. Nor were the lawyers only in fault, since many of the clergy imitated the archbishop's ritual without the archbishop's piety. To the multitude, difference in outward observances will always seem more important than doctrinal disputes. The huge majority, who were not ill-pleased to see Puritan ministers silenced for dooming them all to everlasting misery because they did not take the trouble to assent to their teaching, kicked when they were forbidden to loll in the seats, or to walk about and discuss crops and prices during the prayers; and disliked being obliged to take their part in worship and to kneel for communion before the eyes of their fellow-townsmen.[1]

The archbishop was asking too much of his countrymen. To persuade them to decorous worship would be the work of time and gentleness. He strove to hurry it on;[2] and he would fail, for the present moment; until the cold severity of Puritanism,[3] repressing all bright amusement, and exacting profession of a profound personal religion which most men could not feel, would drive the

[1] Laud allowed that it was legal to communicate in pews if the worshipper knelt (*Works*, vi. 478). He was most anxious that they should be quietly persuaded to come to the rails (*Accounts of Province*, 543). For irreverence in church, *cf. State Papers*, vol. 154, No. 94.   [2] Sir P. Warwick, 90.

[3] In Mrs. Hutchinson's *Memoirs* of her husband she tells us that she, like other godly persons, disliked every kind of amusement (i. 27, 94).

nation back thankfully to the gentler teaching of the Church. Therefore, though the visitors were usually well received and readily obeyed,[1] a certain bitter taste remained in several districts, and the archiepiscopal visitation was undoubtedly one cause of the growing unpopularity of the Government.

But perhaps the want of careful supervision in the conduct of the visitation, and the absence through the province of that conciliatory spirit which Laud had shown in winning over the Puritans in his former diocese of London, and which he still employed in dealing with his own diocese of Canterbury, was in the main due to the archbishop's being occupied through these years in the reform of the administration of the Treasury. Wentworth, crippled and hampered in his work of building up Irish prosperity, was continually denouncing the Lord Treasurer Weston, now Earl of Portland, to his friend.[2] Laud himself was perplexed and irritated by complaints of corruption at the Treasury, bribes taken from monopolist companies, difficulties put in the way of merchants who would not offer presents to the Treasurer. While Weston lived nothing could be done ; his easy ways and readiness to produce the necessary money made him agreeable to the

---

[1] *State Papers*, 1635, etc., *passim*.

[2] *Strafford Letters, passim.* Laud's *Works*, vii. 102, 115, 130, 162, etc.

king, and popular with the queen.   But on the 13th
of March, 1635, Weston, the " Lady Mora "[1] of the
Laud and Strafford letters, died, and Laud, fearing
lest Cottington, "the Lady Mora's waiting-maid,"
as they called him, and as unprincipled as Weston
himself, would become treasurer, most unwillingly
accepted a seat on the Board of Commissioners
for the Treasury.[2]   Even the active mind of the
primate, indefatigable in his attention to the
smallest matters, could hardly supervise the
details of the visitation, while he superintended
his diocese and the ordinary business of the
Church, reformed the Universities of Oxford and
Dublin, interested himself in the Church affairs of
Scotland and Ireland, watched the religious condition of the regiments in foreign service and the
English communities abroad, attempted to reconcile in Germany Lutherans and Calvinists,[3] and
settled the necessary reforms of the Treasury.
" To manage all was no better than a glorious
burden."[4]   The details of the visitation, and these
were all-important since they affected the interests
of great numbers of individuals, fell into the hands
of Brent, and the consequences we have seen.

---

[1] This was the name given to Weston, Earl of Portland and
Lord Treasurer, because of his dilatory ways, by his two fellow-
ministers.   [2] *Diary*.

[3] Laud's *Works*, vi. 410, vii. 112, and *State Papers*, 30th January,
1634.

[4] *State Papers.*   Letter from Nicholas on Laud's appointment
to the Treasury.

Laud threw himself vigorously[1] into his new duties of finance; he was determined to free the king from debt; in the quiet of his palace at Croydon he took counsel with prominent merchants, whom he admitted to his friendship, as to the best means of developing trade.[2] For the Treasury was on the verge of bankruptcy; each year closed with a deficit; an immense floating debt crippled any settlement; and yet a fleet was necessary to vindicate England's supremacy over the seas, and to show France and Holland that she was still a power in Europe. The Parliament which could so easily supply the funds the king refused to hear mentioned. Economy was therefore the first requisite,[3] and Laud began by securing a thorough investigation of the royal accounts in spite of the opposition of Cottington, who was Chancellor of the Exchequer. The new First Commissioner had a weekly report of the finances laid upon the Board. He secured a proper adjustment of the expenditure to the receipts. His hand was seen in all the dealings of the Treasury.

But he could not carry his point in all the disputes at the Treasury Board. Windebank, an old

---

[1] See *State Papers* in March, 1635, for the remarkable stir in every department of Government.

[2] Every year part of the king's debts was paid off (Clarendon, *Life*, i. 21-28; *cf. State Papers*).

[3] Fuller, iii. 475. *State Papers.*

pupil, and appointed by his recommendation Secretary of State,[1] one of his dearest personal friends, deserted him in the crucial division on the rival soap companies,[2] which came about in this wise.

All Englishmen in those days agreed on the importance of keeping to England the manufacture of English soap. But in order to secure this, Weston had set up a soap company of his own friends who were to pay the king openly £20,000 a year, and himself secretly £2000. As this company was largely composed of Romanists, the soap was called Popish soap, and was most unpopular in London. The older soap manufacturers, now Weston was dead, offered to form a new company, and to pay the Treasury £40,000 a year; they were vigorously, even passionately, supported by Laud; but Cottington, suave, full of wise expedients, perfectly self-controlled, carried the day against the archbishop, whose zeal in insisting upon his convictions was already making him somewhat imperious in manner and overbearing in argument. The Popish soap was not a success, if we may trust the defeated minister; he told Wentworth that his clothes washed in it "smelt mighty ill". But these wrangles over the monopolies were at least public enough to show the people that individual

[1] See letter ccxxxvi. *Works*, vii. 43.
[2] *Diary*, 12th July, 1635.

ministers found in them a source of personal profit,
and that the specious reasons urged in defence of
them, about the improvement of manufactures and
keeping the profits of England for the English,
were not the sole motives in their creation. The
monopolies became continually more discredited
and unpopular. Wentworth often persuaded
Laud that they could only serve to build up
private fortunes for royal courtiers; but it was
difficult to change the system.

It was still more deplorable to Laud that
other ministers were encouraging the king in
heavy expenditure at Richmond Park. "I am
alone," he writes to Wentworth, "in those things
which draw not profit after them." Hamilton,
Holland[1] and the rest were using their influence
with the king to fill their own pockets. At last a
specially flagrant case of attempted corruption
brought on a pitched battle between the archbishop
and the Chancellor of the Exchequer. Cottington
saved the briber from prosecution, but he lost the
treasurer's staff, which by Laud's advice (as Wentworth could not leave Ireland) was given to Juxon,
Bishop of London, on the 6th of March, 1636. The
king announced that he chose Juxon as a clergyman, because he could trust the clergy; and that
he had selected him among the clergy, because
he had no children, and therefore less private

[1] *E.g.*, Lord Ormond paid Holland £15,000 to secure his support to his marriage with one of the king's wards (Carte, i. 8).

ends to serve. Laud was delighted. "No churchman," he writes in his *Diary*, "had it since Henry VII.'s time. I pray God bless him to carry it so that the Church may have honour, and the king and the State service and contentment by it, and now, if the Church will not hold themselves under God, I can do no more."[1] Juxon proved an admirable treasurer: he was popular with men of all parties.[2] Now, at last, no one doubted that every shilling of the taxes found its way into the national treasury. His modest diligence is shown by his instruction to a high permanent official to arrest and criticise anything which he considered novel and detrimental in the treasurer's own acts.[3]

But his appointment was a fatal success.[4] Forest courts had been set up to compel men who had encroached upon the forests to pay fines to the king. As gentlemen and small squatters paid their fines they cursed the episcopal Lord Treasurer. Ship money was now being exacted from every county in England, illegally as many thought, though the law courts upheld the royal claim. The tax added to the unpopularity of the bishops. Was not a bishop treasurer, and the archbishop the

---

[1] *Diary*, 6th March, 1636.

[2] *Strafford Letters*, letter from Garrard, ii. 55, and Sir P. Warwick, pp. 93-95. He was not molested even by the Long Parliament.

[3] *State Papers*, and Wood's *Athenae*, ii. 1145.

[4] May, *Long Parliament*, p. 33.

king's most trusted counsellor? A new book of
rates for customs was brought out and enforced ;
it increased the king's revenue by £70,000 a year,
and was far less troublesome to the merchants.
But what right had the Crown to alter the rates
without consent of Parliament? Everywhere men
complained that power had fallen into the hands
of the Church ; and the scrupulous honesty of the
new administration made no amends to the laity
for the loss of influence. The Church was rising
as a mighty power to suppress wickedness and to
defend the weak ; but it was objected that Christ's
commands were carried out, not as He desired by
persuasion and example, but by force and coercion.

The results which the new energy of the
Government could show were undoubtedly magnificent. The monopolies were curtailed ; and courtiers
compelled to surrender patents which checked the
free development of trade. [1] A postal system was
gradually created to carry letters at fixed rates
through England, and even into Scotland, and to
foreign countries ; [2] an invaluable aid to men of
business. New companies were founded to organise fresh routes for commerce, and to attract
to England the carrying trade of the world. [3] Embassies to distant potentates in the East opened

[1] *State Papers*, March, 1635.

[2] Macpherson's *Annals of Commerce ;* Rushworth, ii. 145 ; *State
Papers*, vol. 291, Nos. 114 and 294, No. 62.

[3] Macpherson's *Annals of Commerce, sub anno* 1630, etc.

opportunities for English merchants in many new markets.

But if this progress was to be maintained, it was evidently necessary to make England respected abroad. Turkish pirates from Sallée, and Flemish privateers from Dunkirk, preyed on English traders, and made the very Channel itself dangerous to navigation. [1] France and Spain and Holland sneered at a kingdom which had no fleet to protect its ports or to vindicate its claims to the sovereignty of the seas. It was annoyance at the refusal of Parliament to support him in foreign enterprise which had originally alienated the king from the House of Commons. His pride demanded that England should again become a great power. A paper prepared by Secretary Coke at the wish of the king and Laud in June, 1634,[2] a few months before Portland's death, exhibits the dissatisfaction which they felt at the feebleness of the foreign policy of the kingdom. This they were now determined should be gloriously reversed. Noy's suggestion about ship money supplied them with the necessary means. In 1635 a great fleet was equipped ;[3] year after year it put to sea ; the Turk-

---

[1] *State Papers*, vol. 279, No. 106.   [2] *Ibid.*, vol. 269, No. 51.

[3] Laud's *Works*, vi. 498, 513. Garrard to Strafford. Baker's *Chronicle*, 455. Howell, i. 256. A description published at the time tells us that the great ship launched at Woolwich soon after and called the *Sovereign of the Seas* was 1637 tons, 128 feet long and 48 feet broad. The ship cost £80,000, and carried ninety-six guns. *Cf.* Gussone's *Relations*, 1635, quoted by Ranke.

ish pirates were driven from the Channel; the Dunkirk privateers were severely punished for their attacks upon the post boats and the coasting craft;[1] finally the pirates were pursued, in 1637, to the African coast; at Sallée, their dreaded harbour of refuge, they were obliged to accept the terms dictated to them, and thousands of unfortunate captives were restored to their homes in England.[2] The French and Dutch were compelled to strike their flags to the royal admiral of England,[3] who had now recovered for his master the sovereignty of the narrow seas. Behind the fleet the train bands, now improved in discipline and efficiency by constant exercise, and well armed from the royal arsenals, defied foreign invaders,[4] and provided a force which, being officered by the nobles and the gentry, could not be dangerous to English liberty, but could make the king a redoubtable ally to any of his great neighbours.

---

[1] *State Papers*, vol. 295, No. 65. For their ravages, *cf.* vol. 162, Nos. 62 and 83.

[2] *State Papers*. Baker's *Chronicle*. *Accounts of Province*, 1637. Laud took special interest in the proper reception of the released English slaves (Laud's *Works*, vi. 498, 513).

[3] The Dutch were compelled by the new fleet to pay £30,000 for the right of fishing, and to acknowledge the English sovereignty of the narrow seas. *Cf.* Mason's *Norfolk*, 261, for the protection given to the commerce of the eastern counties by the Whelps.

[4] There was some fear of a French invasion in 1635 (*State Papers*, vol. 298, No. 63). For train bands, see *State Papers*, vol. 310, Nos. 44 and 45, vol. 287, No. 55.

But this unparalleled prosperity [1] earned for the Government no gratitude; rather it gave men leisure for discontent. It was free play for their own talents in ruling, and free discussion of their opinions political and religious, that the gentry and merchants wanted. But the bishops held power, and the bishops tuned the pulpits, and the bishops regulated the press.[2] Everywhere men, when they found themselves in collision with authority, encountered ecclesiastics, and these ecclesiastics, they were taught by nobles like Lords Saye and Brooke, by angry country gentlemen and suppressed lecturers, had resolved to give them over tied hand and foot to Rome and the Inquisition.

[1] Extract from Roberts' *The Merchant's Map of Commerce*, published 1638. "When I survey every kingdom and great city of the world and every petty port and creek of the same, I find in each of them some English prying after the trade and commerce thereof." English traffic used to be confined to the export of the staple merchandise of the country, "such as are cloths, lead, tin, some new late draperies, and other English real and royal commodities"; now England was become the emporium of the world, and its ships the world's carriers. England had superseded Venice and actually supplied that city, and took the traffic of India, Arabia and Persia to Italy and to France. Manchester and the cotton trade were rising into importance; Manchester also manufactured linen. Here we have the first mention of its manufacture in England. England rivalled Holland, and supplied Scandinavia and Muscovy, and its goods were to be found throughout France and Spain.

The Capuchins write to Italy, "England is an abundant country and hath no taxes" (p. 309 of *The Relation of Their Mission*). *Cf.* Clarendon's *Rebellion*, and even Ludlow, i. 174.

[2] Every book had to be licensed by the archbishop, the Bishop of London, or one of the universities.

Besides, as the Puritan lords and gentry were always repeating, the bishops and priests were " base-born, "[1] and nobles had an hereditary right to rule England. The clergy were believed to be grasping at all the great offices ; one was named as future Master of the Rolls ; another as Secretary of State ; a third as Chancellor of the Exchequer.[2] Nor was the Government popular at Court ; the courtiers detested its economy, and longed to dip greedy hands into the money bags of the State, and persuaded the queen to become the head of a party opposed to Laud. Only the working classes rejoiced to find that their oppressors were controlled ; and heard with amazement and delight that the judges on circuit had special directions to see them righted ;[3] and that many of the worst oppressions had been severely punished in the Star Chamber. But the working men were not yet a power in England ; and their sympathy would avail Laud little.[4]

It was still possible and most important to conciliate the professional classes : from their ranks the clergy were drawn ; they benefited

[1] Mrs. Hutchinson, i. 133; Lord Saye's *Speech against the Bishops*, and Prynne, *Cantorburie's Doom*.

[2] Garrard to Wentworth, *Strafford Papers*, ii. 2.

[3] Rushworth, ii. 294, for Lord Keeper Coventry's *Instructions to the Judges on Circuit*.

[4] See Baxter's *Autobiography*, p. 30, and Ludlow's *Memoirs*, i. 121, for hostile testimony to the affection felt for the Government by the common people.

greatly by the universal prosperity ; many of their
number were promoted to office ; and the Government was most diligent in encouraging and
developing education. But they were to be
alienated by some severe and barbarous punishments, which now agitated people's minds ; and
as peace and prosperity afforded leisure for attention to events which in stirring times pass unheeded,
news writers, and historians after them, have been
compelled to enliven the dull years of quiet progress
by giving exaggerated prominence to a few legal
sentences ; and thus the uniformly merciful
government of Charles I. gained a name for
cruelty and oppression, while few remember the
executions under Elizabeth, or those in the Reign
of Terror under Harry Vane and Oliver Cromwell.[1]

---

[1] Guizot, blindly following Neale's *Puritans*, a valuable work,
but one requiring careful handling, has written a description of
these prosperous years of Charles I. in his *English Revolution*
which is no better than a parody.

For the navy, see Note B on p. 295.

The two principal authorities for this part of Laud's life are
Anthony à Wood, as quoted above; and Laud's *Account of
his Chancellorship* (Wharton's edition, pub. 1700). The letters
to Vossius are often very valuable.

CHAPTER VIII.

*Toleration of Opinion—The Chancellorship of Oxford—
Repression of Indiscipline—Cultivation of Eastern
Languages—The Learned Press—Royal Visit—En-
couragement of Mathematics and Science—Resignation.*

No part of the voluminous Laudian literature is
so interesting or so delightful to the student as the
history of his dealings with the University of
Oxford. Indeed, here and here alone, we can
study the free working of the great archbishop's
will. For in the university he was supreme ; and
in the university he worked with kindred minds,
of whom most loved him as a friend, while all
followed him as their leader. In State affairs the
imperious will of Buckingham or of Strafford
constantly swayed his judgment ; the intrigues
of Cottington and the obstinate delays of Weston
hindered his reforms. Even in Church affairs
bitter and ignorant opposition or the faultiness
of irreligious instruments hampered, as we have
seen, the free play of his far-reaching ideas, and
introduced an intolerance which was foreign to his
nature. Therefore it is to the university that we
see him turn for refreshment ; it is with the uni-

versity officials that he opens his mind in correspondence.   To gain privileges for the university
seems to him like a personal victory.   His
collections of coins and manuscripts and objects
of interest are for the university.   The university
is his "dear mother".   When his admirers and
flatterers propose to call the university institutions
after him, he instantly checks the project; there
shall on no account be alterations in the old
familiar names.   And in the busiest and most
anxious weeks he always finds time to plan and
execute schemes and reforms for the prosperity of
the university.   At Oxford Laud had raised
himself to be leader of the Liberal party, if that
word may be justly applied to the body of men
which fought for the advance of learning, and the
progress of free opinion.[1]   He had never lost
touch with the heads of the university; and when
the chancellor, Lord Pembroke, died in 1630, the
most influential men at once pronounced that
Laud was the only magnate able to raise the
university to its former high renown as one of the
great centres of European learning, to restore its
discipline, and by his influence with the Government secure full scope for its development.   The
Puritan party did indeed bring out a rival in the
person of the new Earl of Pembroke, one of the
most empty-headed and self-seeking men of his
time.   But the prestige of Laud carried all before

[1] Clarendon's *Life*, i. 55-66.

it, and the chancellorship was offered to him and accepted at London House in May, 1630. His religious policy in the university is well expressed in a letter which he wrote to Vossius in the preceding year :—[1]

" I have always made every effort that those rough and difficult subjects should not be discussed before the crowd ; fearing that under pretence of truth we should injure piety and charity. I have always laboured for moderation, so that passionate minds, to whom religion is far from being the first love, should not disturb the rest. And this, perhaps, has not made me popular, but I remember how earnestly our Saviour commended charity. How cautiously and patiently the apostle advised men to deal with the weak! If the craft of men destroy me, and I become the prey of the victor in the strife, my reward is with me, nor shall I look for comfort outside myself except in God.

" It is better to pray against the self-wrought ruin of the reformed Church in England and Holland, which I fear, than to predict its coming. For I do not wish to be a true prophet on such a condition. But I will say no more, lest dealing with the troubles of the time I should utter feelings which I specially wish no one to know. Only one thing will I tell you. God helping me, I will do my best that truth and peace may kiss each other."

The university was intended to be a place of

[1] Laud's *Works*, vi. 265.

religious training and of liberal learning, not of purposeless, dogmatic discussion.   How is it, my lord, he writes to the Bishop of Winchester[1] during his chancellorship, that while " so many good scholars come up from Winchester to New College," that college breeds " so few eminent men " ?   And he begs him as visitor to see into it : being convinced that the explanation will be found in the character of their course, in which letters, logic and mathematics are neglected, while undergraduates have to find their staple food in Calvin's Institutes, a very useful book among others, according to Laud's judgment, for a divinity student, but utterly unfit to be a foundation of general learning.

He at once proved his intention to be completely neutral as chancellor between the contending parties of Puritan and Anglican ; for in the first weeks of his office the vice-chancellor is directed to censure two preachers ; one for attacking the Calvinist Synod of Dort, another for denouncing Anglican ceremonialism in religion.[2]   If it can be, he says, he will not allow the terrible and bloody scenes[3] of recent religious controversy in Holland to be reproduced in England : and for this purpose he forbids heated public discussion : men may think and hold what they will, but they shall not

[1] *History of his Chancellorship*, p. 82.
[2] *Ibid.*, p. 8.
[3] Lord Herbert's *Autobiography*.

publicly stir popular passions. In pursuance of
this policy, individual Puritans were constantly,
through the eleven years of his chancellorship,
treated with the greatest gentleness. A proctor
who had scruples about wearing a surplice was
advised to find a substitute at the university communion. Even fierce sermons were forgiven to
men who acknowledged their breach of university
good manners. The regius professor, Prideaux,[1]
was admitted to Laud's friendship, and invited,
though inclined to Puritanism, to supervise Chillingworth's defence of the Church against Rome,
which was being composed and published at
Laud's instigation. Only when there was a deliberate rebellion, and an attempt to pit the vice-
chancellor against the proctors, did Laud grow
severe to the offenders. Then he struck hard,
and quickly quelled opposition.

The University of Oxford became once more
the chief home of learning in England : and
naturally the scholars, writers and poets of the
day took the side from which they received patronage and sympathy, while the one notable exception proved by his own career the blighting influence of Puritanism on the inspiration of
literature. Those works of John Milton, which we
read and love, were written either during the
government of Laud, or after the Restoration.

---

[1] *Cf. State Papers*, vol. 174, No. 45. For Prideaux's high opinion
of Laud see Warwick, p. 88.

11

But few lines are rescued from oblivion in the mass of his compositions under Puritan rule ; and a Presbyterian or Anabaptist press censor would have made short work with *Paradise Regained* or *Paradise Lost*. With much that was noble, exhibiting in many cases a deep sense of duty, and in many cases evincing an intense devotion to God and a consciousness of His immanent presence, the Puritan party was in its very nature obscurantist.[1] It might draw to itself for a moment the lovers of liberty, because, though it was for government by a single person in Holland, in England it happened to be on the side of government by Parliament ; and some of its higher ideals might attract noble and educated minds ; but these were sure sooner or later to find the uncongenial alliance impossible. There was no free play for the intellect within the iron-bound prison of the doctrine of Divine decrees, and the mind which had enslaved itself to this pitiless fate would rest content without further progress in learning ; while all fresh discoveries or speculations could only upset the comfortable repose of the soul which had been convinced of its own exceptional favour in the sight of God.[2]

---

[1] "Ordered that all such pictures at Whitehall as have the representation of the Second Person of the Trinity or of the Virgin Mary upon them shall be forthwith burnt" (Parliamentary Ordinance of 1645). And the writer in *Pictorial History* says : "Music must be considered as having lain dormant in England from the death of Charles I. till his successor mounted the throne" (p. 566).

[2] See refusal of Puritan schoolmasters to teach Latin gram-

For many years Puritanism had been dominant at Oxford; and though much had been done in Laud's earlier days for the revival of learning, the university still groaned in the trammels of the Institutes of Calvin. Discipline was of the laxest, and it was a favourite amusement for undergraduates to poach the king's deer at Woodstock. There were 300 ale-houses in the town of Oxford; university dress had dropped out of use; the proctors were treated with contempt. The chancellor set to work in earnest;[1] 200 ale-houses were closed; drinking in college common-rooms was checked; graduates and undergraduates were compelled to wear cap and gown, "in order that," as a distinguished teacher put it, "having these perpetual monitors about us, we may not be forgetful of the places wherein we are, and the end for which we came hither, *viz.*, to grow in piety and good letters". The proctors and other dignitaries were to be treated with respect. A riding school which had become a centre of rowdiness was put out of bounds: Mr. Crofts "is to carry back his great horses as he came". Candidates were mercilessly rejected at the examinations. There should be no more ignorant graduates, nourished only on the Institutes of Calvin, sent out to be blind teachers of the blind, men often "who could not distinguish *quisquis* from *quisque*," as

mar, because it contained the names of pagan gods (Laud's *Works*, folio, i. 546). [1] *Cf. State Papers*, vol. 203, No. 90.

they sat opposite their examiners on the new
raised seats which the chancellor caused to be
provided, answering the questions amid a crowd
of onlookers, delighted at their helpless flounder-
ing.   It became a real distinction to obtain the
B.A. degree.   Before they could even qualify for
examination, students had to prove attendance at
lectures in grammar and rhetoric, in the ethics,
politics and economics of Aristotle, in logic,
moral philosophy, geometry and Greek ; while for
the M.A. degree, three more years had to be
spent in studying geometry, astronomy, meta-
physics, natural philosophy, Greek and Hebrew.

Nor were these requirements merely nominal.
No one should be excused examination.   A
doctor of divinity in those days had to be a
real divine.   Young noblemen, who, trading on
their high birth, dared to transgress discipline,
were ruthlessly sent down, for Laud did not care
how great and proud their fathers might be ;
"the base-born archbishop," as the Puritan press
insolently called him, was for equality.

Upon this foundation of careful instruction he
raised his edifice of deeper learning.   The Hebrew
professor was provided with a canonry at Christchurch, so was the public orator.   An Arabic
lectureship was endowed with the archbishop's
own meagre savings.   The famous Pococke, the
first lecturer, was sent to the East to perfect
himself in the language, and to bring home manu-

scripts.[1]   In future, the Bible would be seriously
studied and criticised in its own tongues, with all
the assistance that history and philology could
afford.[2]   It was a special direction to the new
lecturer to treat Arabic in its relation to Hebrew
and Syriac.   The archbishop could feel that while
ignorant sectaries might draw their reckless
conclusions from phrases in the English translation, and from dangerous notes in the Geneva
edition, at least they would have scholars at hand
to correct them.

Hundreds of manuscripts in every tongue,
Chinese, Persian,[3] Turkish, Arabic, Armenian,
Russian among them, as well as Greek and
Latin, were presented on various occasions to the
library by Laud.   Any one who wanted to find
favour with him knew the sure way was to send
a new and rare manuscript for Oxford ; it was the
weak spot through which unworthy and self-
seeking men could obtain his favour.   Time and
money he lavished on the collection.   He eagerly
hoped to recover the lost work of Clement of
Alexandria, the *Hypotyposes*.   It was a delightful
recreation to turn from the dry business of the
Treasury or Board of Trade in the company of

---

[1] Twells' *Life*, 67, 72.

[2] *Ibid.*, 38.   Syriac was studied by all the leading scholars of
that time.

[3] Lord Denbigh's mission to Persia in 1631 opened a connection between that distant country and England (Lodge's *Life*).

Weston and Cottington, Coke or Vane, to discuss the date and history of some new-found manuscript. He was constantly regretting that he had so little time for the diligent study which had been a characteristic of Bishop Andrewes of Winchester.

But, above all, he had set his heart on what he describes as a learned press. In 1631 he obtained from the king a patent for the university to print books, a privilege already possessed by Cambridge; and the university, agreeing with the Stationers' Company that they would waive their right to print the Latin grammar and the Bible for three years on an annual payment of £200, devoted this sum at his direction to the manufacture of type in Greek and Eastern alphabets. Rich nobles who were admitted doctors of law at the king's visit to the university were summoned to read a thesis, or to pay £20 as a fine to the learned press. Printers were brought over from Holland; and special officers appointed by the university to superintend the work.[1]

It was felt to be essential to discipline and to steady progress that the vast undigested mass of university statutes should be arranged and published under the chancellor's supervision. A short summary of those affecting the daily life of under-

---

[1] The publication of the Parisian Polyglot Bible in 1633 had stirred Laud to greater emulation (*Works*, vi. 337).

Henry Jacob was helped by Laud to retain his Merton Fellowship (*Works*, vi. 462) because he was an Oriental scholar.

graduates was printed in a little book, and presented to them at matriculation ; lest, as the archbishop said, they should unwittingly perjure
themselves in their oath to observe the university
laws.   His digest of the statutes remained in force
for more than 200 years ; it was considered almost
sacrilege to alter it.   The letters about Oxford in
these eleven years give the clearest impression of
the zeal for learning, the patient attention to detail, the calm, clear judgment, the strong, unshaken
will, the indefatigable diligence of the archbishop
chancellor.   He corresponded on terms of friendship with all the great foreign scholars, and constantly sought their advice and support.

Perhaps it was the proudest moment of his life
when the Court visited the reformed university in
1636.[1]   The king and queen with their princely
nephews of the palatinate lodged in Christchurch.
There plays were performed before them : the
" Persian Habits," procured for one of these plays,
caused special delight : the queen could not be
satisfied without seeing them again at Windsor.

The mornings were occupied in visiting the
city and the colleges, many of which had been
restored and enlarged in these years of learning.
They walked in Lord Danby's new " Physic
Garden " by the banks of the Cherwell, which the
chancellor exhibited as a welcome stimulus to the
scientific studies which he desired to foster.   They

---

[1] *History of Chancellorship*, 102-105.   *Cf.* Evelyn.

noted the handsome marble pavements in Queen's
College Chapel, and its excellently designed wains-
cotting : Magdalen Chapel too had been put in
beautiful order : in the chapel windows the gorgeous new painted glass produced a play of
gemmed colour and reverently subdued light.
But the crowning joy of the archbishop was to
entertain his sovereign in the hall of the splendid
new quadrangle which he himself had added to his
own college of St. John the Baptist, and to show
the artist king the beauty of the architecture and
the careful arrangements for serious study.

The chancellor remained after the king's
departure in consultation with the heads of the
university. There was Dr. Prideaux, soon to be
bishop in the Puritan reaction ; Dr. Duppa, the
future tutor of Charles II. ; Dr. Baily, once the
bitter personal foe of Laud, now promoted by his
forgiving influence to be president of St. John's ;
Dr. Frewen, the vigorous reforming vice-chancellor ; his godson Chillingworth, doubtless, the
great controversialist ; and many another soon to
be distinguished as scholar, saint, apologist, or
administrator through the fiery persecution, or
when the good times returned. The archbishop
was at his best ; genial, full of wit and humour,
entering into learned jokes, and stimulating the
scholars to fresh discoveries. He was delighted
with the good discipline, the studiousness and the
reverence of the university.

In one direction of study he considered Oxford still somewhat unenlightened,[1] and he urged upon the authorities of St. John's the pursuit of mathematics and physical sciences, for which he had provided facilities in his new buildings. This zeal for scientific study infected many of his disciples, who became the founders of the Royal Society. On leaving Oxford he slept a night with his friend Dr. Bancroft, the bishop of the diocese, at his new episcopal residence in Cuddesden, which he had done so much to secure for the see. Then making provision (how characteristic it is of the man's consistent attention to the details of his duties!) that his steward should immediately pay every item of the expenditure he had incurred in Oxford,[2] he returned to the busy cares of Lambeth—intent, all too unsuccessfully, on securing for the metropolis that same learned peace and calm liberty which had appeared to him so happy in the atmosphere of Oxford.

But Oxford was never long out of his thoughts. Every week he received a report from the vicechancellor. Friends wrote on all matters of importance; nothing escaped him. The printer shall be dismissed if the Romanists get hold of Chillingworth's sheets before they are published. A Jesuit has seduced an undergraduate and carried him off to St. Omer; the chancellor will not

---

[1] Laud's *Works*, vii. 192, 434, 612, etc.
[2] *Chancellorship*, 121.

be satisfied till he has the boy back in Oxford, and settled in the true faith. An Arian under the hypocritical cloak of a private tutor is leading men astray; he must be exposed and expelled. The Westminster supper at Christchurch ought to be discontinued, for it is making factions in the college.

No wonder the university grew and throve. From 2000 in 1611 the number of students had increased in 1638 to over 4000, and was multiplying year by year. The care bestowed upon the grammar schools[1] provided an ever-growing supply of eager undergraduates who delighted in the studious atmosphere of the beautiful city. Oxford was full of learned men, who were carrying their newly-acquired knowledge through the length and breadth of England; flaunting it, perhaps, too often in the faces of ignorant and powerful squires, who vowed to pay off the score when they sat snug and omnipotent in the House of Commons at Westminster.

Then, just as the great work is accomplished, comes the final scene. The chancellor is in the Tower; Pym is all-powerful; the censorship of the press is practically at the mercy of Prynne. Learned inquiry is hateful to the majority of the Commons. Oxford is accused of Popery. Laud's

---

[1] For Laud's attention to Westminster School, see Stanley's *Westminster Abbey*; for his foundation at Reading see Heylin; for his help to Winborne, *State Papers*, vol. 291, No. 28 (*cf.* vol. 219, No. 55).

day is done, and he resigns his chancellorship.
Let them elect some other chancellor who can
protect them a little ·in this deluge of Puritan
narrowness, and pray for happier times. So the
curtain falls on a work which could neither be
destroyed nor forgotten ; Oxford still cherishes
the memory of her great *alumnus*.

Empty-headed Pembroke becomes her chancellor. War turns her scholars into soldiers. A
victorious Parliament sets to work to reform her ;
and in its reformation almost reforms Oxford and
learning with her off the face of the earth : till
Laud's pupils return to rebuild the edifice he had
so painfully and carefully erected. The history of
Laud's Oxford chancellorship makes it clear
enough why the forces of art and literature, of
learning and scientific research, came to be
marshalled on the side of the Anglican party
and to play so great a part in the Restoration.

CHAPTER IX.

THE OPPOSITION, 1637-1639.

Development of the Opposition—New Antagonists—Star Chamber Cruelties—Their Failure—Laud's Dejection — Attack on Bishop Williams — The Roman Propaganda—Romanists and Puritans.

WE have seen how successful and how liberal was the policy which Laud shaped and practised in educational matters ; and how deeply his religious ideas had already struck their roots into the national life ; nor can we withhold our admiration from the stern economy which he had tried to institute in the management of the Treasury, and from the vigorous impetus which his sympathy and patronage had given to trade. But in the ordinary administration of the Government he had by 1637 come into dangerous collision with the most powerful classes and the most thoughtful political minds in the nation. It was not the Puritans in particular who desired that Parliament should take its place as the leading factor in our English Government. Rather the wiser leaders, who appeared at this time to be leagued with

Puritanism, were only using that religious movement as a means to arouse the enthusiasm of the
nation against the Stuart system of government.
And there remained but two methods by which
the growing indignation against the king's ministers,
which the memoirs of the time help us to trace
among the thinking minority, could be successfully
abated.   One method was a severe policy of repression such as Richelieu had organised in
France, such as Wentworth might easily have
organised in England.   It would have required
the creation of a standing army ; but for this
Wentworth felt the means were not difficult to
find.[1]

Happily for the liberties of England there were
two insuperable obstacles to such a policy in the
condition of things then existing.   One was to be
found in the gentle, placable nature of the king :
"there is a *mare pacificum* in that breast,"[2] says
Laud, more than once, writing to Wentworth ;
and a king who dallied for two years with the
Scottish revolt was hardly likely to consent to a
policy of blood.[3]   But the far more serious obstacle lay in Laud's own character.   He considered
it a religious duty to forgive his enemies.   Even
when he was convinced that his own life was in

---

[1] *Strafford Papers*, i. 173, ii. 136, 250, etc.   Probably he would
have removed the lord-lieutenants and put the trained bands into
the hands of creatures of the Government.   [2] *Works*, vii. 425.

[3] *Cf.* Lilly, *Life and Death of Charles I.*, and the king's own
words on the scaffold.

danger from some "secret Felton," he assures
Wentworth that, though the law of libel and the
precedents of Udal, Penry and others under
Queen Elizabeth would more than justify the
execution of a prominent libeller, "for my part
I desire no blood";[1] and as a matter of fact the
first marked step towards political toleration in
England was taken by Laud, when, during his
administration, he took care that no man should
lose his life for politics.   In this respect the eleven
years of Charles' so-called arbitrary government
contrast most favourably with the fifty years which
followed them.

But if Laud would not suppress the rising
opposition, could he be made willing to conciliate
it?   Edward Hyde, now climbing into prominence as a barrister, seems to have had hopes that
he could persuade the archbishop, and through
him the king, to attempt once more a policy of
periodical Parliaments.[2]   But this the king absolutely refused; he would hear nothing of Parliaments; and among the artistic pleasures of
Whitehall he never ceased to feel that all was
going well.   Nor was Laud himself hopeful of
seeing a House of Commons which would allow
religious toleration.   Therefore the Government
was still carried on without the assistance of the
king's natural counsellors.   But there were no
preparations against a possible rebellion.   The

---

[1] *Works*, vii. 329.   [2] Clarendon's *Life*, i. 70.

old English system of police and military forces
remained unaltered.   A few officers of justice
executed the writs of the courts, and were obeyed
rather from habit than from any fear which they
could inspire.   The only serious force at the disposal of Government consisted of the trained
bands of London under the city magistrates, and
the county militia under the gentry and great
nobles, composed of the classes in whom dislike
of the Laudian theology was most prevalent,
and officered by the natural members of the two
Houses of Parliament.[1]   Such a system made
tyranny impossible, for it left the king at the
mercy of his people.

Unwilling to repress and unable to conciliate,
the minister, who in spite of all his influence was
seldom allowed to work his own will, was placed
in an impossible position.   He was obliged to
admit that something must be done : and if the
great leaders, Saye and Brooke, Warwick and
Bedford, Pym and Holles, were left to plot in
peace, the libellers at all events must have their
pens checked ; and severe chastisements must
prove that the Government would not be insulted
with impunity.   Hence came about the most startling severity of the period, which is so graphically
related for us in the pages of Fuller,[2] and which,

[1] There is an excellent account of the constitution of this
force in Mason's *Norfolk*, 247.

[2] Fuller's *Church History*, iii. 386.

more than anything else, has made Laud so unpopular with posterity.

On 30th June, 1637, three pillories had been erected in Palace Yard. They were for members of the three learned professions, William Prynne, a lawyer; Henry Burton, a clergyman; and John Bastwick, a physician. An immense crowd had assembled to see how these libellers would face their punishment, for the Star Chamber had decreed that, after standing in the pillory for some hours, each man was to lose his ears by the knife of the executioner. Burton was the first to suffer; the pillory made a good pulpit for the nonce; and all felt that a man who was willing to face such shame and pain for his opinions must at least be worth listening to. "Methinks," he said, "I see Mount Calvary where the crosses were erected. If Christ was numbered amongst thieves, shall a Christian think much for His sake to be numbered among rogues?" Soon his head was smothered in blood under the executioner's knife, but he endured manfully and did not flinch. The crowd "howled," some with fury, some with compassion as they saw his sufferings. Bastwick followed with equal courage. "Indeed," he said, "I wrote a book against Antichrist the Pope; and the Pope of Canterbury said it was written against him. But were the press open to us, we would scatter his kingdom, and fight courageously against Gog and Magog." "Mrs. Bastwick got a stool, kissed him, his ears being cut off she called for them, and put them in a clean handkerchief and carried them away with her." [1]

Prynne was the last to face the knife. "Rather," said he, "than I would have my cause a leading cause to the depriving of the subject's liberties, which I seek to maintain, I choose to suffer my body to become an example of this punishment." The words imply that he had deliberately refused to use his right to appeal from the Star Chamber to the ordinary law courts, because he either had no confidence in the soundness of his case, or distrusted the impartiality of the judges. The sayings were repeated and remembered. These men had suffered, it seemed, for religion, for freedom of opinion, for personal liberty. It is true that the libels were atrocious,[2] and the punishment the usual reward of libel, but the crowd had assembled to listen and see, not to reason.[3] The archbishop, men said, was mean and cruel to use the law for his own personal revenge; this was shamefully inconsistent in a minister of Christ, and

---

[1] *Strafford Papers*, letter from Garrard, ii. 85.

[2] Bastwick had published a blasphemous litany (Baker, p. 457); and he had called the bishops "servants of the devil" (*Parliamentary History*, ix. 60). He had been cautioned and then fined previously in the High Commission (*State Papers*, 261, fol. 97 and 178). Burton and Prynne had used much the same language. Burton is said to have been made an enemy to the Court by not getting the high preferment he had expected; he had been attached at one time to Charles' household (Sanderson's *Life of Charles I.*, 218; *cf.* Salmonet, i. 88). [3] Wallington, i. 90.

especially in one who so vigorously vindicated his claim to be a successor of the apostles.

Nothing is more dangerous to rulers than to be thought guilty of a spiteful use of power. Laud indeed had refused to concur in the sentence on Prynne, Burton and Bastwick; "because the business hath some reflection on myself, I shall forbear to censure them and leave them to God's mercy and the king's justice".[1] But these words prove that he must take his share of responsibility for barbarous and useless punishments which he might undoubtedly have prevented. The thought certainly crossed his mind that Prynne could legally be sentenced to death for his constant libels. Such action would have been cruel; it might have successfully checked attacks on the Government. As it was, the punishments were worse than useless. To the leaders of the Opposition the imprisonment of three noisy followers, who could exercise far more influence by their sufferings than by their talents, caused no inconvenience. Such troublesome allies were well out of the way: and concerning John Lilburne, one of the two or three other libellers who suffered about the same time, Henry Marten, the wittiest of the members of the Long Parliament,[2] remarked "that if there were none living but himself, John would be against Lilburne and Lilburne

---

[1] Laud's speech in Star Chamber.   [2] *Cf.* Ludlow, iii. 91.

against John ".[1] When the time came for action
a very subordinate part would be assigned
to these virulent writers.   But their punishment and their popular triumph had exposed
the weakness of a Government which had not
guards enough even to drive away a mob from
Palace Yard.[2] Their sufferings, enormously exaggerated, and spoken about as if they were being
inflicted every day by the brutal myrmidons of
tyrannical rulers upon the upholders of liberty,
were described with fullest details in pamphlets
spread broadcast over England ; and became the
topic of conversation in every alehouse where
men met.   The punishments inspired no dread
because they were so infrequent and in themselves
not sufficiently terrible ; and the Star Chamber
grew to be hated without being feared.   Elizabeth
with her wholesale massacre of Roman priests,
hardly strong enough to mount the ladder after
the constant application of the rack ;[3] Cromwell
with his awe-inspiring scaffolds, where bands of
splendidly equipped cavalry surrounding the condemned [4] made patent the strength of the Govern-

[1] Forster's *Lives*, iii. 217, but Wood's *Athenae*, ii. 174, attri-
butes the words to Judge Jenkins. *Cf.* Hutchinson, ii. 160.

[2] See *Relation of Capuchin Mission*, 346, "The king hath no
guards," and Ranke's *England*, ii. 66, "Foreigners were surprised
to see how completely the king was in the hands of his people,
that there were hardly any fortresses to which he could fly for
safety in time of need ".

[3] See Howell's contemporary comparison of the policies of
Elizabeth and Charles, iv. 450.

[4] *Executions of Charles I., Hamilton, Holland, and Capel*, pub. 1650.

ment and the weakness of its opponents, knew
how to evoke a well-calculated terror.   The
secret prisons, the tortures, the burnings of the
Inquisition, to which the proceedings of the
Laudian bishops were sometimes absurdly compared.[1] made men's blood run cold with fright.[2]
But no Englishman in those rough days[3] feared
the loss of a little blood, or a few minutes' pain
which would leave him active as ever for the future.
And, indeed, no one took the trouble to express
pity for the ordinary petty criminal, or for the
poor Papist Pickering who lost his ears in the
pillory a year later "for saying the king was a
Papist at heart and the Protestants devils".[4]

Laud seems to have been perfectly conscious
that the policy of the pillory had proved a mistake.
He laments to Wentworth its failure as a deter-
rent ; nor could Wentworth give him any sound
advice as to how he should check the libels.[5]   Perhaps it was the feeling that no one was frightened
by the pillory which caused the Star Chamber to
inflict that horrible cruelty of a public whipping upon
Lilburne in 1637, which blots its usually gentle
list of sentences.   The archbishop often speaks,

[1] Russel's *Life of Spottiswoode*, xliii., quoted by Ranke.

[2] Howell's *Letters* describe this, i. 218.

[3] *Cf., e.g.,* Howell's *Familiar Letters*, i. 25 and 28, and iv.
493 ; Cromwell, *Letters*, xcix. and ci.; and the acts of the Scotch
Presbyterians.

[4] Garrard to Strafford, July, 1638.

[5] *Strafford Papers*, ii. 119.

in the constant succession of lengthy cyphered despatches which he sent to Dublin, of the evil days which he is sure must be expected, unless they could carry "Thorough" through quickly. His health was becoming more and more uncertain; and he felt himself growing old, for at sixty-four[1] (he was born in 1573) most great men of those days were worn out; Andrewes had died at sixty-one; Salisbury at forty-eight; King James at fifty-eight; Richelieu would only live to be fifty-seven; Pym to be fifty-nine; Oliver Cromwell to be fifty-nine. It was time for him to be retiring, and to spend his last years in devotions as Lerma had done in Spain:[2] for his elasticity was gone, and his endurance was becoming exhausted; but he had no successor ready to hand. He had lost by this time that bright, genial manner which had won the hearts of the young Oxford Fellows; had captivated the royal courtiers at Whitehall; had made him the intimate friend of Buckingham; and had even persuaded the citizens of London to open their money bags for the restoration of St. Paul's. Men complained now of the rough impatience of the primate; at Lambeth he had become inaccessible to visitors from the country, or sent them home offended by his harsh and hurried rejection of their

---

[1] Letters to Strafford prove that he expected his death in this year.

[2] Howell, i. 111.

courtesies. He had mortally wounded by his rude-
ness the self-love of Argyle,[1] who was to repay
him by becoming the most cunning engineer of his
ruin. He himself felt the change that had come
over him as he spoke with Edward Hyde in the
Lambeth Gardens about the unintentional sharp-
ness of his voice and manner.[2] His letters to
Wentworth lose the quaint humour and the love
of amusing anecdote[3] which are so characteristic
in the early days of their intimacy. Overwork
had strained his nerves. Now the tone at best is
a humorous melancholy. "I prophesied, and it
proves most true, that the old wife of Canterbury
would prove a notorious shrew to me. And I'll
tell you a pretty tale by-the-bye, and 'tis true.
When I first came to Lambeth there were in the
walks song-thrushes which even began to sing in
February, and so continued, and the nightingales
followed in their season. Both of these came my
first year, I think to take their leave; for neither
of them hath appeared ever since : and I presently
said I should have a troublesome time in that see,
and so it proves."[4]

And a few months later he writes in the same
key : "Oh, my lord, I am grown old and extreme

[1] Sir P. Warwick, p. 90.

[2] Contrast his reception of the Dutch ministers of English
congregations in September, 1635 (*State Papers*, vol. 297, No. 21),
with Clarendon's *Life*, i. 71, and *State Papers*, vol. 314, No. 67.

[3] Laud's *Works*, vii. 70, etc.   [4] *Ibid.*, vii. 416.

weary of this my pen, yet I am willing to endure all, if not more, than I am able (for very crazy I was last week, and my frequent letters to my Lord Marquis of Hamilton by his Majesty's command lie heavy upon me) to give you a full, true and real account of all your business.   And now, my lord, I shall conclude sadly.   It is not the Scottish business alone that I look upon, but the whole frame of things at home and abroad, with vast expenses out of little treasure, and my misgiving soul is deeply apprehensive of no small evils coming on.   God in heaven avert them ; but I can see no cure without a miracle, and I fear that will not be showed."[1] The ill-health of statesmen has often exercised a decisive effect on the course of politics, and made them fear imaginary perils so vividly as to leave them blind to their real dangers.   A serious mistake of Laud's at this time well illustrates his irritable and fatigued condition.

Williams, Bishop of Lincoln, had been deprived of the Great Seal early in the reign of Charles, and had retired to Buckden, his diocesan residence.   As lord keeper he had used his influence at the close of James' reign to attempt the overthrow of Buckingham, who had been the original architect of his fortunes : disgrace had naturally followed detection.   But the king could not be satisfied until he was ruined.   Williams

---

[1] Laud's *Works*, vii. 456.

had always been Laud's enemy and Laud's rival :
and entries in the *Diary* prove how much jealousy
and apprehension Laud had felt regarding him,
till the archbishop had gradually persuaded himself that with Williams religion was only a ladder
for ambition.   Of this he was so convinced that
when the Bishop of Lincoln became involved in
lawsuits with the Crown he persistently refused
to appeal to the king on his behalf.[1] It is noticeable
that while Charles and Laud forgave their personal
enemies as a religious duty, the enemies of Buckingham could never recover their favour.   Eliot
had expiated by his death in the Tower the eloquent words which the king believed were the
cause of Felton's crime.   And the treatment of
Williams was certainly unwise ; it was probably
unjust ; for there is no real proof that Laud was
correct in saying : "The Bishop of Lincoln has been
the root of all the mischiefs which have befallen
Church and State for many years past".[2] Consequently they allowed the Opposition at this time
the spectacle of a bishop, learned, diligent, capable,
to all outward appearance devout, imprisoned in
the Tower on a charge of tampering with witnesses
in a lawsuit.   Even before this their harshness

---

[1] Laud speaks of many intercessions made by him for
Williams with the king, but they certainly ceased at this time.
There is no proof that he had owed his advancement to Williams
in any way. This rests on a story in Hacket which has naturally
quite a different explanation.

[2] Laud's *Works*, vii. 396.

had driven Williams into the arms of the discontented nobles.[1] At Buckden he had brought up the sons of several great peers; at Buckden he had somewhat ostentatiously set the example of what a prelate should be who was not cumbered with the affairs of State, hospitable and genial, affording to his guests the cheerful refreshment of artistic and musical services, strict in his ordinations, zealous in his superintendence of his clergy, broad and liberal in his ecclesiastical policy, friendly to men of all opinions and all classes.[2] From Buckden came the only pamphlets[3] and books which could in the judgment of the learned answer the weighty and witty defence of Laud's system which his chaplains issued at his direction. Thus Bishop Williams in the Tower seemed to stand forward as the natural mediator between High Church and Low Church. Men could point to his principles as the true alternative to the present plan of government, and assert their fidelity to the Church while they assailed the archbishop. It was this prosecution of the Bishop of Lincoln, following upon the pillorying of Prynne and his friends, which seemed to give colour to the charge spread by seditious tracts broadcast over England that the archbishop had laid a deep and dark design to

---

[1] Hacket's *Life of Williams.*

Compare his friendship with Nicholas Ferrar.

[3] Fourteen hundred copies of Williams' book on the altar were sold immediately after publication (*vide Strafford Papers*).

reintroduce Popery. Specious evidence was not
lacking ; the Lord Treasurer Weston was believed
to have died a Papist ; Secretary Windebank was
suspected of Popish leanings ; some of the bishops,
notably Goodman and Montague, were accused
of negotiating with the Papal envoys ;[1] Romanism
was spreading at Court, and had gained many
converts.[2] The queen[3] had even dared to take the
young Prince of Wales to mass. The Papal
envoys were received by the king ; and instead of
executing Jesuits the Government was doing its
utmost to persuade the recusants to take a modified
oath of allegiance.[4]

So far as Laud was concerned, never had he
been so active and so resolute in his opposition to
Rome, though he always refused to persecute the
Roman Catholics.[5]   At the council board,[6] and at

[1] See *Life of Laud* by a " Romish Recusant ".

[2] *Capuchin Relation*, pp. 314-343.

[3] For the bitter hatred felt for the queen by the Puritans see
Ludlow's comment on her death, iii. 226 ; and *cf.* Tillières, p. 205.

[4] *Clarendon Papers*. See the whole question in Berington's
Panzani.

[5] Epistle Dedicatory of *Book against Fisher*. The system
seems to have been this. The priests and Jesuits were arrested
and convicted according to law ; but then released on bonds given
by their friends that they would come before the courts for sentence
when required (*State Papers*, vol. 308, Nos. 66, 68, 69, 70; and *cf.*
Berington's *Panzani*).

[6] *Diary*, 22nd October, 1637 ; Laud's *Works*, vii. 379. The
" Romish Recusant " absolutely acquits Laud of intrigues with
Rome, though he accepts the evidence against Montague. See
Con's *Letters*.

private interviews with the king, he was constantly
demanding that English men and women should
not be allowed to attend the queen's chapel.[1]   At
this time he republished his *Book against Fisher,*
the Jesuit.   His efforts to reconcile the recusants
to the English Church and "to break the bonds
which united them to the chair of St. Peter"[2] were at
times so successful as to call out the jealous watchfulness of the Roman Curia.[3]   He had been deeply
offended when emissaries from the Pope pressed
upon him the offer of a cardinal's hat,[4] pointing
out that in reunion with Rome lay the real safety
in the struggle against the Puritans.   The Roman
claim to be the only and the original Church of
Christ struck him as not merely ill-grounded, but
even ridiculous; "there is no greater absurdity
stirring this day in Christendom than that the
Reformation of an old corrupted Church must, will
we nill we, be taken for the building of a new;
the Catholic Church of Christ is neither Rome nor
a conventicle;"[5] and though he was perfectly con-

[1] Englishmen were driven from the chapel by force.   *Cf.*
Lilly, *Life and Death of Charles,* p. 146.

[2] Salmonet, i. 226.   [3] Evelyn's *Diary.*

[4] *Diary,* 4th and 17th August, 1633.   Père d'Orléans, the
Jesuit historian, is confident that Abbé Siri spoke without evidence
in stating that Laud intrigued with Cardinal Barbarini, ix. 260;
while on the other hand the "Romish Recusant" tries character-
istically to throw doubt on the offer of the cardinal's hat to Laud.

[5] Epistle Dedicatory of *Book against Fisher.*   *Cf.* sect. xxvii.
2 of the book, where he comments on the absence of the Greeks
from Trent.

scious that his adhesion was worth any price which
the Papacy could pay, he always showed the most
profound distrust and dislike of the Papal court.
" So long as the Jesuits write and maintain
that 'faith given is not to be kept with heretics,'
and the Church of Rome leaves their doctrine
uncensured (as it hath hitherto done), A. C.
shall pardon us that we come not to Rome,
nor within the reach of Roman power, what
freedom of speech soever be promised us."   Rome
is "a very safe place, if you mark it, for us to
come to ; just as the lion in the apologue invited
the fox to his own den ; safe perhaps for coming
thither, but none for coming thence ; *vestigia nulla
retrorsum* ".[1]

   Rejected and thwarted by the archbishop, the
Romanists had proceeded to organise an opposition party in the Court.   It was headed by the
queen,[2] who detested Laud's economy, and was
continually urging the king to extravagant building
and to lavish gifts ; all too successfully, since Laud
complains to the Irish deputy: "We will spend on
and not be sensible of our wants till extremities
seize upon us,"[3] and again : " As for the king's
coffers, the lock of them is too much at command
and there be many keys ".[4]   Cottington sup-

---

[1] *Book against Fisher*, sect. xxi. 7.

[2] Laud's *Works*, vii. 172, 334, etc.   *Cf.* Hobbes' *Behemoth*
and Lilly.

[3] *Ibid.*, vii. 451.

[4] *Ibid.*, vii. 511.   For royal extravagance see *State Papers*,
vol. 288, Nos. 11, 51, 100, vol. 289, No. 70, etc.

ported her with his skilful knowledge of political
life : Holland, Jermyn and Percy, hungry for
grants from the Crown, besieged the ears of the
king with complaints of the archbishop's meanness.
Hamilton had his own interests to serve, and exercised his preponderant personal influence with
the king on their behalf. Windebank was afraid
to support the archbishop. And soon a new
Secretary of State, Sir Henry Vane, bringing
about a malign alliance[1] between the party of the
queen and the party of the Puritans, would finally
place the archbishop " between two factions, very
like corn between two mill-stones,"[2] and in so
doing seal his fate. The instability of the king's
character, though he was firm enough when in
the archbishop's company, made him incapable
of resisting the blandishments of his charming
and beautiful wife, and the insinuations of some
of his accomplished courtiers ; and added to his
minister's embarrassments. " I believe nothing
in Court but what I see done,"[3] Laud writes one
day ; and another day : "'Tis a wonder to see
the king so constant".[4] The ground was slipping

---

[1] The alliance was all the more dangerous because it was not
avowed. Each party was intriguing against the minister. Further
Baxter (*Autobiography*, p. 76) gives it as his opinion that the Papists
hatched several of the sects, and that there were secret Papists
in the Parliamentary army. Cromwell later on had Jesuits in his
pay ; see " History of Penruddock's Rebellion " in Ludlow, iii. 514,
and *cf.* Hutchinson, ii. 178.

[2] Laud's *Works*, vii. 380.   [3] *Ibid.*, vii. 421.

[4] *Ibid.*, vii. 181.

from beneath his feet. Jesuit and Puritan alike were persuading the people that he was a tyrant. He was detested by the great nobles and country gentry because he had checked their oppressions and severely punished their vices ; [1] while the Londoners and other commercial communities disliked him because he was opposed to Parliaments, and was levying taxes which they considered to be illegal.

But the charge of Popery was the most deadly of all those which were whispered against him ; [2] for the hatred of Rome had become by this time firmly engrained in the character of the whole English people. " I was born in 1588," said the Earl of Oxford to a Romanist who tried to bring him over, "and christened on the 5th of November." [3]

---

[1] Lilly's *Life and Death of Charles I.*, p. 162.

[2] Nehemiah Wallington's *Historical Notices.* May's *Causes of the Civil War* and Hobbes' *Behemoth.* Foley's *Records of the English Province, Society of Jesus*, appears to show fewer English enrolled as Jesuits during this period.

[3] Fuller's *Church History*, iii. 309.

NOTE.--The Count de Tillières, who was for some time intendant of the queen's household, gives us full details in his memoirs of her political action. He blames her secret alliance with the Puritan chiefs and her opposition to Laud, and explains it on p. 201 (ed. 1863): " Soit qu'elle fut fachée qu'un autre qu'elle gouvernât son mari, soit qu'il lui donnât les mêmes sujet de plainte qu'avait fait l'autre (*i.e.*, Weston : this refers to the queen's extravagance), soit qu'étant jointe à la cabale des Puritains, elle voulut choquer un homme qui n'était pas dans leurs intérets ".

CHAPTER X.

Friendships —Neile — Buckingham—Noy — Windebank—
Wentworth—Hyde—The Household—The Ferrars.

SINCE the archbishop had no domestic interests to divert his thoughts at Lambeth from the dangers which threatened his policy, and no family affections to console him for the loss of popularity, it was natural at times that he should be bitterly depressed by the rising storm of opposition. His father and mother had died while he was a young man at Oxford; of his half-brothers and sisters, who apparently had settled in London, he saw little,[1] and most of them died before he rose to power;[2] for his nephews and nieces he did as much as the heavy ecclesiastical calls upon his purse would allow him, though he refused to benefit them by his public patronage.

---

[1] This did not arise from his neglect, but from the difference of interests; he would now and then drive straight from Whitehall to visit them (*Diary*, 3rd January, 1625).

[2] Letters to Wentworth.

(191)

He had deliberately adopted the celibate life, and persuaded his friend Juxon, his successor in the see of London, and lord treasurer, to follow his example, because he considered that without family he gave no hostages to fortune, and left himself free to carry out the work of reforming the miseries of the Church, to which he believed God had specially destined him.[1] His affections therefore could only find an outlet in friendships and in that kindly interest which, as his *Diary* shows us, he always took in the affairs of his servants.[2]

Of his early friendships we know little. From 1608 to 1640 he lived in the closest intimacy with Dr. Neile; and when that prelate became Bishop of Durham Laud made Durham House his London home, until his own elevation to the metropolitan bishopric. The patronage which Neile bestowed upon him he repaid with interest, as his own power increased; and he persuaded the king to appoint his friend, first to the see of Winchester, and then to the primatial throne of York. But no letters, and only a few bare entries in his *Diary*, remain to prove their terms of friendship.

It is when Buckingham appears on the scene that we are first admitted to the affectionate warmth of Laud's heart. That magnificent noble,

---

[1] Fuller, *Church History*, iii. 476; and *Trials and Troubles*, 161.
[2] *Diary*, 23rd July, 1624; 26th October, 1635, etc.

whose personal beauty dazzled the nation, whose
easy grace made him for some years the darling
of the House of Commons, so calmly self-con-
fident that he could be courteous to the meanest
of the people, and never forgot his politeness[1]
under the most savage invectives of Eliot and of
Coke (both at one time his clients and his
admirers), exercised a similar fascination upon
Laud.   From the 9th of June, 1622, when, as he
records, "My Lord Marquis Buckingham was
pleased to enter upon a near respect to me.   The
particulars are not for paper," until the 24th of
August, 1628, when "the news of the Duke of Buckingham's death came to Croydon, where it found
myself and the Bishops of Winchester, Ely and
Carlisle, at the consecration of Bishop Montague
for Chichester with my lord's grace," Buckingham
is the central figure in his thoughts.   Sometimes
we come upon a letter to the duke, as on the 13th
of December, 1625 :[2] "I am heartily glad to hear
your lordship is so well returned and so happily as
to meet so great joy.   God hath, among others
His great blessings (and I know your grace so
esteems them), sent you now this extraordinary
one, a son to inherit his father's honours, and the
rest of God's blessings upon both.   So soon as I
came to the end of my journey I met the happy
news of God's blessing upon your grace, and it

---

[1] *Parliamentary History*, vii. 42.   *Cf.* Clarendon's *Rebellion*.

[2] **Laud's** *Works*, vi. 247.

seasoned all the hard journey I have had out of Wales through the snow." Sometimes there are entries in the *Diary* meant for no eye but his own, as on the 11th of January, 1623: "My Lord of Buckingham and I in the inner chamber of York House"; the 16th of May, 1624: "I watched with my Lord of Buckingham. This was the first fit that he could be persuaded to take orderly;" and the 22nd of May: "My Lord Duke of Buckingham missed his fit"; the 3rd of January, 1625: "The duke brought me to the king. There I was about an hour and a half reading papers and talking about them with his majesty and my lord duke;" the 23rd of January, 1625, Sunday night: "The discourse which my lord duke had with me about witches and astrologers"; Sunday, the 4th of September: "I was very much troubled in my dreams. My imagination ran altogether upon the Duke of Buckingham, his servants and family;" the 25th of September: "I was told that the Duke of Buckingham had a son born, whom God bless with all the good things of heaven and earth".

After Laud's appointment to London, and the great increase of his power in the State, his letters have been preserved to us in large quantity. From these we learn of several very intimate friendships which cheered the period of his administration. Of Noy, the famous attorney-general, he writes: "I have lost a dear friend in him, and the Church the greatest she had of his

condition since she needed such".[1] Sir Thomas
Roe, Sir Henry Wotton and Vossius are in constant
correspondence with him.   But two were specially
close friends : the first was Windebank, an old
pupil at St. John's, whom he persuaded the king
to make Secretary of State in June, 1632.   He an-
nounces the appointment in a characteristic letter :—[2]

To Secretary Windebank,
S. in Christo.

MR. SECRETARY,—For though you will think
perchance that I am apt enough to jest, yet I know
you will believe these enclosed.   And this present
day in the afternoon at council, Secretary Cooke
is by his Majesty's special command to declare it
to the Lords.   So now you have a second cure to
attend as well as your son-in-law.   The name of
the parish is S. Troubles.   And now I return you
your prayers for me : God send you as much
health as you may have business.   I have sent
Dr. Ducke to bring you the news, that the women
may abuse him for his last week's knavery.   I
pray you make haste up, and follow the directions
of this enclosed.   And among other benefits I
doubt not but the very naming you to this place
will make them at Oxford look well to your son.
So in great haste I leave you to the grace of God,
and rest,

Your very loving friend,
GUIL., LONDON.

[1] *Diary*, 10th August, 1634.   [2] Laud's *Works*, vii. 43.

But Windebank gradually deserted his patron, evidently under the influence of the queen's chaplains, who, in their constant intrigues against the archbishop so soon as they realised him to be the strongest barrier against the restoration of Popery, persuaded the secretary that his only safe alliance was with the queen's party. Little by little a coldness grew up between the former friends, which Laud felt bitterly.

His other most intimate friend was Thomas Wentworth, afterwards Lord Strafford. The outspoken consistent bishop had for some time distrusted the new minister who had been so lately the leader of the Opposition. But on the 21st of January, 1631, took place that conversation "in my little chamber at London House"[1] which bound the two men in the most intimate alliance, only to be severed by death. Laud constantly requested his friend to burn his letters, but happily his wishes were disregarded, and from them we obtain the most distinct picture of the archbishop's life in the years when he ruled England. The first portion of a letter to be transcribed shall be that in which he thanks his friend for congratulations on his appointment to Canterbury :—[2]

"Now, my lord, why may you not write as whilom you did to the Bishop of London? The man is the same, and the same to you; but I see you stay for better acquaintance, and till

---

[1] *Diary.*　　　　　　　[2] Laud's *Works*, vi. 312.

then you will keep distance. I perceive also my predecessor's awe is upon you, but I doubt I shall never hold it long; and I was about to swear by my troth, as you do, but I remember oaths heretofore were wont to pass under the Privy Seal, and not the ordinary seal of letters. Well, wiser or not, you must take that as you find it; but I will not write any long letters and leave out my mirth, it is one of the recreations I have always used with my friends, and 'tis hard leaving an old custom, neither do I purpose to do it; though I mean to make choice of my friends, to whom I will use it." The next[1] shows the overwhelming character of the work described in chapter vii.:—

"I can scarce keep open my eyes, it is so late; therefore I end abruptly, and with hearty wishes for your good, answerable to that you do for God and His Church, I leave you and yours to His blessed protection". The next two extracts refer to some presents which Wentworth had sent him :—[2]

"Therefore truly I suspect that either they use worse salt to the eels than to other fish, or less than such great fish require, or else there is some incorrigible muddiness in the eel while 'tis fresh. Your lordship sees what a skilful fishmonger I am grown. But this learning I have all the Lent long, and a kind of unmannerliness which accompanies it, contrary to the proverb of

---

[1] Laud's *Works*, vi, 360.   [2] *Ibid.*, vii. 331.

a gift horse, whose mouth should not be looked into. But now Easter is coming you shall see I shall be more civil. I have also received the cap which you sent me ; but I cannot tell you how it may be to my liking (for that is the thing you wish) because, to deal truly with you, I have quite forgotten whether it be to be used for winter travel in the daytime or for the night. But sure the perfume is so strong that whether I use it by day or by night it will fill me with headache, and if it be for night use, quite mar my sleep. But your lordship must needs be at the pains to send me word how I must use it. As for the pad-saddle and the martin's fur, I will stay your own leisure for them ; yet this I'll tell you, and you may be sure of it, I will not use my great horse till I have that saddle. And if you think that I will not ride him then neither, the matter is not great." And again :—[1]

"I thank your lordship for my lamp. I have not yet had leisure to try it, but I will as soon as I can, and then give your lordship an account of it, as now I give you thanks for it. Within two days after I received the lamp, I received from you a rich saddle, the Dutch pad which you spake of to me. And the first opportunity I can get to step to Croydon, I will, God willing, try that also, and see how easy it will prove. All the fear I have of it by view is, that it rises too high

[1] Laud's *Works*, vii. 418.

)efore.   But it may be that it is my fault of skill
hat judges so ; but, however that prove, you have
)een at too much cost with me, for the saddle is
oo rich, this being not an age for any bishop to
go, or ride, or almost do anything else like him-
elf."

Then we come to more serious matters mixed
vith humorous comments.[1]

" I am sorry to hear you say that the gout will
lot leave you.   And yet that is no wonder ; for
here is not one of a thousand that once comes to
lave it in his feet that can ever shake hands with
t afterwards and bid it farewell.   You make a
good use of it when you think of Cosha.   But
lure your thoughts would grow wild there.   And
nore service a great deal may you do at the
council table, so long as the gout hangs in your
leel and lets your head alone.   But your next
houghts please me very well : that you will never
vithdraw from the king our master's service in a
itorm, though I am not of opinion that any valour
)f yours could make anything stir but your tongue,
vere you fettered indeed with the gout.

" I'll assure you I was very proud of my justice
n the sentence which I gave concerning the hung
)eef.   And it was well executed : for it did as
vell deserve to be hanged as any beef in England.
\nd now I see your lordship's approbation of my
ientence given in that very weighty controversy,

[1] Laud's *Works*, vii. 532-3.

it doth very much encourage my justice : as I doubt not you shall find in your cause the next term, if it prove as good and justifiable as this did, otherwise you were best look to it. As for your promise of sending me more, I like it well. And the condition better, that no Scottish Presbytery might be permitted to eat of it at my table. For I'll assure you, I will ne'er admit a lay elder of them all, if I may know him, much less will I teach any of them the way to your house for more. Only, I pray, take heed they do not find the way of themselves, for as yet, to my apprehension, I do not see 'thorough ' in anything.

"And this last line of mine is answer enough and too much to the next passage of your letter. For as for your half a dozen men that would set their hearts upon the business, you shall do well to send Diogenes with his lantern to look for them. Not but that I think there are more than so many to be found ; but because my eyes are dim and cannot discern them. And I pray God, you do not prophesy, that there will be no thinking of 'thorough ' till things come to greater extremity. And then, for aught that any man can promise, it may be too late. As for the trained bands, there are many disputes raised which you shall have more at large in my side paper if I can come to any certainty."

From other letters we see him at Lambeth, swinging a book in his chamber for exercise ; or

pacing up and down the great stone gallery, and
longing for the company of his friend, Lord
Scudamore ;[1] or delighted with a present of a cat
which Lady Roe has sent him from Germany ; or
worried with the volume-like letters which he has
got to answer from Scotland and Ireland; or gliding
across in his barge to Whitehall to have a long talk
on business with the king after dinner, or to discuss deep philosophical questions with him and the
students and artists of the Court.[2]   Then in the
spring he is looking for the reappearance of his
pet tortoise.[3]   Or the famous Hales comes to
visit him, and walks with him in the garden at
Lambeth, till they thoroughly understand one
another, and part—Hales astonished at the archbishop's learning, and satisfied that the troubled
times require prudence in what is written and
published ; the archbishop planning what he can
do to reward the philosopher, and make work
easier to him by driving away the *res angusta
domi*.   Or Edward Hyde comes in, and, as they
pace among the shrubberies, tells Laud what a
bad name he is getting in the city of London, and
how the country gentry complain of his want of
courtesy, when he hurries them out of his Lambeth
study on discovering that they have only come to
flatter him.   There was little time for pretty com-
pliments in those busy days when he was "late to

---

[1] *Works*, vi. 367.   [2] *Diary*, and *Works*, vii. 283.

[3] Benson's *Laud*, p. 11.

bed," and "extreme weary"; but no one on reading the *Diary* and *Correspondence* can fail to see the sincerity of the man, the greatness of his purpose, his keen sympathy with affliction, and his true attachment to his friends.

Any spare time and attention had to be given to the supervision of that huge household of chaplains, gentlemen, servants and friends, who occupied at this time "the ninety-seven chambers" in the palace of Lambeth and were organised for work and prayer, study and public writing in a manner which evoked admiration and made it possible for the archbishop to supervise every department of State business, except the one which the king jealously withheld from his cognisance, the office for Scottish affairs.

A visit to the archbishop at Lambeth by an unknown scholar shall conclude the chapter. We have seen the deep interest which Laud had taken in the community of Little Gidding: Nicholas Ferrar had died in December, 1637; but at Easter, 1640, his nephew Nicholas, who at the age of twenty-one was already master of twenty-four languages, came to London to present a polyglot Bible to Prince Charles. Laud introduced him to the king, sent him to Prince Charles, and then received him and his father at Lambeth, on the morning of Easter Eve.

After a few words with the young man, he[1]

[1] See Rev. J. E. B. Mayor's *Two Lives of Ferrar*.

'took his father aside and said : ' Let your care
now cease for your hopeful son, or for his future
preferment, or estate, or present maintenance.
God hath so inclined the king's heart, and his
liking to your son, and the gifts God hath en-
dued him with, that having been informed of his
virtuous pious education, and singular industry
and Christian deportment, and of his sober incli-
nation, he will take him from you into his own
protection and care, and make him his scholar and
servant ; and hath given me order that after the
holidays being past I should send him to Oxford,
and that there he shall be maintained in all things
needful to him at the king's proper charge, and
shall not need what he can desire to further him
in the prosecution of those works he hath begun
in matter of languages; and what help of books, or
heads, or hands he shall require, he shall not be un-
furnished with : for the king would have this work
of the New Testament in twenty-four languages
to be accomplished by his own care and assistance;
and to have the help of all the learned men that
can be had to that end.   Assure yourself he shall
want for nothing.   In a word, the king is greatly
in love with him, and you will, and have cause to,
bless and praise God for such a son.'

"So John Ferrar, being ravished with joy, in all
humble manner gave thanks to my lord's grace.
And they returning to Nicholas Ferrar, my lord
embraced him and gave him his benediction.

Nicholas Ferrar, kneeling down, took the bishop by the hand and kissed him.   He took him up in his arms and laid his hand on his cheek, and earnestly besought God Almighty to bless him and increase all grace in him, and fit him every day more and more for an instrument of His glory here upon earth and a saint in heaven, 'which,' said he, 'is the only happiness that can be desired, and ought to be our chief end in all our actions. God bless you!   I have told your father what is to be done for you after the holidays.   God will provide for you better than your father can.   God bless you and keep you.'   So they parted from his Grace."

The correspondence of Laud and Wentworth here becomes in-valuable. Carte's *Life of the Duke of Ormond;* Baillie's *Letters and Journals; The Verney Memoirs;* Nehemiah Wallington's *Historical Notices; The Hamilton Papers;* Sir Ralph Verney's *Diary;* Mentet de Salmonet, *Histoire des Troubles de la Grande Bretagne,* ed. 1660; May's *Causes of the Civil War,* Maseres' edition; Lilly's *Life and Death of Charles I.,* Maseres' edition; *Mémoires du Comte Leveneur de Tillières.*

CHAPTER XI.

POLICY IN IRELAND AND SCOTLAND—THE FIRST
DISTURBANCES—1633-1639.

*Wentworth in Ireland—Reform of the Church and
University—Ministers for Scotland—Laud's Mistake
about the Clergy—Secrecy in the Scotch Office—The
Army on the Frontier—Pacification of Berwick.*

LAUD and Wentworth had always realised the
dangerous complications in which the existence
of two semi-independent nationalities within the
empire might at any time involve their system.
If they were to maintain the Tudor plan of government, by the king for the people, they must be
free from dependence on the will of Parliament ;
and war or rebellion would necessitate the raising
of funds which Parliament alone could supply.
They therefore turned anxious eyes upon Ireland
and Scotland.

Ireland Wentworth took into his own charge.
There to some extent he could carry out his ideal
of a strong and beneficent executive, drawing to
itself the affections of the people by its financial
probity, its industrial energy, its sternly impartial
administration of justice ; and there he never
forgot to listen with attentive sympathy to every

complaint made by Parliament in the name of the people; for Ireland was far from the Court and from the harpies who fed upon the gentle-natured Charles.[1]   Laud's share of this work had been to defend the Irish administration at the council board.   Had it not been for his influence the recall of Wentworth would on several occasions have been certain; and he had brought the Irish bishops, clergy and university into alliance with the lord deputy.[2]   As Chancellor of the University of Dublin, to which office he was elected in 1634, and by his personal influence with many of the prelates, the archbishop had materially aided Wentworth in the pacification of Ireland.   Irishmen could be made, and were made, contented and happy by a strict police and by the protection and development of commerce and industry, such as secured to every man the fruits of his labour, and opened to all fresh opportunities of advancement; and never were Irishmen less brow-beaten by "the great ones"[3] than in those prosperous years.   But neither statesmen considered these measures a full solution of the Irish difficulty.   A rich and thriving community would agitate for freedom, and for a share in the government of the empire. Then the differences of education, of habits, of

[1] Carte's *Ormond*, vol. i.

[2] Laud's *Works*, vii. *passim*, and Carte's *Ormond*, i.

[3] *Strafford Correspondence*, ii. 93.   Carte's *Ormond*, i.   See *Lives* of Strafford.

religion, would threaten a schism between the two
countries.   Prosperous Ireland would become a
peril to the imperial interests of England unless
the Irish could be absorbed in the English race;
unless the educated classes could be imbued with
English ideas, and English principles, and English
ambitions ;[1] while the cultivators of the soil, and
artisans, and smaller traders came to practise
English habits and to live with English surround-
ings.[2]   Thus it was an article of Wentworth's
political creed that the university and the Church
must mould the future.   Romanist Ireland would
never be loyal Ireland ; Laud in the University
of Dublin was to do for the Irish gentry and professional men of the new generation what he was
doing so successfully for England through Oxford.
Meantime an able and popular clergy might with
the support of the Government teach the Irish
peasantry to love the Prayer Book and to look to
the Church as their protector ; and thirty years
might see them weaned from Romanism with a
success as complete as that attained in England.

A good deal was achieved in this direction.
The Irish bishops and clergy were compelled to
reside each in his diocese or benefice, and were
allowed on no pretence whatever to hold preferment in England ; there was no playing with duty

[1] *Strafford Papers*, i. 299.
[2] The Irish children were to learn English (Laud's *Works*,
vi. 374). *Cf. Irish Narratives* of 1641, Camden Society.

for the coadjutors of Laud and Wentworth.
Pluralists like the Archbishop of Cashel, who held
sixteen livings, were compelled to disgorge.   Lay-
impropriators received equally severe treatment ;
of one of the greediest of them Laud writes :
" Dermot O'Dingle hath a mighty swallow,"
" three vicarages at once and not one stick
by the way ".[1]   Everywhere neglected and im-
poverished parishes were being put into working
order.   The Irish articles, which were strongly
Calvinistic, were repealed by convocation, and the
English accepted in their stead.   The new bishops
were carefully selected at Laud's advice by the
king ; and the lord deputy himself was authorised
to appoint to all inferior dignities.   Moreover, as
it was found that the episcopal chancellors were
both ignorant and corrupt, and able to hinder
many of the reforms of devoted bishops like the
saintly Bedell,[2] directions were given by Laud's
desire to the lord keeper Coventry to choose in
England suitable lawyers of repute for these difficult appointments.   Meanwhile the Romanists
were watched with a jealous eye, and their propaganda diligently repressed.[3]   Things had gone so
well that the deputy ventured to assemble a

---

[1] Laud's *Works*, vii. 69.   Carte's *Ormond*, i. 72.

[2] Bedell, with Laud's support, translated the Bible into Irish ;
it was just ready for print when the Great Rebellion broke out and
stopped their plans (Heylin's *History of the Reformation*).

[3] *Strafford Papers*, i. 187, and *passim*.

Parliament and obtained Parliamentary sanction for all his plans. From Ireland there would be no danger so long as Wentworth's hand controlled it.[1] But if resolute government was withdrawn, the outbreak would be all the more terrible, since every evil-doer of every party felt and found his liberty of action curtailed, and was burning with regret for the wild anarchy of former times.[2]

Scotland required still more delicate handling; but this Scotland had not obtained. It was an axiom with Charles that Scotland must be ruled by Scotsmen; and there were few Scotsmen of influence likely to endanger themselves for the plans of a Government which was intent on curtailing the greatness of the local magnates. Two classes of men stand out prominently during these years in the history of Scotland. There were the successful preachers, men usually of noble personal piety but devoted to the most extreme principles of their Reformation, and by the narrowness of their experience unable to extend sympathy in any degree to those of different training and of different nationality. Scotland under their guidance would prove to be her own worst enemy; and would fall for the first time in her stormy history under a foreign tyranny supported by a standing army which she herself was compelled to pay. Side by side with these estimable men, and employing them continually as cat's-paws to pull

---

[1] Carte's *Ormond*, i. 88.   [2] Wallington, ii. 216.

out their chestnuts, were the leaders of the
Scottish nobility ; Argyle, whom Laud had personally offended ; Rothes, whose ruined fortunes
required the chances of a revolution ; Montrose,
who was annoyed by the king's reception of
him at the Court of Whitehall ; Loudoun, and
many others like them brought up in an atmosphere of intrigue, educated to consider the
advance of their personal power in their own
districts the one object worth striving after, and
now discontented because the Crown was seeking
to deprive them of their oppressive privileges.[1]
To the nobles the Episcopal Church was most
hateful because they held many acres of the
bishops' lands ; while the Presbyterian preachers
shrank from the bishops and the liturgy because
bishops and a liturgy existed in the Roman Church.

James I. had succeeded in partially restoring
the royal authority in Scotland by skilfully playing
off the preachers against the nobles ; he had
gradually acquired greater power than his predecessors and had set himself to strengthen this
by establishing a new episcopal hierarchy which
he had endowed with some control over the
clergy, and which he employed as a local counter-
poise to the nobles.   After his accession to the
English throne he had prepared the way for the
reintroduction of a liturgy.   But he died just as
his schemes were ripened.

[1] Rushworth, ii. 392.   Baillie, i. 7.

Charles, who had left Scotland when he was two years old, knew little of the Scottish character, and had no sympathy with Scottish habits ; but in his father's Court he had imbibed strong Scottish prejudices which induced him to refuse to discuss at the English council table the details of any of his Scottish measures.   Laud and Wentworth managed Ireland ; they were almost entirely ignorant of the affairs of Scotland, and at first had no conception of the serious nature of the Scottish outbreak.[1]   The part of chief adviser for Scotland was assigned to the Marquis of Hamilton, a man who shared the tendency of his famous house toward a tortuous and irresolute policy ; he had gained the king's affections by his skill in tennis and in hunting,[2] but he was universally disliked and distrusted ; " the air of his countenance," said a shrewd observer, " had a cloud upon it ".[3]

But though Laud was never allowed to interfere with the Scottish administration, his ecclesiastical

---

[1] Laud's *Works*, vii. 402, 426, 468, prove this.   " The secret is between the Marquis of Hamilton and the king," writes Laud to Wentworth so late as 30th July, 1638 ; *cf. Strafford Papers*, ii. 325 ; Clarendon's *History*, i. 172.   See also the defiance sent to France in the middle of the Scottish troubles; when Richelieu asked for English neutrality during his attack on Dunkirk (Père d'Orléans, ix. 264), Charles answered that he would send a fleet and 15,000 men to defend it.   This shows how little ministers dreaded Scottish outbreaks.   *Cf.* Carte's *Ormond*, i. 88.

[2] Sir P. Warwick, 104 ; and Burnet's *Hamilton*, p. 4.

[3] Charles was afterwards convinced of his treachery (Ludlow iii. 260, letter to the queen).

policy was so cordially admired and accepted by the king that in the general direction of the Government his principles were constantly followed and his advice occasionally invited.[1]   And Laud flattered himself that the king could use the Church of Scotland as he was using the Church of England to be the foundation of rule for the good of the people.   In thinking the influence of the Church great upon the life and politics of Scotland he was right enough ; but he had misjudged the feeling of the popular preachers towards episcopacy and towards England. Anxious to bring the Scottish Church into line with the Church of England, and thus to draw more closely the bonds which united the two countries, on his two journeys to Scotland, once with James I. and again for the coronation of Charles, he had allowed his predilections to mislead him as he visited the towns and talked with the leading men, and had been too strongly impressed when at the coronation of Charles no serious difficulty was raised by the clergy or onlookers about the wearing of the episcopal and clerical robes usual in the English Church.[2]   Therefore he had determined to persuade the king to give the bishops a share in the administration, and on the first opportunity the chancellorship had been conferred on Archbishop Spottiswoode of St. Andrews.

[1] See his letters to Scotch bishops, etc., *e.g.*, *Works*, vi. 438, 444.   [2] Salmonet, i. 4.

Several of the great nobles, seeing the direction in which the wind was blowing, offered to restore Church lands in Scotland if they might receive in exchange richer properties in England. To this also Laud persuaded the king, and imagined that it proved a real desire to restore the wealth and authority of the Church. " Conformity," he knew, " must be the work of time ;"[1] but conformity, he had no doubt, could be secured by patience. Other acts of the executive, and new laws passed by the Parliament of Scotland, tended to check the authority of the nobles. And, bitterest of all, the purified administration of the English Treasury had stopped the leaks through which so much English money had found its way into the pockets of the great men in Scotland, who began to think that the English opposition was not likely to prove so jealous a guardian of the money-chest.[2]

Meanwhile Richelieu was troubled at the growing power of the King of England ;[3] French schemes for aggrandisement were frequently hindered, while a mighty fleet, the product of ship-money, held the Channel. There is sufficient proof that French agents entered into communication[4] with the discontented in Scotland, France's

---

[1] Laud's own endorsement of *State Paper*, vol. 286, No. 16.

[2] Lord Warwick made a great fortune out of the Rebellion. According to Walker's *History of Independence* many others took large sums for themselves when they got power. *Cf.* Mason's *Norfolk*, 306 ; Ludlow, ii. 513 ; Hutchinson, i. 263 ; Holles' *Memoirs*, and Milton's *History*.   [3] Martin, *France*, xi. 484, etc

[4] Baker, p. 469. According to Andreas de Habernfield, the

old ally,[1] as well as with the discontented in England who were chafing at the exaction of ship-money and the discontinuance of Parliaments. To the cardinal-minister, the interests of the Papacy were of no account.[2] "No Popery" he found would be a valuable political cry in Scotland; and it was easy to put a brave colour on this cry by misrepresenting events in England, or by partially revealing some of those secrets of the English Court which many of Charles' most trusted courtiers betrayed to France. England should be occupied at home; it had been peaceful already too long for the interests of its neighbours.

Nor did the Scottish nobles and clergy fail to find sympathisers in England. The leaders of the English Opposition had kept up correspondence with them since they had accompanied Charles on his magnificent journey into Scotland for his coronation. And when finally it appeared to the Scottish bishops that the fitting moment had come for the introduction of a liturgy, preachers and nobles saw their opportunity to recover political power.

French and the Jesuits were at the bottom of the whole disturbance (Wharton's edition of Laud's *Works*, i. 573). In 1638 Richelieu was very much troubled at the reception of Marie de Medici in England, and redoubled his intrigues in England and Scotland (*Hist. de Louis XIII.*, par P. de Griffet, iii. 155). *Cf.* Rushworth, ii. 840. Père d'Orléans, ix. 264. Clarendon, ii. 137. Carte's *Ormond*.

[1] See Tillières, pp. 206-261, for French intrigues in Scotland in 1628, on the ground of the former alliance.

[2] See Martin, *Histoire de France*, xi. 511, *seq.*, for scheme of a Gallican Church under a patriarch and independent of Rome, considered by Richelieu.

The Scottish bishops had given them every right to protest. The new Prayer Book had been authorised neither by synod nor by Parliament; in spite of Laud's counsel,[1] constantly repeated, it had been carefully kept from public knowledge until the day appointed for its first use.[2] All that was officially known was that it was modelled upon the English liturgy, with some alterations which had been approved, slanderous tongues did not hesitate to say suggested, by the Archbishop of Canterbury. It was easy enough to go a step further and assert that the new prayers had been seen and were full of Popish doctrine;[3] street gossip was sure that they were to be used as a first step to reintroduce Popery.[4] The passions of the populace were skilfully stirred; they were inflamed by the stupid secrecy of the responsible men; every conscientious Presbyterian was made anxious and filled with alarm. And thus it was natural that at the very first reading of the Prayer Book on the 23rd of July, 1637, a riot broke out in the cathedral of Edinburgh.[5] Well-informed persons were confident that the whole thing had been organised by nobles and great ladies.[6] At all events by

---

[1] *Trials and Troubles*, 168, etc.　　　[2] Baillie, i. 2.

[3] *Accounts of Condition of Province*, p. 551.

[4] *Cf.* Clarendon, i. 165.

[5] Laud's *Works*, vi. 554; vii. 374, 390 and 490, show his disgust at the mismanagement in Scotland.

[6] Clarendon's *History*, i. 162-175; *Strafford Papers*, ii. 264, etc.; Guthry's *Memoirs*, p. 20. *Cf.* Salmonet, i. 29.

a clever precaution the women took the lead in
the open assault upon Episcopacy; it was they who
disturbed the service by their outcries and missiles;
it was they who nearly murdered the Bishop of
Edinburgh in the streets; then as the weakness
and irresolution of the Government became evident,
ministers, nobles, merchants, citizens and farmers
followed in their wake.[1]   The Solemn Covenant
was signed in the Grey Friars Churchyard; the
royal castles were captured; and the authority not
only of the bishops but of the king himself was
broken in a few weeks.

That the Rebellion originated largely in the
anger of the nobles at the resumption of Church
lands[2] and at the growing power of the bishops
is clearly proved by the articles afterwards exhibited by the Scottish commissioners against
Archbishop Laud; they prove also how cleverly
national and religious bigotry had been aroused
against the interference of the English bishops
and the supposed intention to introduce Popish
practices.   One specimen is enough; Laud was
seriously accused of directing the Scottish priests
to represent the Deity by turning their backs
upon the people in the communion service, and
the reference was given to Exodus xxxiii. 23.[3]

---

[1] Guthry's *Memoirs*, and Baillie's *Letters and Journals*.

[2] *Cf.* Skinner's *Life of Monk*, p. 15, and Salmonet, i. 11, etc.

[3] Laud's *History of Trials and Troubles*, 116; letters in *Works*,
vi. 494, 503.

But for many months neither Laud nor Wentworth anticipated any serious results from the Scottish disturbances.[1] Negotiations were being conducted by Hamilton and others who kept the despatches to themselves; and it seemed impossible that the Royal Council in Scotland should be so incapable as to lose control over the kingdom without a struggle. The English Opposition were better informed, and they were not likely to lose such a chance of guiding the flames of discontent into England also.[2] For it began to look as if the king would have no further need of Parliament. Under Juxon's economical management debts were being fast cleared off;[3] and the ordinary revenue more than sufficed for the expenditure.[4] Only a few months before the riot in Edinburgh the judges had decided in February, 1637, by a small majority that ship-money might legally be collected from the inland counties without the consent of Parliament; this would maintain the fleet. The forest courts under Lord Holland, the chief justice in Eyre, were continuing their demands of heavy fines from those who had encroached, often scores of years before, upon the

---

[1] This is evident from the little attention paid to them in the correspondence; and the first allusion to Scotch troubles in the *Diary* is 29th April, 1638.

[2] Wood's *Athenae*, ii. 30, etc.   [3] *State Papers.*

[4] The ordinary revenue and expenditure of these years was about £600,000 a year. The taxes in France reached £5,000,000; and debt grew there.

ancient boundaries of the royal forests ; here was an income for the queen and courtiers. And the Treasury had resorted to several expedients, hardly illegal in themselves, but all pointing to a resolution which the king was said to have formed never again to summon a Parliament. Many conscientious people declared that the king intended to find laws authorising him to take what he chose from his subjects with no Act duly discussed and voted by the representatives of the people. [1]   And as the power of the Government, though, as we have seen, it had no armed force at its disposal, still appeared too strong for open resistance, the only course the Opposition could adopt was to persuade men to delay the payment of ship-money,[2] to resist the removal of the communion table from the nave, which Bishop Williams of Lincoln now maintained was its legal position, and to claim and assert their right to receive the communion standing. But, after all, such measures might annoy, they could not overthrow the Government.

How then could the passionately ambitious leaders, who had always determined to rule

---

[1] Simonds d'Ewes.

The first writ of ship-money issued in 1635 was paid up speedily (*State Papers*, vol. 302, No. 45). In later years collection proved more difficult. It was often unjustly assessed by the sheriffs ; this was one cause of its unpopularity. A few, like Hampden, refused to pay on political grounds, but most of the complaints were of unfair assessment (*State Papers*).

England and who believed that Laud was fast
leading them to Rome, throw away the opportunity offered by Scotland? They opened negotiations with the Scottish leaders ; Lord Saye and
Sele, Lord Brooke and others promised the Scottish ministers to establish the Presbyterian system
in England ; they caressed the nobles with the
assurance that they should obtain practical independence in their own districts and the sole
influence in the central Government ; they stimulated resistance by their avowed belief that the
king had not popularity enough to raise an
English army, nor money enough to pay it, and
that the English people would support the Scots.

So the months rolled on with negotiation and
intrigue. Laud's voice was raised resolutely for
peace ; not that he had any doubt of the power
of the king to repress the rising ; in England he
was sure that public opinion sided with the
Government ; the press was in the hands of the
Church,[1] and the curtailment of the lectureships
gave the bishops the disposal of the pulpits through
which they would exercise the strongest influence
upon the congregations. In Ireland Wentworth
held ready an army which might at any time
form the nucleus of a force to be used against the
Scots. But the archbishop detested war ; he says :
" Differences in religion I conceived might better

---

[1] See measures to suppress unlicensed printing in 1637
(Heylin, 341).

be composed by ink than by blood"; [1] and "all those domestic evils which threaten a rent in Church or State are with far more safety prevented by wisdom than punished by justice". [2]   He had always urged upon the Scottish bishops the importance of strictly legal action; if they had now violated the law, the new service book, so he advised, ought to be publicly withdrawn.

But, as we have seen, Laud had little influence upon the conduct of Scottish affairs.   He has no responsibility for the vacillating character of the negotiations.   And, though, as matters grew more serious, it became necessary to consult the English council, he was by no means omnipotent at Court.   The queen desired war; the courtiers represented to the king that he was being insulted; and as by the advice of Hamilton and other Scottish counsellors[3] Charles absolutely refused to make terms with rebels and insisted on an armed demonstration in 1639, Laud finally recommended him to call upon his people for an army and for supplies.   This plan was adopted.   The nobles and gentry were summoned to lead their retainers in person to the North in order to repel the threatened invasion of the Scots; the clergy took

---

[1] *Trials and Troubles*, 167.

[2] Epistle Dedicatory of *Book against Fisher*.

[3] The Earl of Lanerick was Secretary for Scotland; he was Hamilton's brother; he was only twenty-one. See list of other Scotch nobles at Court in Heylin, pp. 354 and 355.

the lead in contributions of money ; the diocese of Norwich, which was supposed to be the hot-bed of Puritanism, sent £2000 ; the Archdeaconry of Winchester gave £1300 ; and money flowed in from all sides.[1] Only a few of the Puritans held aloof, and with them the larger part of the Romanists dissuaded, so it was said, from supporting the Anglican king by a special letter from the Pope.[2]

The action of the Government proved its complete assurance that it possessed the support of public opinion ; and that the nation would place its arms and its money at the king's disposal.   And Laud's confidence was justified. Lord Warwick had long been looked upon as the head of the Puritan party, in spite of his dissolute private life ;[3] but even he did not venture to fail in mustering and despatching to the front the train bands of Essex, of which county he was lord-lieutenant.[4]   Only Lord Saye and Lord Brooke showed any sign of disaffection ; they refused the military oath when they reached York and were sent back contemptuously to their homes.[5]

Lord Essex, on whom the Opposition thought they could count, accepted the office of lieutenant-

[1] Heylin's *Life*, 358; Laud's *Works*, vi. 558 ; Rushworth, ii. 819. Rossingham News Letter, 1st April, 1639.

[2] Rushworth, ii. 821.   *Cf.* Rossingham News Letter, 1st April, 1639.

[3] Lodge, *Life of Lord Warwick.*   [4] *State Papers*, 1639.

[5] Heylin, 362.

general to the new army; nor was his support
merely nominal; his rapidity of movement and
skill secured Berwick,[1] though Scottish councillors
flying from Edinburgh assured him, when they
met him as far south as York, that Lesley and his
hosts were close at their heels.[2]   He was desirous
to strike a blow at Edinburgh quickly before the
enemy was prepared.   A powerful army soon
gathered on the frontiers; Lord Arundel, the
greatest and proudest of the ancient nobility, was
at its head.   The Court favourite, Lord Holland,
had command of the horse, appointed against
Laud's advice to please the queen;[3] the minister felt
that here lay the weak place, for he dreaded the
intrigues of such courtiers who preferred their own
personal advantage to the interests of Church and
State, and, to gain popularity with the Puritans,
muttered to their confidants that the war was a
bishops' war.   But there was a loyal spirit in the
army as a whole;[4] the men were eager to come
to blows with the ancient enemy;[5] we see, in the
letters written from the camp by Sir Edmund
Verney, that the troops, insufficient and ill
equipped at first,[6] gradually grew into a compact

[1] *State Papers*, April 3, 1639, Coke to Windebank.

[2] Heylin, 363.   [3] Laud's *Works*, vii. 523.

[4] *State Papers*, vol. 423, No. 67, shows some disaffection but
more loyalty.

[5] *State Papers*, vol. 417, No. 65, and Heylin, 360.

[6] *Verney Memoirs. Court and Times of Charles I.;* letters from
the army. *Cf.* Baillie and *Hamilton Papers.*

and powerful force,[1] in which the brilliant feudal cavalry of the great nobles and wealthy gentry, numbering some 8000 men, vied with the well-drilled infantry which Wentworth had sent over from Ireland in order to form the backbone of a somewhat raw mass of soldiers, selected from the train bands of the counties. The generals and experienced officers were confident that by a vigorous advance they could drive Lesley's army before them and restore the royal power in Scotland by force ;[2] while the blockade of the Scottish ports, which Wentworth and Laud advised as a gentler alternative, must soon have compelled the insurgents to submit themselves to the king.[3] The fleet held the narrow seas and made it impossible for the friends of the revolt in Holland and France to land the arms which they had prepared.

But Charles was surrounded by Scotsmen who could not be expected to welcome an English invasion nor to rejoice in the pros-

---

[1] *Verney Memoirs. Cf.* Warwick, 129; Heylin, 363 to 367; Baker, 466; Hutchinson, i. 175. See *State Papers*, 4th April, 1639, the account of arms, ordnance, and ammunition that day despatched from the dockyard; and vol. 422, No. 63 ; and Rossingham News Letter, 1st April, 1639, for the sums of money sent to the army.

[2] For comparative strength of armies, *cf. State Papers*, vol. 424, No. 50, and vol. 421, No. 60. Col. Monk (afterwards Duke of Albemarle) always gave it as his opinion that throughout the war and even after the Battle of Newburn on 28th Aug., 1640, when the Scots had obtained arms from abroad, the English forces were decidedly the stronger (Skinner's *Life*, p. 18). Baillie, i. 210, puts the Scots at 12,000. Heylin and Baker say " they had not 3000 musquets amongst them ". [3] *Strafford Papers*, ii. 234 and 235.

pect of an English success ; Scottish lords-in-waiting insinuated excuses into the royal ear ; Scottish gentlemen of the bedchamber searched the royal pockets in the night and sent the most detailed information across the border ;[1] Scottish nobles at Court spread rumours of the enormous force with which Lesley was advancing, and for a time gained credence, as the Verney papers prove to us.[2] The Marquis of Hamilton had no desire that his countrymen should be crushed ;[3] lying in the Forth with a royal fleet, he carried on negotiations with the popular leaders ; he allowed Montrose to capture loyal Aberdeen and to scatter the Gordons ;[4] in a constant flow of letters he assured the king that the Covenanters would submit peaceably.   Hamilton had probably begun already that double game of treachery to both sides which eventually brought him to the block ; but his younger brother, Lanerick, now Secretary for Scotland, exercised an influence over the king all the more dangerous because of his sincere belief that the Covenanters were genuinely desirous for peace.   Bright, open, sprightly in conversation, this nobleman had learnt from his strong-willed mother[5] to be a firm Calvinist as

[1] *Strafford Papers*, ii. 325. Guthry's *Memoirs*, 47. *State Papers*, 417, No. 85.

[2] *Cf.* Rushworth, ii. 909, and Heylin, 363.

[3] Guthry, 48, and vacillation shown in *Hamilton Papers*. *Cf.* Burnet's *Hamilton*.   [4] Salmonet, i. 69.

[5] See *State Papers* for the part taken by old Lady Hamilton at this time (vol. 420, No. 121, etc.).

well as a devoted servant of the throne : persuaded himself, he persuaded the king that it was
only the irritating mistakes of his counsellors
which had produced the revolt.[1]   His arguments
were supported by Holland ; as general of the
horse he held the command of a reconnaissance
into Scotland and had retreated in disorder at the
news that a strong body of troops under Lesley
was preparing to attack him.   The disgrace of
this repulse Essex was eager to blot out by an
advance in force ; but Holland, who in Laud's
absence exercised the strongest influence with the
king, wished to cover his discredit by posing as
the mediator of a successful compromise.   Always
irresolute, Charles gave way ; in spite of the en-
treaties of Laud and Wentworth, necessarily
weakened by distance, he agreed to the Pacification of Berwick on the 15th of June, 1639.   He
dismissed his troops, who returned home full of
contempt for his vacillation ; Arundel felt himself
discredited ; Essex considered that he was despised, since the king had rejected his advice and
now sent him away without thanks for his services ;
other great nobles like the showy and chivalrous
Newcastle had received personal rebuffs ; it would
be hard indeed to assemble such an army again.

The terms of the Pacification of Berwick
proved the dread which the English army had
inspired ; for the Scots agreed to surrender to the

---

[1] See Lodge, *Life of Lanerick.*

king the principal fortresses, and to restore the expelled and plundered royalists. But all they desired was to gain time ; time to supply themselves with munitions of war from Germany and Holland ; time to drill an army ; time to make themselves friends in England and to organise an English opposition against a king who had proved himself irresolute and incapable before the eyes of the assembled leaders of both nations.[1]   In the friendly meetings with Scotsmen at Berwick many an English nobleman came to see the profit he might make by the ruin of the Church and the pillage of her property.   Their strong feelings of patriotism had been dangerously played with and weakened in spite of the archbishop's advice.[2] Scores of little borough votes would be marshalled by great landowners against king and bishops at the next opportunity; and the little borough votes controlled the Parliament.[3]

It was soon made evident that the Scots had no intention of observing the Pacification of Berwick ; they refused to keep their promise of restoring the property of the bishops ; everywhere the royal authority in Scotland was still disregarded, and a powerful Scottish army was assembled on the frontier where the deluded king had left the English fortresses ungarrisoned at the mercy of the foe.

[1] Heylin, 367; Clarendon, i. 197.

[2] *Trials and Troubles*, 168.

[3] See *Verney Memoirs* for smallness of constituencies.

If there was to be a war under such dangerous conditions there was only one minister who would be likely to conduct it successfully. The pacificator of Ireland must try his hand at pacifying Scotland. Therefore the long-felt desire of Laud that the Irish deputy should be summoned to England[1] and put at the head of affairs was now gratified; and Wentworth became Earl of Strafford and chief counsellor to the king in January, 1640.

Laud's Premiership was at an end; the vigour with which he had arranged the mustering of the great army and had equipped it with ordnance and money[2] proved that he held England perfectly under control; but nothing would induce him to imitate Richelieu and take that part in actual fighting which he considered incompatible with the clerical office. Therefore he was absent at the crisis of his career; the courtiers for the moment obtained the upper hand; Charles failed to carry through his purpose; and the fatal loss of prestige endangered the settlement of the English Church, and the unity of the British Empire. What would have been the change in the course of history if the English army had crushed Lesley, had advanced to Edinburgh and dictated peace to Scotland, with Essex as the king's general and Laud as the king's counsellor?

[1] *Works*, vii. 177, 273.   [2] *Hamilton Papers*.

For the comparative strength of the armies on the frontier, see Note C, p. 296.

CHAPTER XII.

THE SHORT PARLIAMENT OF 1640.

The Elections—Laud's Hopes—Temperate Character of the New House—Pym's Skilful Leadership—Hyde's Compromise—Abrupt Dissolution—Laud's Expectation of Death.

THE new Earl of Strafford had no hesitation in persuading the king that it was necessary to summon a Parliament. He was personally familiar with the arts by which a majority could be formed in the Commons whether for opposition or for the support of the Government; and he was convinced of his capacity to manage both electors[1] and elected.[2] The archbishop gave him his cordial support;[3] they both disliked the doubtful legality which hung round many of the expedients of the Treasury, and considered it most important that

---

[1] There is no proof of royal interference in these elections, but the Government certainly did not leave Pym a free hand as they did in the autumn.

[2] As a rule there was no representation of the minority on committees, *e.g.*, in Long Parliament (*Parl. Hist.*, ix. 45, 496).

[3] *Diary*, 5th December, 1639.

(230)

these questions should be publicly debated and
settled in the great council of the nation.[1]

Nor did the time seem to observers to be unfavourable.   Many of the bitterest speakers of
1628 were dead.   The success of the administration during the last eleven years, which had proved
that the Government could be carried on without
a Parliament, would make members all the more
unwilling to risk another breach with the Crown,
while the revelation of the intrigues detected between the Scots and France must stir resentment
in every English patriot.   To make concessions
in order to maintain the union of Britain under
one sovereign would be creditable to the popular
leaders ; while the minister who could re-establish
good relations between king and Commons would
deserve renown.   Laud thought that Strafford was
peculiarly well adapted for this task, on the accom-
plishment of which he had set his heart.

But they both forgot how different the conditions in England were to those of Ireland ; at
the English council table Laud and Strafford
counted for only two votes among many.   The
king, vacillating between their advice and the
queen's persuasion, liked at times to show his independence of his chief ministers.   He obliged them
to share with Hamilton, whom they now distrusted

---

[1] Laud's *Book against Fisher*, pub. 1639, speaks strongly of the
supremacy of Parliament, p. 211, *e.g.*, "The statute laws which must
bind all subjects cannot be made and ratified but in Parliament".

and despised, the counsels for the Scottish campaign and the Scottish negotiations.[1]   In spite of their fulsome protestations of affection for Strafford, the haughty Arundel, the mindless irresolute Northumberland, and other great nobles in the council claimed in their hearts the supreme power as the due of their high birth, and disliked his overbearing manner, while they ridiculed Laud as a parvenu.   Holland and Cottington were intent on their own interests and would always cut the shape of their policy to enlarge their pockets ; they were already intriguing with the Opposition.[2]   The most serious point of all was to decide upon the representative of the Government in the House of Commons.   This office was left to the new Secretary of State, Sir Henry Vane the elder, who had been appointed against the advice of Laud and by the influence of the queen ; the two leading ministers could not now succeed in obtaining his removal.   Vane had proved himself an adroit diplomatist on foreign embassies, but he was without Parliamentary experience ; he was an hereditary rival of Wentworth's family, was a dependent of Hamilton and Holland, and belonged to that Court clique which they directed against the honest administration of the Treasury, and to which the Jesuits'[3]

---

[1] They were called the Junto of Three (Lady Carlisle's letter, quoted by Lodge, vii.).   [2] *State Papers.*

[3] Baker, p. 470, asserts that Con had aided Richelieu's chaplain,

hatred of Laud had given substance. His strong-willed and capable son was the intimate of Pym and Martin, and combined the Puritanism of the first with the latter's aspirations for a republic ; he was already betraying secrets of the Court to the group of politicians who had promised the Scots that they would wreck the Parliament.

On the 13th of April, 1640, the Commons met. On the whole the elections had gone well for the archbishop's hopes.[1] Though Puritan and Jesuit[2] had had their influence in the constituencies, the House was mainly composed of moderate men, vexed certainly at many of the measures of the last few years, prepared neither to support to the full Laud's Church policy,[3] nor the system of taxation constructed by Weston and Noy, and full of many grievances ; but possessed of a strong feeling that a compromise between king and Parliament should be attempted if possible.[4] Laud and Strafford had expected no more than this ; they were themselves most anxious to redress the numerous personal and local wrongs of which an arbitrary Government hears nothing

Chamberlayne, in stirring up the Scotch troubles. Carte, *Ormond*, i. 89, speaks of the Jesuits as swarming over from St. Omer at this time to stir trouble. Just here, when we should have been so grateful for information as to the proceedings of the Roman party, "the Romish Recusant" gives us none, in his *Life of Laud*.

[1] See his fears in *Works*, vii. 502 and 513.

[2] *Works* (folio), p. 584.   [3] *Parliamentary History*, viii. 397-457.

[4] May, in *The Causes of the Civil War*, speaks indignantly of "the obedience and compliance" of this Parliament.

till a storm of discontent breaks out against its
agents.   The redress of private and public
grievances they considered the first duty of every
Parliament.   They had also prepared the king's
mind to surrender ship-money, which the judges
had only justified as a temporary expedient; to
admit that his right to tonnage and poundage
rested on Parliamentary grant alone; and to
reform the Earl Marshal's Court.   All these
concessions were promised or implied in the lord
keeper's speech when the king opened Parliament.
But they were determined to insist that under the
critical circumstances supply must for once take
precedence of grievances; if the Commons would
vote subsidies to replenish the Treasury, so that the
Scottish army could be confronted with a strong
force, and the northern garrisons of Berwick, Newcastle and Carlisle set in order, the king pledged
his word by their advice to continue the session
until Michaelmas, so as to give full opportunity to
discuss necessary reforms in the administration.
The lord keeper was instructed to point out that it
would be disgraceful to leave the northern counties
at the mercy of their ancient enemy, and that the
Scottish nobles had gone so far as to send an invita-
tion to the French king to interfere on their behalf.

The Commons elected Glanvill, a moderate
constitutionalist, as their speaker; they proved
their temperate intentions by a stern rebuke
administered to a member named Peard who

spoke of ship-money as "an abomination";[1] the tone of the speeches[2] contrasted strikingly with those violent claims to settle the doctrine of the Church and those savage invectives against the ministers which had brought about the catastrophe of 1629. But Pym and his friends had promised the Scots that they would break up the Parliament;[3] after several speeches from others on the grievances of Englishmen and the necessity of keeping well with the king, the great leader of the Opposition rose in his place; no one knew better than he the temper of his audience or was more capable of varying his tone to suit their feelings of the moment; and if he was already possessed with the idea that to the House of Commons and not to the king belonged of right the control of the destinies of England, no one had been more quick to perceive that this House of Commons was not prepared for so great a revolution: with measured and temperate utterance he recalled to their minds their ancient privileges, violated, as he maintained, by the law courts in 1629; he dwelt upon the hardships imposed upon men of sincere religion by the Declaration of Sports, by compulsory kneeling for communion, and other innovations; he concluded with those

[1] Clarendon's *Rebellion*, i. 208.

[2] See those of Waller and others in *Parliamentary History*, viii. 441.

[3] Clarendon, i. 218.

pecuniary grievances which were sure to inflame the mass of new members ignorant of the neces- sary expenses of Government and familiar with the meaningless cry that the king should live of his own.[1] When he sat down he had taken captive the imagination of the wavering members; they had been as sheep without a shepherd ; this was the man they would follow. All applauded the mildness and clearness of his principles. There was no Wentworth[2] in the House to rise on the other side and to set forward against the long catalogue of petty annoyances some great concep- tion of imperial Government. Vane sat silent and allowed himself to be swept along with the stream ; suffering the great body of moderate members to feel that the Crown intended to insist upon its usurpations, and leaving them to forget the defenceless North and the public interests of England.

Under Pym's leadership the votes of the House began to show that it was resolved to give precedence to the redress of grievances, and had no immediate intention of granting supplies. Still, men like Edward Hyde, who began his political career in this Parliament,[3] and Glanvill,

---

[1] The growing expenses of Government had long made this impossible. There was no separation as yet of the civil list from the military and civil expenses.

[2] Wentworth's sickness during the Short Parliament kept him even from giving full instructions to the privy councillors in the House.　　　[3] See his *Life*, i. 83.

he Speaker, made their influence felt as the days
vent on ; and Pym did not venture to throw off
he mask and to open those direct attacks upon
ninisters which in the next Parliament were to
nake him famous.

After several feebly-conceived efforts to per-
uade the House to vote supplies, Vane was
ommissioned to go down with a definite proposal.
The king would give up ship-money, allowing
he judgment of the judges to be called up before
he Lords on a writ of error and to be reversed, if
he Commons would vote him twelve subsidies.
Ne are told that this was done against the advice
of Laud and Strafford, and that they had so far
nodified the resolution of the council as to get
Vane authority to accept eight subsidies.   Hamp-
len, most popular from his resistance to ship-
noney, rose in his place to oppose the motion ;
uch a grant, according to him, would crush the
ax-payer to the ground ; but when Glanvill,
peaking from the floor as the House was in
:ommittee, pointed out how small would be the
um payable by individuals, even of large estate,
nd Hyde interposed with an amendment that
he House would consider the proposal, it became
:vident that the Moderate party was likely to
rove the stronger.   Many members, while
efusing to throw out the proposal, thought that
he king should make further concessions before
hey granted so large a sum.   Vane stiffly repeated

his former statement; the king would take no less, and grant no more; but it is said that Herbert, the Solicitor-General, a persuasive speaker, held out hopes of conciliation. The second day's debate lasted from 8 A.M. till 5 P.M., and then the Opposition could only succeed in securing an adjournment. What malign influence could they find to convince the king and his council that the Opposition would be victorious, and so make definite the breach between Crown and people?

Vane hastened to Whitehall; he informed the king that the House would grant him nothing; he out-talked the Solicitor-General, who always distrusted his own judgment, and he thoroughly incensed Charles against the Commons. The king agreed to summon a council at 6 A.M. the next morning, the 5th of May, and then declared his decision to dissolve a Parliament whose members evidently cared nothing for their country. Vane repeated his statement that the Commons " would not give one penny," and seems also to have persuaded the king that they would vote the war with Scotland to be unjust.[1]   Strafford and Laud, who arrived late, owing to a mistake about the hour, had no opportunity of forming an opinion on the possibility of working with the House of Com-

---

[1] The *State Papers* show that Pym had intended to raise this question in the hope of confusing the issues.

ions, and found that the king's decision was already settled without their advice.[1]

So strangely does the personal character of comparatively unimportant men decide the course of events. In the early days of the Covenant, Montrose had taken no very high position among the leaders in Scotland; his adhesion to the cause had been short-lived; yet it was his enthusiasm and skill which by crushing Aberdeen and the Gordons had made the rising a success.[2] And now Sir Henry Vane, hitherto an almost unknown man, had broken down by his misrepresentations the last hope of agreement between king and Parliament in England. Royalist writers accused him of a deliberate treachery such as that by which he afterwards destroyed his personal enemy Strafford; but it is at least possible that he had lost his head in the debate and had fancied himself peculiarly well informed, through his son, of the intentions of the members. Pym had gained the day; the Puritan leaders listened with smiles of joy to the royal speech dissolving Parliament; Oliver St. John expressed the thoughts of all his friends when he said that day to Hyde: "All is well; and it must be worse before it is better; this Parliament would never have done what was necessary to be done".[3] For if they could now prevent the

---

[1] *Trials and Troubles*, 78, 79; *cf.* Clarendon's *Life*, i. 84.

[2] *Cf.* Salmonet and Baillie.

[3] Clarendon's *Rebellion*, i. 218.

king from assembling the forces of England, and could bring a Scottish army into the northern counties before the next elections, the disgrace and the danger would ensure an irresistible majority to overthrow Church and State, and give the Government of England once more to the aristocracy.

The Moderate party were overwhelmed with sadness. Edward Hyde, like many others, had left the House on the night of the 4th of May, without a doubt that he could carry a compromise. Now the Government appeared to have cast away all moderation, and to have embarked on the most arbitrary course.

It has seemed important to describe so fully the history of the Short Parliament,[1] because we see in it the serious effort made by Laud and Strafford to rule England with a Parliament, and the reasons which frustrated their attempt. The Scottish rising had compelled Charles to listen to counsels to call the Houses together which he had previously refused to entertain; and had afforded the most natural opportunity for the reconciliation of all classes of Englishmen. Now the archbishop's policy had been defeated, he hardly knew how; and he felt as a man groping in the dark.[2] The whole blame of

[1] Its history is very difficult to trace, for Rushworth is almost a blank.

[2] *Works* (folio), p. 579.

the dissolution was cast upon him though he had no hand in it;[1] and he was bitterly grieved that all these moderate men in whom he had felt such real confidence, and about whose character he had learnt so much from Hyde, were now going home to tell the country that the king must be brought to his knees, or he would take away their liberties.[2]   There were serious riots in London, culminating in an attack on Lambeth which had to be repelled with armed force : and the archbishop felt painfully the libels which were constantly brought to him.   Evidently, to use Laud's own words, Charles "was a mild and gracious prince who knew not how to be, or to be made, great". Skilful Puritan opposition, and secret Jesuit intrigue, had driven him into his present course, in which he was rushing to destruction.

Laud had always known that his enemies would be satisfied only with his blood.   It now remained for him to define and strengthen the Church position which he believed essential for the future of English Christianity ; and to continue his life-long strife against ceremonial Puritanism ; for he was "still of opinion that unity cannot long continue in the Church when uniformity is shut out at the Church door.   And of all diseases I have ever hated a palsie in religion, well knowing that too often a dead palsie ends that disease in

[1] See libels mentioned in his *Diary*.
[2] See Heylin, 396, and Barnard's *Life of Heylin*, p. 118.

16

the fearful forgetfulness of God and His judg-
ments."[1]

With the second attempt to subdue Scotland,
and the circumstances which compelled the calling
of the Long Parliament, the biographer of Laud
has no special business. The tale of Charles'
vacillation and of Strafford's broken health has
been often told and needs not to be repeated.
The archbishop's share in the Government was
no more than a general support of the policy of
Strafford, and an attempt to satisfy men's minds
that the English Church had no desire to
Romanise ; for which end he directed the publication of a defence of Episcopacy written by Bishop
Hall, one of the moderate Puritan bishops, and
also of a treatise in explanation of the Scottish
liturgy. He was too great a man to feel the
slightest jealousy of a colleague who had superseded him in work for which he considered him
better fitted than himself ; and to Strafford he
willingly left the conduct of the campaign, and
the direction of State policy.[2]

---

[1] *Trials and Troubles*, p. 224.
[2] Lady Carlisle to Lord Leicester. Lodge, vii.

The *Trials and Troubles* of Archbishop Laud, by himself (Wharton's folio edition); Laud's *Answer to Lord Saye and Sele;* *The Book of Devotions;* Prynne's *Canterbury's Doome;* County Histories.

CHAPTER XIII.

THE CONVOCATION OF 1640. THE FALL OF THE ARCHBISHOP.

Character of Convocation—Divine Right of Kings—Enforcement of Conformity — Etcetera Oath — Church Policy Defined — Electioneering in 1640 — Scottish Army in England—Attack on Strafford and Laud—Impending Reaction.

THE Convocation of Canterbury had been summoned as usual to meet simultaneously with the session of Parliament; and the archbishop, anxious at this crisis that the ecclesiastical policy of England should be more thoroughly defined, had obtained the royal permission to frame new canons. But the Lower House of Convocation was an elective assembly, chosen freely by the clergy of England. Fifteen years of Laud's government could hardly have allowed time to shape even the chapter members and the official members to a blind conformity with his will; while a large proportion of the House was selected by the votes of the beneficed clergy in each diocese, who, being presented by lay patrons

(245)

for the most part, were certainly in no danger if they opposed the bishops.

Laud's own account of the matter is that "no canon in that convocation was surreptitiously passed by any practice of mine or without due consideration or debate. Neither was there anything in that convocation but what was voted first or subscribed after, without fear or compulsion of any kind. And I am verily persuaded there never sat any synod in Christendom wherein the votes passed with more freedom or less practice than they did in this." [1]

Nor, when we read the story of the resistance which these same clergy offered to the stern tyranny of the Presbyterian and Independent divines, can we imagine that such an assembly of well-born English gentlemen and learned scholars would have bowed to the will of an archbishop, however resolute and imperious. Therefore it may be assumed that the seventeen canons, which were passed by them unanimously after careful debate, represent the reasoned opinions of the English clergy in 1640. This is confirmed when we remember that the lead in the Lower House was taken by such cool-headed men as Sheldon, now rising into prominence, and that violent counsels for repression of Puritan opinions were strongly reprobated by the vast majority.

It was natural that the first place should be

[1] *Trials and Troubles*, p. 155.

given in such troubled times to the teaching of
the Christian Church about the civil power ; it
was equally certain that any weighty opposition
to the ideas now prevalent among the bishops
would find sufficient support from the House of
Commons then in session.[1]   But the canon on the
supreme power of the king, which was passed
before Parliament was dissolved, caused apparently no displeasure to thoughtful men ; and
indeed its language was studiously moderate.
Kings were declared to be responsible to God
for the right government of the Church, and to
possess the sole right to summon councils.
Subjects were warned by quotations from the
New Testament not to bear arms against their
lawful sovereign ; on this matter the example
and the opinion of the martyrs of old and
of the fathers under the early empire were
brought forward and endorsed.   It was pronounced to be the duty of subjects to supply the
king's necessities, and of kings to protect their
subjects' goods.   In short, the Divine character of
the office of the king, consecrated by the Church,
accepted as sovereign by the popular shout
according to the old English custom, was here
insisted upon.   But the king was declared to

---

[1] Heylin says that Laud attempted to get a conference arranged between a committee of Convocation and a committee of
Parliament, so that the laity might be thoroughly satisfied about
the doctrine taught by the clergy (Barnard's *Life*, p. 117).

govern under restrictions imposed upon him by his coronation oath and the statutes of the realm, and defined by the decisions of the law courts. If it was a fair objection that those courts had recently strained the rights of the prerogative as they were soon to strain the powers of Parliament, and Laud himself points out that there was serious danger in leaving the common law un-written,[1] the clergy might justly answer that it was no business of an ecclesiastical synod to dictate to the judges how they should administer the law.

Thus was solemnly set forth the English Church principle of the relations between Church and State. The bishops and clergy acknowledged that the Government was a Divine institution, sanctioned by God to administer justice between man and man ; just as really as the Church could claim the exclusive right to declare doctrine, to preach the Gospel, and to administer the sacra-ments. To emphasise this close relationship, special services of prayer and praise in every church were to solemnise the day of his Majesty's most happy inauguration.

Church and State, being thus bound together, were to enforce upon all men a certain uniformity. Here it is evident that the theory of the seventeenth century and the theory of the nineteenth part com-pany. Yet few men at this period, certainly not Hen-derson the Presbyterian champion of Scotland, nor

---

[1] *Trials and Troubles*, 151.

Burgess and Marshall so soon to be the spiritual dictators of England, nor the leaders of the Long Parliament, questioned the right and duty of Church and State to combine in order to secure conformity.[1]

Three excesses in religion, as men felt them, were to be repressed, but by argument rather than by force; Papists were to be summoned to conferences, conducted by the bishops themselves, in which the errors of Romanism should be exposed; and all measures short of actual persecution were to be used to bring back into the English fold the 150,000 recusants. A similar method was to be adopted against the growing Socinianism which had tainted so many of the Puritans;[2] and against the Anabaptists, Brownists, Familists and other similar sects who were calling in question the doctrines held universally by the Church since the days of the apostles.[3]

An oath was to be taken by every clergyman and member of the universities to give a general adhesion to the government of the Church by "bishops, deans, archdeacons, etc.," and to its doctrines as set forth in the articles; this oath was soon to be represented to the archbishop's astonishment as an intended instrument of tyranny;

[1] See Bacon's essay, *De unitate Ecclesiae.*

[2] *State Papers, passim.*

[3] *Cf.* Laud's *Speech in answer to Lord Saye and Sele.*

and the somewhat careless words *et cetera* were supposed to be the veil under which men would swear away their liberty.[1]

The next canon concerned some of the rites and ceremonies about which there had been such heart-burnings of late, particularly the position of the communion table at the east end of the church. " We declare " said the canon, " that this situation of the holy table doth not imply that it is or ought to be esteemed a true and proper altar whereon Christ is again really sacrificed ; but it is and may be called an altar by us in that sense in which the Primitive Church called it an altar and no other." Unless the bishop should specially direct otherwise, all communicants were to come up to the chancel and kneel at the altar rails for the reception of communion.   Bowing on entering the church was declared to be profitable and edifying, but it was not to be compulsory.

The remaining articles dealt with the manners of the clergy, and reformed and restricted the powers of the ecclesiastical courts which the lawyers had constantly used as a means for exaction. Further, the Convocation passed a resolution to make an improved translation of the Bible into Welsh, in order to stimulate in that part of the country a more vigorous spiritual life.

The legality of these canons was at once called

---

[1] *Vide* Baxter's *Autobiography* for proof that the oath was genuinely dreaded, and Nehemiah Wallington.

ere n question. Laud had felt grave doubts whether
ld ne Convocation could legally continue to sit after
the dissolution of Parliament;[1] but he had been
es overruled by the Crown lawyers, and was doubtless
h glad of his opportunity.

Thus did the Church of England under the
archbishop's guidance fortify its position and marshal its powers when the rising storm seemed
certain to sweep it out of existence. "When
the foundations of faith are shaken, be it by
superstition or profaneness, he that puts not to
his hand as firmly as he can to support them
is too wary and hath more care of himself than
of the cause of Christ."[2] Laud, like Strafford,
was convinced that his enemies would not be
satisfied till they had taken his life ; both perceived
that there were secret influences about the king
which would attempt to overthrow the best com-
binations they could arrange by a repetition of
the intrigues which had been so often successful.
Strafford's system was destined to perish with
him. But Laud knew how deeply his principles had
taken root in the country, and he believed they
would survive ; by the promulgation of these
canons he was able to give substance to his ideal
of the Church ; barriers were erected against
Popery, Socinianism and Sectarianism ; the duty of
supporting the established government was set

---

[1] *Trials and Troubles*, 282.
[2] Laud's Epistle Dedicatory to *Book against Fisher*.

strongly before Churchmen, while they were taugh
to take the lead in reforms of the administration
to insist upon equal justice for all, and to defenc
liberty of opinion so long as it did not overthrov
outward unity.

In the evil days which now came upon the
Church such an authoritative declaration of policy
could not fail to be eminently useful ; it would
bind together faithful minds, and would keep
before them the ecclesiastical system which they
ought to strive to restore.   By Sheldon, Morley
Cosin, and Ward, all of them Laud's disciples
these principles would not be forgotten in the
great Convocation of the Restoration; and while
these bishops of the future did not slight the
warnings given by their master's failure, neithe
did they forget the magnificent conceptions which
he had set before them.

The Convocation was closed on the 29th c
May ; on the 3rd of November, five months later
the Long Parliament had assembled.   The Scottis
army had invaded England; the king had rejected
Strafford's advice, and, persuaded by some of th
great nobles, had entered into treaty with them
" The ancient enemy " remained in the country
encamped at Newcastle, ready to draw sword a
any time in the service of the English Puritans
who skilfully combined the disasters of the king
with the success of their Scottish allies to secure
majority in the new House of Commons.   Grea

as the change in the faces and great the change
in the sentiments of the men who now replaced
the moderate members of the Short Parliament.

There is no matter on which our curiosity is
more aroused than the conduct of this important
election; on no matter has our curiosity been more
completely baffled.[1] The *State Papers* give us
no help.[2] We know that the freeholders alone
enjoyed the franchise in the counties,[3] and that
the country gentry could always have their way in
these constituencies; the great Puritan peers did
not hesitate even to use threats to secure seats for
their friends.[4] We know that in the boroughs
the franchise was sometimes very limited; at
Buckingham twelve burgesses could elect whom
they pleased, and at Aylesbury and Wycombe[5]
the voting strength was little greater, while many
small boroughs were in the hands of great lords
like the Earl of Pembroke and the Earl of Bedford, both gained to the Puritans. Leicester
decided that it was more important to please

[1] For Thetford where two Puritans were returned the candidate gives no hint of his intentions in his address (Mason's *Norfolk*,
279).

[2] Hardly a single document bearing on this election appears
to exist in the Record Office. So absolute is the dearth of information that Dr. Gardiner says nothing about the elections.

[3] In the populous county of Norfolk 1500 votes headed the
poll (Mason's *Norfolk*, 251).

[4] See Lord Warwick's proceedings in Essex at the former
election (*State Papers*, 31st March, 1640).

[5] Sir R. Verney's *Diary*, p. 3.

Lord Stamford[1] than to conciliate the Chancellor of the Duchy ;[2] and petty local questions often, as they do to this day, decided the choice of men who were to sway the destinies of England for years. The town of Lynn afterwards suffered severely for its Royalist opinions, but two Puritans represented it in Parliament.[3] Oxford city was decidedly Loyalist ; but it had private quarrels with the university, and, rejecting Secretary Windebank, sent two members who long supported the Opposition. Even the university, though it was devoted to Laud, elected Selden, the great Opposition lawyer, to Parliament, evidently quite unconscious of the sad consequences to itself. Pym found a seat for one of Lord Bedford's boroughs ; he and his friends took the greatest pains to exclude men who, like Gardiner, the Recorder of London, were suspected of moderate opinions. Yet even thus, when both sides appealed to arms, more than half the county members (and the county elections best represented the opinions of the nation) ranged themselves on the side of Church and king ; while the measures taken by the majority to invalidate many elections,[4] and

[1] For Lord Stamford's Puritan politics cf. State Papers, vol. 424, No. 28.

[2] History of Leicester.

[3] Mason's Norfolk, 282, where we see its own members attacking it.

[4] At least fourteen Royalist members were unseated, and replaced by extreme men of the other side (see lists in Parliamentary History, vol. ix.). Wallington, i. 221, talks of fifty.

their arbitrary suspension of outspoken supporters
of the Crown,[1] combine with the petitions signed
by thousands of electors against interference in
the Church government to prove how little the
House agreed with the people on Church questions.
Perhaps the consciousness that they did not
really represent the nation was the reason why
the great body of members usually followed with
sheep-like docility the decisions of a few strong
men.   Only gradually did two parties develop
themselves in the Long Parliament, and then
almost for the first time we find divisions taken.[2]

The first object of the Puritan majority was to
ensure the disbandment of the royal forces at
York, and to retain the Scottish army in the
country by a fixed monthly payment.   Thus
England lay by the choice of the Commons at the
mercy of a foreign army,[3] ready to march south-
wards if the organised mob[4] of London should
fail on any important vote to coerce the Peers, lay
and spiritual, or the constantly increasing Royalist
minority in the Commons.   The king, having no
force to oppose to the city apprentices, submitted
helplessly to the dictates of the Puritans; and to
the Puritans it seemed that the troubles of Eng-

---

[1] *Parliamentary History*, ix. 237, 328.

[2] There were two divisions on the impeachment of Buckingham
in 1626, but these stand by themselves; and also one or two in
the Short Parliament of 1640.

[3] Baillie, i. 283, and Salmonet, i. 126.

[4] Pennington, the Lord Mayor, had a system for marching
down the city apprentices to Palace Yard (see *Parl. Hist.*, ix. 248).

land were due to Laud and Strafford.   Hamilton, who had at one time been the most unpopular of the three, had deserted his master and made terms with his enemies ;[1] but, as he said himself, "the earl (Strafford) was too great-hearted to fear, and he doubted the other (Laud) was too bold to fly".[2] These were the two men pointed out by the popular finger as the counsellors of that final breach with the last Parliament which, cunningly or stupidly, Sir Henry Vane, father of one of the most eloquent Puritan leaders, had brought about. On the 11th of November, Strafford was impeached and sent to the Tower.[3]   The attack upon Laud had to be deferred until the 18th of December ; he was then accused of high treason by the Scottish Commissioners, and impeached in the name of the Commons of England by Denzil Hollis, a prominent Puritan member, who hoped to save his brother-in-law Strafford's life at the price of the abolition of the bishops and the sacrifice of the primate.   Black Rod was ordered to remove the archbishop in custody until detailed articles of accusation should be presented.

Thus this great experiment of ruling England for religion and by religion had been tried and had failed.   Never again would a bishop be Prime Minister or chief counsellor of the Crown.

---

[1] Baker, p. 470, says he helped Vane to get the Short Parliament dissolved.   Was this the first part of the price of his safety ?

[2] Clarendon, i. 239.   [3] Baillie, i. 275.

The Church, having been consolidated, would soon enter on a safer and truer course, exercising a dominant influence upon the development of the nation; exhibiting a power which it was dangerous to provoke; stimulating charity, education, devotion, literature; until the cold hand of the Whig party nearly choked out its life in the eighteenth century. But for the moment the public feeling had been shocked by seeing the coercive power employed under the direction of ministers of the Gospel. As Christians the bishops seemed to have no right to avenge the most atrocious libels; as magistrates and rulers they had no choice but to punish insults or allow the Government to fall into contempt. Therefore, bishops must cease to rule the State; and the animosity against them carried men away so far that their retention in the Church became matter of debate. Presbyterian ministers, sectarian laymen, fanatical soldiers, were now to try their hands in succession at other forms of theocracy; but their attempts would end in the derisive laughter of the nation over the ridiculous failure of Barebones' Parliament. The bishops had at least taken some measure of human nature: under Laud religious government had been learned and liberal, bright and artistic; the equality of all men had been vindicated by the law, and freedom of opinion had been jealously safeguarded; while the Bishop Treasurer Juxon had administered the finances with such scrupulous

17

rectitude and good sense that no charge whatever could be found against him.   But in Puritan England, learning would be banished from the universities ; mirth would be suppressed ; the most pious and the wisest teachers, Barnabas Oley and Cosin, as well as Hales and Chillingworth, would be reduced almost to starvation ; and if the Government made itself respected abroad it would be much more dreaded at home, where Presbyterian Scots and Romanist Irish and Episcopalian English shuddered at the memory of the massacred and murdered, or longed for news of friends sold into slavery in the plantations of the West Indies.[1]

These two great failures would make it clear that England must not be ruled by a religious party ; the second failure would, in addition, make Puritanism detestable to every class of the people, and produce the dissolute society of the Restoration.

In politics Laud's failure was now decisive. He had been led dangerously near an attempt to make the king autocratic, and therefore it was fortunate that he had failed.   To what extent his Church ideals would survive depended upon the immediate future.   No doubt the time had come when Episcopacy might have its wings clipped. It had always been a principle with the Anglican divines that each national Church had a right to

---

[1] Ludlow, *Memoirs*, ii. 553, 559; he speaks of Cromwell transporting "whole droves at a time".

shape its own policy; but they had so far added
the conditions that each Church must remain
within the traditional lines of episcopal rule and
apostolic succession, of liturgical worship and of
sacramentally imparted grace; and Laud as a
practical statesman had given this conception its
most distinct form.   But would not the theory of
national independence in Church matters now be
pushed further?   By the loss of Strafford Ireland
was to become definitely Romanist; the failure of
Hamilton's Government left Scotland determined
for Presbyterianism.   Could the ancient form of
the Church be maintained any longer in England?
Would it not be right and wise to set up presby-
teries throughout the whole island?

The peculiar character of the English people
imposed certain plain conditions.   A fair opportunity would be given to the new rulers if they
were moderate; but persecution would provoke an
irresistible opposition.   Then opinion would swing
back again to the side of the ancient Church, provided that the chief men of the Church party showed
sufficient endurance, and such faith in their own
principles as to suffer and, if need be, to die for the
cause.   If the leaders of the Long Parliament pushed
their victory to extremes, and insisted on destroying
their rivals; if the great statesman now in the
Tower would face the block deliberately, rather
than betray Episcopacy; if the infirm and aged
primate should be ruthlessly martyred; if the king

should be publicly executed for insisting on the maintenance of bishops, then a safe future would be ensured for the National Church.

Laud's behaviour in prison became therefore a matter of the greatest moment to his followers, dismayed but not in despair. They were prepared to face the terrible and searching trial through which their doctrine of peaceful submission to the powers that be must now lead them. And just as Laud had always opposed at the council board any armed interference for Episcopacy in Scotland, so they refused to raise the standard of revolt so long as the king remained with the Parliament; for it would be disgraceful that the ministers of Christ should hesitate to suffer shame for their Master's sake. And the Puritans found it difficult to persecute their opponents at first, because there was no resistance to the most violent oppression of opinions and of principles. The clergy stirred up no war to maintain the bishops' right to sit in the House of Peers, or to liberate them from illegal imprisonment in the Tower, or to alleviate their own constantly increasing wrongs. Only when the Parliament broke into two parts, and the votes proved less than a majority to be present at St. Stephen's, and the king set up his standard at Nottingham in defence of his divine right, did churchmen deliberately take their side in arms. So potent was the influence of the teaching of Andrewes and

Laud against civil war upon the clergy and laity of the Church of England. It was this teaching which gave patience to the great mass of the nation through the oppression of the military government of Cromwell, when Henry Vaughan wrote, giving voice to the feeling of his fellow-churchmen :—

> But seeing soldiers long ago
> Did spit on Thee and smote Thee too;
> Crowned Thee with thorns and bowed the knee,
> But in contempt as still we see :
> I'll marvel not at aught they do
> Because they used my Saviour so;
> Since of my Lord they had their will
> Thy servant must not take it ill.

FURTHER AUTHORITIES.

The authorities for the last chapters are Laud's own *History of his Trials and Troubles;* Heylin's *Life of Laud;* Fuller's *Church History;* and Rushworth's *Collections,* while details have been added from the memoirs and histories of the time.

CHAPTER XIV.

IMPRISONMENT AND TRIAL, 1640-1645.

*Leaving Lambeth—In Prison—Execution of Strafford—
Insults from Prynne—Meekness of Laud in Prison—
Devotions—Effect of his Patience—Trial and Sentence
—Religious Bigotry.*

Though committed to custody in the morning of
the 18th of December the archbishop obtained
leave to spend the rest of the day at Lambeth,
arranging his papers and settling his affairs, and
thence, when the short December day was done,
to cross to his prison at Black Rod's residence.

That evening the aged primate knelt at his
devotions for the last time in the dimly-lighted
chapel of Lambeth. The daily services of the
Church had been his constant stay; and now he
noticed with thankfulness how appropriate was the
consolation of the psalms for the evening.[1] The
chapel itself was alive with memories. It had
been built by a foreign primate, Boniface of
Savoy, the uncle of King Henry III., at the
command of a great Roman Pope. Was the
ruin of the one free Church in Europe now

---

[1] The *Diary*.

presaged by his own departure? and would the
colossal figure of Rome, the great enemy of his
life, and now rejoicing in his overthrow, step in as
master?   There, in that same chapel, Parker had
knelt for consecration, and had often thought out
upon his knees the principles which were to steer
the Church through the early storms.   There
Whitgift and his friends had asked for God's
guidance before they framed the Lambeth articles,
whose incubus it had been Laud's duty to remove from the spiritual life of the nation.   Out of
it opened two rooms, simple and dark, which
Cranmer had constructed for himself: Cranmer,
whose martyrdom had destroyed the Roman yoke.
Could his own sufferings and death mark an epoch
like the death of Cranmer, and become a dyke
on the other side walling in the pure stream of
English Christianity from the desolate morass of
Puritanism?   To Laud this chapel had always
been an object of the deepest interest; he had
restored the beautiful painted glass of the windows
with diligent affection;[1] they were soon to be again
shattered by the now dominant faction.   The ex-
quisite architecture had contributed not a little to
the effect of his own devoutly organised services.
Gorgeous copes and altar ornaments, beautiful
music and elaborate reverence of demeanour, had
heightened the dignity of worship on many a
solemn occasion.   In the garden outside he had

---

[1] Rushworth, ii. 274.

often walked in counsel with Hyde the lawyer,
and Hales the deep thinker, and Heylin, bright
historian and witty pamphleteer, and the narrow
but capable Neile, and the conscientious Juxon.
Now all this was over; he had nothing more to
achieve, only to suffer and to die.

As he stepped down the stairs, under the
so-called Lollards' Tower, to enter his barge, he
was startled by the crowd upon the river shore.
Had the Anabaptists come to hoot and to insult
him? He was deeply moved and comforted when
he recognised the voices of the poor of Lambeth,
to whom for seven years he had been a father, in-
voking God's protection upon his head, and calling
out that they hoped soon to see him at home again
amongst them.[1] Poor folk! they would miss the
munificent charity of the affectionate and self-
denying archbishop.

Prison itself seemed more cheerful after such
a farewell : and in the early weeks of confinement
he was busy and interested with his reply to the
Scottish Commissioners. By these he was accused
as the great incendiary, the schemer for Popery.
His carefully prepared answers penetrate and destroy with trenchant argument their accusations :
they prove the archbishop's vast learning, and the
clearness of his intellectual power, even in old age.

But it was not in the open arena of a struggle
against Presbyterian preachers and grasping nobles

[1] *Diary.*

that the archbishop had to fight his last battles. Week passed after week, and he was not brought to trial. The victim was safe enough in his prison until the chosen hour of the sacrifice should come. There was no law in England which could override the will of some 160 banded members of the House of Commons; no court would dare to give Laud the benefit of Wentworth's Petition of Right. The archbishop might chafe at the illegality of his imprisonment; he would have to suffer in patience.

After several weeks he was moved amid the angry shouts of the London apprentices to the Tower. He saw his friend Strafford led out to die: Strafford, whom, as he said, no law could be found to convict, until a new lawless law[1] was framed specially to destroy him. Strafford, being denied an interview with the imprisoned archbishop, had sent a message to beg for his blessing as he was taken to execution. The long imprisonment had shattered Laud's health, and he fell fainting when Strafford turned to take his affectionate farewell, and could hardly extend his hand in benediction between the prison bars. To him, Strafford was a martyr for the Church. Archbishop Usher of Dublin, who had prepared him to die, came to Laud's cell to relate how Denzil Hollis had promised to save his brother-in-law's life if he would help in the destruction of Episcopacy. The great

---

[1] Cf. Mozley's essay on Strafford, and Evelyn in *Diary*, and *Capel on the Scaffold*.

minister had haughtily refused, and had died resolute: "No enemy," said he, "am I to Parliaments"; and the Petition of Right and the pacification of Ireland seemed to prove his truthfulness.

Then came the long waiting. Month by month and year by year the archbishop expected his trial. There was a great comfort to him in the public service at the Tower; preachers might and did apostrophise and insult him;[1] but he was in God's house with God's people, and he could pray. Again and again he enters in his *Diary* his gratitude to God for the patience which was granted to him. And, indeed, the fierce outbreaks of temper which were chronicled of him had never been stirred, so far as can be ascertained, by personal ill-usage; it was oppression, or dishonesty, or selfishness which made him use hot words or flame with anger. He was meek enough in his prison, though resolute not to give way a jot to the enemies of the Church.

Prynne was allowed to rifle his papers and to carry off his *Diary*, of which he afterwards published a mutilated and interpolated edition; and had even deprived him of his book of private devotions. The archbishop sat by unmoved, and helped the search. To Prynne he presented a pair of gloves which, as he said, "the poor man evidently coveted". He believed God had put him there to learn resignation through indignities,

[1] *E.g.*, 15th May, 1642.

so that he should be fit for heaven ; otherwise, in his busy life he might have been unprepared to die.   Naturally men who loved and followed him, but who had been ashamed of his occasional outbreaks of anger,[1] and annoyed at the sometimes hasty and discourteous manner of his later years, and troubled by the severe sentences which he advocated now and again in the Star Chamber, grew to look upon the prisoner in the Tower as a hero and a saint.   A great downfall, after men have enjoyed their scornful triumph over it for a period,[2] first moves pity, and then admiration, so long as the fallen magnate is dignified and patient. The man who had ranked next in England to the king had scanty food to eat ; was meanly clad ; and confined in one bare room.   At times his books were denied him ; no friend might visit him ; his very collection of prayers had been carried off.   Such a spectacle gave food for thought even in those stirring times, and was enough to move any but the hardest heart.   Men told one another tales of his gentleness and patience, and of how he had won the affection of his gaolers. Next to the story of the sufferings of the king as described in the Eikon Basilike, the sufferings of the once powerful archbishop stimulated the rising reaction.

It was in these months that he brought to perfection that course of private devotions which

[1] Fuller's *History*, iii. 474.
[2] Baillie, i. 309, and Wallington, i. 150.

he had used at intervals through the day in the
busiest period of his life, always setting apart due
time for the recollection of God.   Old, and worn,
and weary, he had now no difficulty in treading
the way of the Cross, and from the Cross to the
Resurrection, and from the empty grave of his
Saviour to the open gates of heaven.   The way
had been familiar when he was strong and well,
therefore it was easy now ; every step of it was
already marked with the impress of his feet.   The
book was published when he was gone ; and like
the devotions of Bishop Andrewes became a great
favourite for the use of pious souls.   The archbishop's sermons had converted many ; this post-
humous work, redolent of his own example, would
prepare many more souls for heaven.   He would
teach men and women how to die patiently and
cheerfully.

Several efforts had been made to bring him to
trial, but the accumulated evidence was so insufficient that it seemed impossible to condemn him.
An archbishop could hardly be executed for
restoring St. Paul's, or for reforming the university statutes ; yet these were put forward as
serious charges.   Consequently at one time
opportunities were given him to escape, but
with the temper of a Socrates he refused.

"I thank my good friend Hugo Grotius,"
said he to Pococke, "for the care he has thus
expressed of my safety, but I can by no means

be persuaded to comply with his advice. An escape is, indeed, feasible enough ; yea, I verily believe it is this that my enemies desire. Every day an opportunity is presented to me, a passage being left free, in all likelihood, for this purpose, that I should take advantage of it ; but they shall not be gratified by me in that which they appear to long for. I am almost seventy years old, and shall I now go about to prolong a miserable life by the trouble and shame of flying? And were I willing to be gone, whither should I fly? Should I go to France or any other Popish country, it would be to give some seeming ground to that charge of Popery they have endeavoured with so much industry, and so little reason, to fasten upon me. If I should get into Holland I should expose myself to the insults of those sectaries there to whom I am odious, and have every Anabaptist come and pull me by the beard. No ; I am resolved not to think of flight, but continuing where I am, patiently expect and bear what a good and wise Providence has appointed for me, of what kind so ever it may be." [1]

Another friend who obtained access to his prison found him reading Galen in the Tower, and rejoicing that "so learned a man, who was so addicted to assign all unto nature, should by the admirable structure of a man be so much convinced of the God of nature". Then they fell to talking

[1] Twells' *Life of Pococke,* p. 84.

of his troubles ; but " God," says he, " will season me for these and all other trials ".[1]

At last the Scots grew impatient ; somehow or other he must be put to death. His execution should be the price of their armed support of the Parliament.[2] How were they to justify their rebellion against the king if his great minister had not been adjudged criminal ?

In April, 1644, he was summoned again before the House of Lords. Each day he was brought through the city to be insulted by the mob ; it was hoped that the danger of violence would confuse the archbishop's intellect, or provoke him to some passionate outbreak. Several of the Puritan leaders publicly urged the crowd to tear him in pieces.[3] At the waiting-room of the House of Lords he was kept for hours exposed to the rude attacks of the preachers, and of his accusers ; and this terrible ordeal was continued for three months. But he had learnt patience in too good a school ; all were astonished at the calm courtesy of his demeanour. Few of the peers paid him the compliment of listening to his defence.[4] But, in the presence of the two or three who sat on the benches, point by point he met his enemies. They accused him of introducing Popery ; he recounted the long list of persons whom he had

---

[1] Warwick's *Memoirs*, 166.
[2] Ludlow's *Memoirs*, i. 86.   *Cf.* Hobbes' *Behemoth*.
[3] Wood's *Athenae*, ii. 63.   [4] *Cf.* Baillie, ii. 139.

persuaded to abandon Romanism : the charge of personal corruption he challenged with his poverty. The country was searched through for tyrannical sentences passed by courts of which he was a member ; they were few enough for so long an administration, and even these could not be established.

Then the wretched Secretary of State, Sir Henry Vane the elder, was dragged forward to give evidence that he had advised arbitrary government ; the charge was too ill-grounded to be seriously debated. On every occasion men were forced to admit that his replies were irresistible.

But when it proved impossible to convict him of treason, an ordinance for his death was passed by such a remnant of the two Houses as still sat at Westminster ; only six are said to have voted in the House of Peers, though apparently some twenty were present ; but undeterred by their insignificant number they finally ratified the ordinance on the 4th of January, 1645 ; and the 10th of January was fixed for the execution.

The archbishop was doomed ; for Sir Henry Vane the younger had pledged his word to the Scots that he should die ; and his value as a hostage was gone, now that the king's fortunes in the war were waning. His condemnation was a proof that the nobles and gentlemen who had commenced the revolution had lost the control of affairs to that little group of determined sectaries who had just

formed the new model army.[1] These men, with
their masterful conviction that they were the
chosen of God, and that their opponents were
God's enemies, looked upon the old man's execution as a simple act of justice. Fanaticism was
everywhere casting a cloud of gloom over England. Irish prisoners were being murdered in cold
blood;[2] and Scottish Royalists executed with the
open approval of the Scottish clergymen. Already
the poor victims of ignorance who were accused
of witchcraft, and whom Laud with his bright,
rational ideas of religion had for years defended
from persecution, were being butchered by the
score; all over the country the revolutionary
tribunals passed sentence upon them; in Yarmouth
alone sixteen had been put to death in 1644; in
1645 twenty in Norfolk and no less than sixty in
Suffolk would meet the same sentence;[3] while as
usual superstition went hand in hand with fanaticism, and the leaders of the Long Parliament were
rejoicing that Lilly, the chief professor of the black
art, had foretold a victory in the next campaign
for the army of Fairfax and Cromwell.[4] Evidently
it was time for the old archbishop to be gone.

[1] *Memoirs* of Lord Holles.

[2] Many Roman Catholic priests were also executed in England (Berington's *Panzani;* Baillie, i. 295).

[3] Mason's *History of Norfolk*, p. 303.

[4] Lilly's *Memoirs*.

CHAPTER XV.

THE EXECUTION OF THE ARCHBISHOP.

Tower Hill—Insults—The Last Sermon—Effect of Laud's Death—Burial.

IN the few remaining days Laud was assailed by the arguments of two noted and violent Presbyterian preachers. These he quietly repelled, and set himself to due preparation for his end, fully realising the importance of a final public profession of his patriotism and his faith.

Tower Hill was packed with an immense throng as the Archbishop of Canterbury, the first and last archbishop publicly executed in London, was led out from his devotions to die. In the last days the gibbet, which had originally been decreed, had been exchanged for the axe;[1] this respect after all being shown to his high rank. He had slept calmly that night, and had risen early for prayer; and his face was bright and cheerful. The vast concourse was hushed at the sight of the well-known figure, short and square, with the hair closely cropped;[2] the strong, resolute

---

[1] *Parliamentary History*, xiii. 373.   [2] Fuller, iii. 477.

countenance, now marked with sorrow, and furrowed with sickness, but calm and happy. His enemies had been anxious he should not be heard. It might be dangerous. They pushed even upon the very scaffold.

"I thought," said Laud, "there would have been an empty scaffold, that I might have had room to die. I beseech you, let me have an end of this misery, for I have endured it long." He noticed, when he at last reached the block, that he could see faces through the chinks of the scaffold immediately below it, and with something of his old playfulness he said: "Remove them, lest my innocent blood should fall on the heads of the people".

"What," asked a bitter enemy,[1] "is the comfortablest saying which a dying man would have in his mouth?"

The archbishop, with much meekness, answered: "Cupio dissolvi, et esse cum Christo".

"That is a good desire," said the persecutor, "but there must be a foundation for that Divine assurance."

"No man can express it," replied Laud; "it is to be found within."

"It is founded upon a word, nevertheless," insisted the other, "and that word should be known."

---

[1] Rushworth, vi. 835-840, and Wood's *Athenae*, ii. 69, 70.

"That word," said the archbishop, "is the knowledge of Jesus Christ, and that alone."

But there was something in the man which at last compelled silence ; the preacher who had so often held thousands hanging upon his lips ; the clothmaker's son who by strength of will, and clearness of aim, and power of gaining affection had won his way upward, till his aged life seemed to his enemies a threat of danger to the revolution they had made, knew how to gain and how to hold the attention of that huge crowd who had come to see him die.

Then, from the boards of the scaffold, he preached calmly his last and most impressive sermon :—

"Good people, this is an uncomfortable time to preach, yet I shall begin with a text of Scripture, Heb., xii. 2. 'Let us run with patience the race which is set before us : looking unto Jesus, the Author and Finisher of our faith, who, for the joy that was set before Him, endured the cross, despising the shame, and is set down at the right hand of the throne of God.' I have been long in my race, and how I have looked unto Jesus, the Author and Finisher of my faith, He alone knows. I am now come to the end of my race, and here I find the cross, a death of shame. But the shame must be despised, or no coming to the right hand of God. Jesus despised the shame for me, and God forbid that I should not despise

the shame for Him. I am going apace, as you
see, towards the Red Sea, and my feet are upon
the very brink of it : an argument, I hope, that
God is bringing me into the land of promise ; for
that was the way through which He led His
people. But before they came to it, He instituted
a passover for them. A lamb it was, but it must
be eaten with sour herbs. I shall obey, and labour
to digest the sour herbs, as well as the lamb.
And I shall remember it is the Lord's passover.
I shall not think of the herbs, nor be angry with
the hands that gathered them : but look up only
to Him who instituted that, and governed these :
for men can have no more power over me than
what is given them from above. I am not in love
with this passage through the Red Sea, for I have
the weakness and infirmity of flesh and blood
plentifully in me." He exhorted his hearers to
get themselves also ready for inevitable death.
He denied that he had been hostile to liberty,
or to the Protestant religion established by law.
" But I have done. I forgive all the world, all
and every of those bitter enemies who have
persecuted me ; and humbly desire to be forgiven
of God first, and then of every man, and so I
heartily desire you to join in prayer with me."

After prayer, he addressed a few words to
those who stood on the scaffold, chiefly to his
chaplain, and arranged a signal with the executioner.

Then kneeling by the block he continued praying : " Lord, I am coming as fast as I can. I know I must pass through the shadow of death, before I can come to see Thee. But it is but *umbra mortis*, a mere shadow of death, a little darkness upon nature : but Thou, by Thy merits and passion, hast broken through the jaws of death. So, Lord, receive my soul, and have mercy upon me ; and bless this kingdom with peace and plenty, and with brotherly love and charity, that there may not be this effusion of Christian blood amongst them, for Jesus Christ His sake, if it be Thy will."

There were a few moments of silent prayer as his head lay ready upon the block. Then he said aloud : " Lord, receive my soul ". It was the sign, and at one blow his head was severed from his body.

The huge crowd gazed awestruck on the face, a moment ago so bright, so ruddy, so instinct with life and love ; now pale, and blanched, and bloodless, as the executioner held it aloft.[1] Most were dissolved in tears ; even his bitterest enemies[2] felt as men have felt since, that if Laud had taught them no other lesson, he had shown them how to die. Great multitudes followed his body to its grave in All Hallows, Barking, to hear the solemn service of the Prayer Book, so long discontinued, read over the primate's coffin ; for the

---

[1] Fuller's *Church History*, iii. 472.
[2] Baker, 539, and Salmonet, i. 262-9.

astonished Government did not know how to hinder this. Men comforted themselves as they returned home sorrowing, that his end had been so quick and so comfortable, and spoke together of the resurrection to eternal life.

His memory, treasured in the hearts of the down-trodden majority, lived green and strong till freer times allowed the restoration in England of those devout and beautiful services, and that old apostolic government for which he had so willingly given his life.

Thus died William Laud, executed against the law of England,[1] for his religious principles. It is impossible to condemn a man as wanting in patriotism because he preferred the king to the aristocracy, or as devoid of sincere faith because he did not love the Puritan creed. He worked for grand ideals, and his partial failure in politics was more than compensated by the final triumph of his principles in Church administration.

An extract from the historian of his beloved university will fittingly close the story of his death. After telling how his remains were finally deposited with reverent affection in July, 1663, near to the high altar of St. John's College Chapel in Oxford, Anthony Wood concludes his notice of his hero with these words :—

---

[1] In the ordinance by which he was executed it was specially provided that it should not become a precedent (*Parliamentary History*, xiii.).

"Thus died and was buried the king and Church's martyr, a man of such integrity, learning, devotion and courage, as, had he lived in the primitive times, would have given him another name ; whom tho' the cheated multitude were taught to misconceive (for those honoured him most who best knew him) yet impartial posterity will know how to value him when they hear the rebels sentenced him on the same day they voted down the liturgy of the Church of England".

CHAPTER XVI.

THE DEVOTIONAL LIFE.

The Duty of Forgiveness—Dreams—Ceremonialism—Private Prayers—Special Days—Reasons for Publishing the Devotions—Last Will.

IT will probably have occurred to the reader to ask how it was that Laud was able to set himself such severe limits in his use of power, refused even to think of organising a permanent military force, and did not, while he was able, strike terror into his enemies by such tremendous punishments as those which overwhelmed the opponents of Richelieu in France, or even of Strafford in Ireland. This self-restraint remains inexplicable until we turn to the pages of that book of devotions of which it will be remembered Prynne barbarously deprived him in the Tower. Here we find the secret of his life, and are enabled to look into the deepest recesses of the man's heart.

Writers who have glanced cursorily over Laud's remains in compiling the history of the times have been content to set him down as a

(283)

ceremonialist, full of vulgar superstitions. They have contrasted his merely external religion with the heart-felt religion of the greater Puritans. But superstitious ceremonialists do not leave the impression Laud has left on the religious life of a great people. Undoubtedly this student of the Bible attached some importance to the visions of the night; now and again he sets down in his *Diary* an account of dreams—some which he notes came true; others which startled him as confirming the accusations of his enemies; others again which strangely harmonised with his predominant anxieties at the moment.[1] Nor could this man as a lover of antiquity help being sometimes impressed in periods of difficulty and danger by omens; the fall of his picture at Lambeth on the eve of the Long Parliament seemed to him to coincide appallingly with his own anticipations of evil.[2] These were the superstitions (if we must call them so) of the thoughtful men of his own day; they differ from the superstitions of the nineteenth century, which will in their turn move

---

[1] *Diary*, 14th December, 1623: 30th January, 3rd July, 21st August, 4th and 26th September, 1625; 21st December, 1626; 5th, 14th and 16th January, 9th February, 8th and 27th March, 7th July, 1627; 31st January, 1628; 6th June, 12th July, 1633; 26th October, 1635; 3rd August, 14th October, 20th November, 24th December, 1636; 12th February, 1639; 24th January, 1640; 2nd November, 1642; 10th March, 1643, seem to be the only passages; most of them, it will be noted, occur in periods, and generally at times of ill-health.

[2] *Diary*, 27th October, 1640.

the laughter of equally superstitious ages to come ; they are distinctly marked off from that astrological superstition which tainted many of the leaders of the Long Parliament, such as Hollis and Stapleton and Whitelock, and even had some influence upon Bishop Williams;[1] and it must be remembered that Laud entirely refused to believe in witchcraft.[2] Nor can a man who notes these for possible warnings sent from on high be fairly accused of superstition, when, as in the case of the archbishop, he never allows them to sway him from what he believes to be the path of duty.

As to ceremonialism, he was convinced, we have seen, that grand and dignified worship helped human souls to realise the grandeur and dignity of God. Outward show he abhorred, except at the service and in the house of God ; he rebuked all splendour in clerical apparel and himself set the example of peculiarly simple and inexpensive dress.[3] But he saw how careless men were of religion, and he knew by the experience of his own busy life how hard it was not to forget God in the hurry and bustle of affairs.[4]

To keep his own soul conscious of his dependence upon God, he made a habit of private prayer

[1] See Lilly's *Autobiography*.

[2] At his instigation the king delivered witches in Lancashire in 1633.

[3] In this he was a striking contrast to his rival Bishop Williams (Stanley, *Westminster Abbey*).

[4] See Salmonet, ii. 216, on the value of the English love of Christmas.

seven times every day. For this purpose he compiled a short service, differing with each day of the week. These rapid devotions were almost entirely personal ; he humbled himself in them before his Maker, and entreated to be guarded against his unknown sins and against the failings which he had already detected. Having these written with his own hand in a small book which he carried in his pocket, he was able, wherever he might be, to recollect himself seven times a day in the presence of God. By putting them into writing he ensured immediate concentration. Gathering them from many saints of the past and adding to them devotions composed by himself, he ensured sufficient variety to lay his whole heart bare to God.

It was by this practice of continual prayer that he was able to check mere selfish ambition, to humble his pride, to keep his mind fixed on high aims, and finally to endure with patience the trials of his later life. To be seven times a day quite alone with God was the safeguard of his soul ; "a man who so often made up his accounts with his Maker could not go very far astray ". [1]

But besides these short private prayers at fixed times which, with those of his own model Bishop Andrewes, became the model of devotion to many of the great saints of the Restoration, he regularly attended the public prayers of the

[1] Lloyd's *Memoirs of those who Suffered*, 231.

Church ; and further spent a considerable time every day in intercession for others. His regular devotions, varied no doubt as to their time by the press of business, included special prayers for (1) the Catholic Church and unity, (2) the particular part of it to which he belonged, (3) the king, the royal family and the officers of State, (4) his relations and friends, (5) his servants, to whom he was always devotedly attached, and who repaid him with the most unstinted affection, (6) the sick throughout the Church of Christ, (7) all mankind and especially his own personal enemies ; for he was constantly on the watch to subdue personal rancour against the libellers of his character. These chief private devotions of the day were commenced with a general confession of sin, a thanksgiving and a prayer for usefulness, and concluded with a self-surrender of his life into the hands of God.

He added to them from time to time special prayers which he felt to be necessary. Now all his affairs were going so prosperously that he dreaded pride ; now sickness or adversity was injuring or seemed to be injuring his usefulness. Again his hasty temper and quick, passionate utterance were getting the better of him at a time of ill-health or special difficulty. Then he saw his flock perishing from some all too frequent outbreak of the plague ; or there was war in England, or a time of dearth.

It was his custom also to offer special inter-

cession to God for the poor, so little thought of
in those days by haughty nobles and despotic
gentry, by wealthy merchants and manufacturers :
" O Lord, when thou makest inquisition for blood,
remember and forget not the complaint of the
poor ".

Certain days were observed as fast days for
his own sins and the sins of the people ; some of
them general fast days of the Church ; two days
on which he himself had grievously sinned and
brought discredit upon the Church of God, St.
Stephen's Day and the 28th of July.

Other days in like manner were observed each
year as days of thanksgiving, such as the day of
recovery from a serious accident, and the day on
which he scarcely escaped from the fire at St.
John's College.   On the 11th of April and the 24th
of November, on which his father and mother had
died, he added special prayers for a happy reunion with them in heaven.   The reception of
the Holy Communion was commemorated also
with carefully composed thanksgivings ; for how
could he thank God enough for the benefits He
had done to his soul ?

As the shadows of life close round him the
prayers become naturally more and more pathetic.
Old age is advancing and he has had so little
time for the great work allotted to him.   The
king's ministers are flying abroad from the wrath
of the Long Parliament, and he fears that he too

may be driven from the England which he has
loved so intensely.   Then he is carried to prison
and he must ask with insistence for that Divine
patience which has always been so difficult to his
fiery temper and clear intellect.   He feels his
complete innocence of the charges brought
against him ; but he has foreseen years ago that
his opponents would be satisfied with nothing but
his death ; he would wish, and God alone can
help him to do it, that he may answer the scur-
rilous accusations of his enemies with none of those
bitter scathing retorts which from his keen understanding rose so naturally and so easily to his lips.
The message of condemnation finds him prepared
to spend the last hours of his life in prayer for his
own safe transition through death into life, and
for the many who are in like case.

Probably we owe this beautiful collection of
devotions to the hostility of Prynne.   That un-
forgiving enemy had picked out sentences here
and there and published them abroad with comments to stir indignation against his victim.   Laud,
who, with all his humility, knew how important
a part his personal character must play in the
future of the Church, was most anxious that it
should be well understood that he had died fear-
lessly, and in the orthodox faith of the Catholic
Church as established in England, and therefore
allowed his chaplains to give the book to the
public.

The larger part of the devotions was published as early as 1650, and was warmly welcomed by a people who lay under the tyranny of the small remnant of a Parliament elected ten years before, and of the Westminster Assembly of Divines. Many who were widows and desolate ; many who were imprisoned or doomed to grinding poverty ; many who were longing for devotional guidance, away from the controversial preaching and still more controversial praying of the times, into the very presence of God Himself, welcomed this collection of prayers, and found therein a comfort until better days. After the Restoration, the book of devotions passed through a great number of editions.

No one who has studied with care the devotions[1] and the *Diary* of William Laud can doubt that his religion was personal, deep and strong ; that his sympathies were wide and his ideals high ; that the ceremonial which he advocated was dear to him only so far as it stimulated a more intimate knowledge and love of God ; and that his personal sanctity must have played a notable part in the events of his disturbed and difficult life.

The last words of a book which has tried not to conceal his faults, nor the mistakes by which

---

[1] *E.g.*, 25th January, 1624; 30th January, 1625. "Sunday night, my dream of my blessed Lord and Saviour Jesus Christ. One of the most comfortable passages that ever I had in my life " (19th August, 1636).

he imperilled English liberty, while it showed his real greatness and sincerity, shall be taken from the closing phrases of his will, made on the 13th of January, 1644.

"Thus I forgive all the world and heartily desire forgiveness of God and the world ; and so again commend and commit my soul into the hands of God the Father who gave it, in the merits and mercies of my blessed Saviour Jesus Christ who redeemed it, and in the peace and comfort of the Holy Ghost who blessed it ; and in the truth and unity of this Holy Catholic Church, and in the Communion of the Church of England, as it yet stands established by law.

"I most willingly leave the world, being weary at the very heart of the enmities of it, and of my own sins, many and great, and of the grievous distractions of the Church of Christ almost in all parts of Christendom."

THE PROJECTS OF THE ARISTOCRACY.

THE great nobles in England had chafed under the strongly centralised rule of the Tudors and the Stuarts; this is clear enough from their frequent rebellions and their own constant complaints of royal control. Therefore, when, with the assistance of London and other great cities, they had secured the control of a majority in the Long Parliament, they set to work to re-establish their power. They began by destroying, imprisoning and driving into exile the principal royal ministers; they coerced their opponents in the two Houses, and secured by statute the permanence of the Parliament. Then they demanded that the military control of the country should be placed in their hands.

On the 11th of February, 1642, they drew up a list of men to whom the government of the militia was to be delivered, with commissions giving powers so immensely increased upon any precedent that they left the central Government practically helpless, and which were only to be revoked by Parliament itself (see the ordinance). It was this demand of Parliament which caused the final breach with the king; he saw in it the ruin of the monarchy. In this important list we find that some heads of noble houses were excluded, Newcastle, Southampton, etc., for their known loyalty to the king; some were left out, like Arundel, because of their growing disgust with politics; some, like Hertford, were entrusted with inferior commands; but all the more important lord-lieutenancies were allotted to men who were at once great nobles, and open opponents of the king. These men were to take the place held by the

(293)

semi-independent governors of provinces in France, who had of late years been the chief danger to French unity, and to the coercion of whom Richelieu had devoted so much of his energy.

Northumberland, the head of the Percy house, so famous for its frequent rebellions, was to have command of the two great frontier garrisons of Newcastle and Berwick, with the county of Northumberland and also that of Sussex; and he was to control the communications between England and Ireland by exercising a similar authority in Anglesea and Pembroke. Four counties fell to this great nobleman's share; while Lord Grey de Wark obtained Carlisle, the other Scottish border fortress, and the county of Cumberland.

Pembroke, head of the Herberts, the richest noble in England and possessor of more borough votes than any other landowner, received Merioneth and Carnarvon, and further Wiltshire, Hampshire and the Isle of Wight, which, with the great fortress of Portsmouth, made him supreme in the south of England. Philip Herbert was to be master in Glamorgan, Brecknock and Monmouth, a compact government. Essex, chief of the Devereux, was to administer Yorkshire with the all-important arsenal of Kingston-on-Hull, and also Montgomery and Staffordshire.

To the powerful family of Rich was given the rule of the home counties. Warwick, its head, was to be lord-lieutenant of Essex, and of the wealthy county of Norfolk; while his younger brother, Holland, had Middlesex and Berkshire, with the royal fortress of Windsor. London, and to some extent Bristol, were to be made independent and to have the charge of their own train bands.

Salisbury was to rule over Hertfordshire and Dorset; while Bolingbroke, Paget, Roberts, Bedford, Suffolk, Leicester, Sir H. Vane, Chandos, Wharton, Stamford, Lincoln, Saye and Sele, Brooke and a number of others became masters each in his own county.

On 14th May, 1642, a bill was passed by the House of

Lords to prevent the creation of peers in the future. This would have ensured aristocratic mastery.

This well laid scheme was thwarted by the successes of Charles I. in the Civil War; and finally overthrown by the genius of Cromwell, whose aristocratic leanings were speedily modified as power fell naturally into his hands in the new model army; but its audacious conception is a sufficient vindication of Laud's jealousy of aristocratic authority.

See the list of lord-lieutenants in Sir R. Verney's *Diary*, p. 153, Camden Society's edition, and *Parliamentary History*, vol. x., *passim*.

NOTE B.

THE NAVY UNDER CHARLES I. AND LAUD.

THE fleet with which Blake and Montague won their successes was bequeathed to them by the Government of Charles I. and Laud. James I. had materially strengthened the navy of Elizabeth; Charles I. added eighteen vessels to the royal navy. These were larger and better built than their predecessors. The *Sovereign of the Seas*, launched at Woolwich in 1637, remained for sixty years the glory and the strength of the British navy. It was nearly double the size of any of its predecessors. The great naval architects, Phineas and Peter Pett, trained under Charles, introduced a new style of shipbuilding which rendered the ships quicker and easier to handle.

The first ship-money fleet, consisting of nineteen royal vessels and six merchant ships, left Tilbury on the 26th of May, 1635. The French and Dutch fleets "plucked in their horns and quitted our coasts," as Monson, who was vice-admiral, relates on p. 263 of his *Naval Tracts;* leaving to England "the ancient sovereignty of the narrow seas". Monson goes on to explain the great prestige which England gained and kept till 1640. The fleet in the following years continued to hold the mastery of the Channel, while a squadron under

Rainsborough threatened Sallée in Morocco, and put an end
for the time to the pirate descents upon our coasts; and it
made England once more respected abroad, until the dis-
creditable conduct of the new admiral, the Earl of Northumberland, which was attributed to treachery (Warwick, p. 120),
allowed the Dutch to capture a Spanish fleet in English waters,
on 11th October, 1639.

The stimulus given by this naval supremacy to English
commerce caused an enormous increase in the mercantile
marine; "in short, Britain, which had long aspired to the
dominion of the seas, now appeared in earnest as to the
establishment of her claim; and had not those destructive
events intervened which are too well known, there appears
little doubt that the pursuit in question would, long ere it
actually did effect that purpose, have raised her into the first
rank and power" (Charnock). Under the Commonwealth,
Sir R. Slingsby tells us, there was scarcely one good merchant
ship built; and the mercantile marine was diminished by above
1000 ships, though the navy was much increased (Pepys, Evelyn
and Clarendon).

It must be remembered that Laud was a prominent
member of the Board of Admiralty during the time of the
great shipbuilding.

Cf. State Papers; Charnock's *Marine Architecture;* Monson's *Naval Tracts;* Southey and Bell's *Naval History.*

NOTE C.

THE ARMY AT BERWICK IN 1639.

SOME historians have assumed that the Pacification of Berwick was forced upon Charles by the comparative weakness
of his army. They quote the incidents from the *State Papers*
and memoirs of the time, which prove the disorderly march
of several bodies of soldiers supplied by the train bands;
they bring forward the calculations of Baillie as to the large

numbers of enthusiastic Scots in Lesley's army; and further they assume a general discontent in the royal ranks, because they hold that the country was on the eve of a revolt against the ecclesiastical government of Laud and the exactions of the Treasury.

Laud's reputation as a capable administrator must to some extent stand and fall with his power to muster an English army at Berwick, and in the text I have maintained opinions very contrary to those often set forward, because the general literature of that time has convinced me of the superiority of the king's forces.

I. Several witnesses speak with admiration of the cavalry which the great nobles gathered on the frontier. Newcastle's troop gained their special praise (Clarendon, Mrs. Hutchinson, etc.); but there is no reason to suppose that it was exceptional. Many of the nobles were delighted at an opportunity for action; they were personally attached to the king; and they knew that the war must greatly add to their political importance. Essex, who was certainly not prepossessed in favour of the Government, acted with a vigour, admitted on all hands, which proved his eagerness to vindicate English power; and refused to listen to any approaches which the Scottish nobles made towards him.

The infantry was probably not so good as the cavalry; it was mainly composed of soldiers selected from the train bands of the counties. These, as has been shown on p. 151, note, had been improved of late, and the companies in Yorkshire, where Wentworth had control, were in a specially high state of efficiency; over 12,000 men were enrolled, armed and drilled in that one county (*State Papers*, vol. 310, Nos. 44 and 45). But the flower of the infantry was the force which Wentworth sent over from Ireland (Carte's *Ormond*, i. 58, 98, 103, and *Strafford Papers*), so splendidly drilled and equipped that people said they ought all to be captains (*Strafford Papers*). They were well commanded; they had been prepared by the lord-lieutenant with a view to just such a crisis as had now to be faced. Handled by Essex and other trained generals in the royal camp, they would have found no Scottish troops fit to be their match. The soldiers, who had been ill provided and fed at first, were now satisfied, for £400,000 was sent down to the army on the 1st of April (see Rossingham, News Letter in *State Papers*).

II. The numbers of the Scottish army have been very much taken on trust from Baillie, a country minister who had never seen an army before in his life; and from the reports given by Puritan peers like Stamford, who visited the Scottish camp (*State Papers*, vol. 424, No. 28; their reports were believed by the king, Vane's Letter in Burnet's *Hamilton*, p. 139) and returned with inflated rumours intended to influence English counsels. Other information speaks of small numbers (*State Papers*, vol. 421, No. 60; vol. 422, No. 62; vol. 423, No. 12, and vol. 425, No. 21) and of a conspicuous want of arms (*State Papers*, vol. 420, No. 109; vol. 424, No. 50); we find in Burnet's *History* of his own times (and Burnet's father was a very well-informed and important person at Edinburgh in 1639) a very interesting description of the way in which the Scots extemporised cannon (*cf. State Papers*, vol. 424, No. 50) which would be capable of discharging three or four shots at most. We know that expected supplies of arms were detained in Holland by dread of the English fleet, and that at least one vessel coming over was captured (Burnet's *Hamilton*, 132).

III. There is no proof of any dangerous discontent in England in 1639. Rather society seemed to be better contented than it had been in 1637. Laud reports his province as thoroughly quiet with very little trouble from nonconformity. Neile writes a similar experience from York. It would have been an act of incredible rashness if the minister had ventured to call up the feudal cavalry and the train bands while the country was full of disloyalty; in that case, the English army at Berwick would have been the sure cause of his ruin. In actual fact, even the nobles showed themselves as a body resolutely loyal when there was real danger to the crown and the country (*State Papers*, vol. 423, No. 67). Certainly considerable dissatisfaction existed among the nobility and gentry and was prevalent in the City of London at the discontinuance of Parliaments; and both had felt the arbitrary power of the Star Chamber and High Commission; but the people in general were not more discontented than people constantly are under all governments, and a compromise between the Ministry and the Commons, such as was suggested in the Short Parliament, would have been thoroughly popular. We find in the *State Papers* (*e.g.*, vol. 161, No. 1; vol. 165, No. 38; vol. 303, No. 56) more annoyance at the action of the saltpetremen than from almost every other cause; the domiciliary visits of these officials in search of materials to make gunpowder, for which they often insisted on digging under outbuildings and even under private houses, caused constant friction and complaints to the central authority of their insolence and roughness. Religion, politics, legality of tonnage and poundage, the exaction of ship-money stirred the opposition of only a few here and there, who could not enlist the active sympathies of large bodies of men while the Government maintained its prestige. Taxation was light; local government was very much in the hands of local persons, only restrained from oppressing the poor by the Star Chamber; justice was evenly administered by the royal courts. There was no serious fear of an influential rising in England, in spite of the promises of some of the Puritan leaders. But when a local disturbance in Edinburgh (see Burnet's *Own Times*) overthrew the Government of Scotland, and the king, who shuddered at bloodshed according to his own speech on the scaffold, proved too irresolute to use the great army at Berwick, opinion naturally swayed round against the dominant policy, and the revolution began. Then the old aristocratic claims which had been almost choked by Laud's government sprang up with new vigour, and threatened to alter the constitution (Note A). Evidently the administration was making the English people a laughing stock by its want of decision. It had no confidence in its own strength. To be despised is the surest source of ruin to rulers. After all, as Carte says in his *Life of Ormond*, " Governments often subsist more by an opinion than by the reality of their power ".

If the king could have been induced to carry through the vigorous action, on which he seemed to have determined when he insisted on having an army assembled at Berwick, he would probably have found it an easy task to pacify Scotland ; for his government had not at that time lost its hold upon England and Ireland, and in Scotland itself he had a large party. The Hamiltons and Holland were the real cause of his ruin, when they succeeded in persuading him to prefer their advice to that of the Prime Minister; and once more nursed into life the power of the nobles in England and in Scotland.

INDEX.

INDEX.

A.

Abbot, Archbishop, 12, 18, 43, 73, 83, 109 f., 112, 131.
Abergwilly, 47, 70.
Alington, Sir G., 117.
Allen, Cardinal, 10.
All Hallows, Barking, 280.
Ambrose, Saint, 42.
Anabaptists, 249.
Andrewes, Bishop, 15, 41, 42, 44, 55, 66. 68, 70, 127, 166, 181, 260, 271.
Anselm, Saint, 17, 132.
Argyle, Marquis of, 182, 212.
Aristocratic claims, 6, 37 f., 153, 224, 232, 293, 299.
Aristotle, 14.
Armada, The, 9.
Arminius, 83, 89.
Arundel, Earl of, 82, 224, 227, 293.
Augustine, Saint, 42.
Aylesbury, 253.

B.

Bacon, 54.
Baily, Dr., 168.
Bancroft, Archbishop, 12, 53.
   „   Bishop, 169.
Barneveldt, 14.
Bastwick, Dr., 176 f.
Baxter, Richard, 30, 55, 75, 112.
Bedell, Bishop, 141, 210.
Bedford, Earl of, 128, 175, 253.
Bible, The authority of the, 50.
Berwick, Pacification of, 227, 296.
Brent, Sir N., 135, 141, 144.

Brooke, Lord, 124, 152, 175, 221, 223, 294.
Brownists, 249.
Buckden, 183, 185.
Buckeridge, Bishop, 13, 36, 68.
Buckingham, Marquis and Duke of, 38, 45, 50, 57, 63, 66, 70, 72, 78, 79, 85, 96, 184, 192 ff.
Buckingham, Town of, 253.
Burgess, 55, 249.
Burleigh, 6.
Burton, Rev. H., 176 f.

C.

Calvinism, 13, 14, 18.
Capel, Lord, 46, 179, 268.
Cartwright, 10, 18.
Chalcedon, Bishop of, 84, 122.
Charles I., 37, 61, 173, 189, 227, 241.
Charterhouse, 85.
Childrey, 74 ff., 131.
Chillingworth, 161, 168, 169, 258.
Coke, Sir E., 43, 96.
   „   Secretary, 150.
Coligny, 8.
Commerce, 76, 123 145, 152.
Commons, House of, 37 ff., 64 ff., 85 ff., 93 ff., 230 ff., 253 ff.
Conference with Fisher, 50, 187.
Convocation, 65, 69, 245 ff.
Copinger, 23.
Corbett, Bishop, 138.
Coronation of Charles I., 70.
Cosin, Dr., 90, 121, 252, 258.
Cottington, 82, 105, 144, 145, 188, 232.

(303)

ABERDEEN UNIVERSITY PRESS.